Miles Apart

Miles Apart

Hadley Hoover

Happy Reading!
Hadley Hoover

Writers Club Press
San Jose New York Lincoln Shanghai

Miles Apart

Writers Club Press
an imprint of iUniverse.com, Inc.

For information address:
iUniverse.com, Inc.
5220 S 16th, Ste. 200
Lincoln, NE 68512
www.iuniverse.com

ISBN: 0-595-17044-7

Printed in the United States of America

This one—and all to come—for my one true love.

CHAPTER ONE

Despite his wintry blue-gray eyes, it was California's summer sun that reflected wildly off sunglasses wedged in the stranger's hair. This picture froze in Molly's mind as she watched the whistle that had first signaled his approach now change to slack-jawed astonishment. "What's going on here?" His voice reverberated around her temporary prison.

The words jolted Molly out of her stunned assessment of the tanned face that had suddenly appeared over a grimy rim. Self-consciously, she shook off the debris he had deposited around her. Embarrassment replaced her shock, quickly followed by a flash-flood of anger at being caught in such ridiculous circumstances.

"Well? You're in a dumpster, and I'm wondering why," he prompted. His laugh yanked her back to reality.

With a last slap across a faded denim knee, she turned a stony glare toward the lean face. A carefully trimmed moustache formed an awning over those lips that spouted words as he attempted to carry on a conversation. She bit her answer off and spat the words out like twigs, "I don't owe you any explanations." Fresh-cut grass fell from her sun-streaked blonde hair as she raked her fingers through its tangles.

Molly mentally retreated into her usual method for handling stress, listing-making. *1) get rid of this man, 2) get out of this literal mess, and 3) call the dumpster company.* She took a deep breath and floundered as she realized that the first step on her list for success loomed before her like an unquenchable foe.

Oblivious to Molly's distress, this Adversary dropped his bushel basket and let it bounce off the step stool beside the metal bin. Their gazes

1

locked, her brown eyes held captive by two blue ones fringed with lashes darker than the maple-syrup hair that brushed his neck. "How'd you get in there?"

Wisps of leaves clung to the mass of curly hair that crept out like moss around the edges of his shirt. "It should be obvious enough. The stool's right beside you," she snapped. Exasperation buzzed in her head like the flies circling them. Then self-rebuke sprung up. Why was she yelling at this guy? Anyone finding her here would ask questions.

He gave the stool only a cursory glance. "So you climbed in. But why?" His glance flitted from the Volvo visible through her open garage door and then to Vinnie's Pool Repair van outside a neighbor's wrought-iron fence. "In this ritzy part of town, a person doesn't expect to find folks hanging out in..." Her paralyzing stare finally penetrated. "Never mind; grab hold and I'll help you out." He extended a muscular hair-matted forearm.

A memory flashed like a neon sign, the memory of her ancient jeans ripping as she had climbed in. As if stung, she backed away from him and forced a smile to reshape her stiff lips. "No. I'm looking for something I lost. I need to find it."

"Most people," the moustache quivered suspiciously, "*deposit* garbage in these monsters. Besides, I'm sure the rules are quite clear, right here in this bright yellow paint." He recited dramatically without giving the sign even the slightest glance, "'Danger. Stay Out.' Seems plain enough to me."

Molly leaned closer in a futile attempt to read upside-down over the edge. He continued staring at her, reducing her to the unfamiliar role of air-headed blonde instead of the in-control, take-charge professional woman she was, the librarian with the reputation for being counted on to handle difficult situations with tact and dignity. "So you say."

"Who are you, anyway? A hardened criminal, breaking just one more law?" he asked as a dimple in his left cheek quivered and deepened.

"I didn't...I'm not..."

He interrupted, "Looks like I have to report you! After all, I'm the model citizen, putting trash in its proper place, only to discover," he stepped closer, biting his lower lip as he studied her, "...someone hiding out like a fugitive."

This hyena, Molly fumed, *has the nerve to laugh at me.* She retorted coldly, "Until you showed up, I was just fine."

"*Fine*? You call hiding in here 'fine'? What's a bad day like for you, anyway? Or do you view-of-the-mountains yuppie-types always hit the alley for excitement?"

This clown has never had a serious thought. Zero. He's just a play-in-the-sun guy who should not be allowed to run loose. "Not that it's any of your business, but I was looking for a watch and I heard you whistling and I didn't want..."

"Wait just one minute!" His hand a sword, he sliced the air. "Oops, that's right. No more personal questions from a total stranger!" Clapping dust off his hands, he stuck the right one across the wall of her mold-green prison. "Jordan's the name. Concerned, involved, caring citizen, and native of this great state of California."

His grin was bewitching, but she ignored his hand. "So I gathered. Unless valid birth certificates aren't required to buy one of those shirts," she said with wilting energy.

"You noticed, huh?" He stuck his thumbs in the armholes of a faded tanktop and held it away from an enticingly hair-crowned chest for her to read the inscription *Welcome to California. Now go home* which blazed across the front in fluorescent green letters. "The shirt for genuine natives. Are you one of our rare breed, too?" His hand, again, crossed the dirt-caked rim.

Invisible cords lifted her hand. "No, I'm from Minnesota."

Wow, what a strong hand...shake. Suddenly flustered, she realized that all motion had stopped. *A handshake, by all definitions, Molly, is an activity involving motion.*

She slid her palm free of his grasp, knocking an orange peel of questionable age loose from the dumpster's edge. "Nice to meet you, I'm sure. Now, will you please hand me the stool?"

He shrugged. "Not yet. You're still looking for a watch. Tell me, how did you intend to get back out?" Somewhere in the neighborhood a lawn mower revved into action. He reached out and gently flicked a stray leaf from a strand of hair dangerously close to her mouth.

Mesmerized, she watched the leaf float gracefully down to join others beneath her. "I'm not sure." *Less than five minutes with this man and I've become a blithering idiot.* Sobered, she added feebly, "I guess I acted on impulse."

She watched, dismayed, as he perched one foot atop the stool, settling in for a chat. "My impulses lean more toward chocolate! What did you lose?"

Mister, conversation, even with a pulse-stopper like you, is not a priority right now. Molly sighed, sneezed, and squirmed as a stream of perspiration ran along her spine. "I already told you. My watch. The clasp broke when I threw a bag in here."

"Do you always carry a step stool when you take out the trash?"

The laugh that bubbled up in her throat was a total surprise. "Not usually, no. I repeat: I took out my garbage, my watch fell off, I got the stool from the garage…am I going too fast for you?" she quizzed him, suddenly feeling impish.

"No, no, go on; this is fascinating."

Why did this loquacious hunk of eyes, hair, and grins have to choose today to wander by? "Someone, obviously you, whistled. That truck blocked my view," his eyes followed her hand when she gestured at the guilty vehicle, "so I hid."

"You know, this story just gets better and better."

Pointedly ignoring him, she shuffled her now-filthy dock-siders to signal dismissal, "Well, I don't want to keep you from your work…"

"Funny lady, Minnesota! Nope, you find that watch, and I'll wait around." He continued before she could shape a protest into words. "After all, the reputation of California men rests on me! I really am the culprit in this drama. I whistled..." The lips twitched suspiciously. Oblivious to her stare, he continued, "...and it's my truck..." He nodded in the general direction.

She had to remind herself to swallow. *Molly! Get a grip!*

"...I threw messy junk over you. They should lock me up! I'm a regular menace." He slapped his wrists together and clicked his tongue like a giant handcuff.

"You rarely stop talking, do you?" She snapped back to reality, giving him what her family teasingly called her teacher-stare.

"You really don't laugh much, do you?" he shot back. She bit her cheek to stifle a retort.

Resting his chest against the dumpster's outer wall, he leaned over and dangled an arm into the dumpster. "Pull up the brown bag on top of that big branch. Check under that heap and a couple more and you could be out of this stink-hole in seconds."

No way, buddy! If I bend over enough to move any of these bags, you will get a view that one friendly handshake doesn't license you to have. "Oh, it could be anywhere and take forever." She waved her arms in an all-encompassing swoop.

"Time, I've got lots of. Patience with you, Minnesota, I'm running a little thin on." He could produce a pretty chilly stare, himself. "Why you're so confounded stubborn about leaving this mess is beyond me. If you're afraid I'll drop you, forget it! From what I see," he subjected her to a painfully thorough review, "lifting you is child's play. What are you, 115 pounds?" He flexed his sun-bronzed arms dramatically. His eyes were pools of laughter despite the stubborn set of his chin.

She backed up against the opposite wall and shielded her exposed backside from his scrutiny. "Now *that* really is none of your business. I'll get out. On my own. When I'm ready. Which I'm not. You might as well go." She jutted an equally firm chin in his direction. Anger marched through her veins. *So I don't laugh much, huh?*

"Not ready? What is this, some new millennium hobby I've missed hearing about, this dumpster diving?" He effortlessly snagged the stool and suddenly he was a man in charge, ordering, "Climb up on that and swing yourself up on the rim. Then I'll catch you." Stepping back, he demonstrated how his arms would engulf her when she made the leap he intended.

"Thanks a lot; you probably just smashed my watch when you dropped the stool down here." She poked around in the mess with her foot, flinching as wafts of foul air rose with each movement. "I don't know what you're doing here anyway; you don't live around here."

Any short-lived charm she had mustered now gave way to outrage that sputtered beneath his unwavering grin. Her growing list of complaints against this nervy stranger began with his uninvited presence in her previously well-ordered world and ended with his uncanny ability to bring out the worst in her with every word and grin. In amongst these grievous offenses, trouble rumbled like a distant thunderstorm.

"Begging your pardon! But I think any jury would agree that I was using this container," he pounded the side for emphasis, "more appropriately than the defendant." He snared his bushel basket and brandished his evidence. "I present Exhibit A. Now take you, Minnesota; what do you have to show as proof of your innocence?" He turned and addressed the tree, "Members of the jury, I see only a lady who I'm sure is normally breathtakingly exquisite, who is now knee-deep in gunk and apparently loving it."

They waited, he in triumphant silence, she with narrowed eyes.

"Aha! I rest my case. She produces zilch in her own defense!" He muttered to the leafy jury box, "This sort always manages to land in California."

"My watch *is* in here, and I *will* find it." A lopsided grin released the tension in her body. "Has anyone ever mentioned that you're certifiably crazy? You could be committed to a home!"

"How many clues do you need to guess who would be in the room next to me?" he hooted. "I give the highest compliment I've ever mustered up for a lady in a dumpster, and this is my thanks? I take it all back. Here's my revised version: You look better in dirt and litter than anyone else I know." He shrugged carelessly. "Meanwhile, back at the ranch. Keep searching, Minnesota."

Subdued and chastened, she knelt, keeping her back against the opposite side, and gingerly shook large clumps of garbage. "It's here. Despite your theatrics. Whew, it stinks in here!" *Why did I get up this morning? I could have hired a yard man, but ho-no, old Molly decides raking is such good exercise...*

"Must be an expensive watch. Good Lord, you can get watches so cheap these days. Come on," he grabbed at her T-shirt, "quit being so independent. I'll buy you a dozen watches."

"Can't you understand some things have sentimental value?" She jerked away from him; the sudden movement set the rubble in motion and she fell backwards. She glared up at him from her hole in the debris and felt unwanted tears well up. *Don't cry, you ninny.* She ducked her head from his view.

He howled with laughter that echoed throughout the dumpster. "Hey, I'm the innocent bystander, you're the maiden in distress." Stretching to put a finger under her chin, he tipped her head and grinned into her glistening eyes; his mood changed instantly. "Whoa, Minnesota, I'm sorry. I never meant to make you cry," he said softly.

"You didn't make me do anything. Just go away." She rolled to one side to push herself up.

And there it was.

"Hey! I found it! Now do you believe me?" She blew dirt away, waving the watch triumphantly between puffs.

Stumbling up the step stool, she unwittingly followed his earlier instructions to the letter. Strong arms caught her up, swung her over, and held her a second longer than necessary before releasing her on the ground. "Are you okay?" He bent to peer up into her face and her breath caught on her heart as their eyes met. "You can borrow my shirt if you want to blow your nose. I'm going to burn it anyway."

Defenseless, she burst out laughing. "You know, that's a pretty hard offer to turn down! Thanks, but no thanks. Keep your shirt. It would be a pity to burn it. After all, you natives may only get one per lifetime!" On level ground with him, she realized that he topped her five feet, eight inches by nearly half a foot.

"Let's see this winner of a watch." Hands on his knees, he bent his lanky frame at the waist. "Unless it's a gift from a male brute, I would never dive for this; it's nice enough, but it's a pretty basic watch."

He straightened up and arched his back. Muscles rolled like waves under his skin, her pulse responding like the tide to the moon. Molly bent and gave particular attention to brushing off her jeans.

Diverted, he dropped to his knees to help. "You landed in coffee grounds and some very scrambled eggs." He spun her around; a deep male chuckle erupted as he brushed his way up the back of her legs. "It's suddenly clear why you fought me off like a tiger! What a magnificent rip!" He whistled seductively.

She twisted out of his reach. "Okay, you've played the role of Rescuer to the hilt. Thank you and good-bye. If you get paid by the hour to trim and weed, you're not a very honest worker."

"I'm not a gardener." He struggled to rein in his laughter.

This guy probably laughs hysterically at earthquakes. She seethed inwardly. "Then what are you doing dumping clippings here? Huh? This is a neighborhood dumpster, not one for the whole Valley to use, you know."

"I'm just helping a friend who lives over there." He waved vaguely across the alley, his eyes cruising her face. "Let me at least get the step stool out. Unless you're planning another trip back in! If so," he grabbed her hand and opened her fingers to expose the watch, "I'm not available for my part in the adventure for another couple hours." He wiggled his eyebrows and she looked away from his thinly disguised amusement.

What an infuriating man. "You're a regular homing pigeon, aren't you, once you get going on something you find funny?" Lightening flashed in her eyes and her words sizzled like the first drops of rain hitting hot pavement. "Can we drop the subject and get on with our lives?"

"You never did answer me. Is the watch from a Mafia-type?"

"End of discussion, okay?" she commanded sharply.

"Have the jeweler clean it when he fixes the clasp again, then Brutus will never be the wiser that his special gift has been places you don't want to talk about." His moustache twitched.

"Your assistance and advice are deeply appreciated. I'll add that trip to the jeweler to my list for next week. Thanks so much; I never would have thought to go without your suggestion." He appeared unscathed by her sarcasm.

One final amused sputter echoed inside the bin as he hiked himself up enough to balance on the wall of the dumpster, reach in and effort-lessly swing the stool out. He bowed dramatically as he presented her with his gift. "For you, Minnesota."

She pulled her eyes away from the greasy line that now marked his chest and focused her attention on a point just beyond his head.

"I guess Minnesotans don't exactly find life amusing. Must be that nippy weather just freezes your humor like an icicle. Brrrrrrrrrrr!" He shivered dramatically.

"*What* are you talking about?"

"You need to relax. In the short time I have been with you, you have managed only one chuckle, and maybe two giggles. No, they were more like noisy smiles."

She pursed her lips in and out, in and out.

"I thought *I* was tense, but at least I laugh." She continued to stare off into space, tapping her foot, marking each second he was wasting. With a good-natured shrug, he backed away, waved a casual farewell, and hooked a thumb in the back pocket of his jeans.

He had the trimmest backside she had seen in years. "Wait!"

He looked back over one shoulder and stopped.

"Your basket." She picked it up and walked toward him.

"Oh, yeah." He met her in three strides, retrieved the basket with one finger and slung it over his shoulder to bounce against his brawny back with each step he took away from her. Stray leaves fluttered down that ugly shirt and rounded the bend of that tight denim temptation to the ground behind him.

Molly rocked back on her heels, chewing her bottom lip while chiding thoughts rumbled through her head. *He really is leaving. And I behaved like a petulant child.* An apology bubbled inside but didn't spill out. "See ya." *Oh yeah, classy way to make amends, Mol. You make Emily Post proud.*

He glanced pointedly at the dumpster, then back at her jeans with unabashed amusement in his eyes. Loping back, he gently rubbed a smudge of dirt off her nose, smiling as if he sensed that his light touch sent shivers rippling through her body despite the afternoon's heat. "I doubt it," he said softly. He walked away; his whistle again spun a web between them, a fragile cord floating on the afternoon breeze.

Molly's chin tightened as the unseen gate clanged shut behind him. She kicked at a piece of bramble caught in the legs of the step stool. Overhead, a bird chirped and broke into song. "Oh shut up, will you?"

She choked the stool's leg until her nails dug into her palms, and then stormed across the alley to her gate, crossing the yard in long, pounding strides. "You did it again, Molly. You met a man who piques your interest and then you pretty much destroyed any chance of ever seeing him again." *Seeing him again? Where did that absurd thought come from? Why on earth would I even want to see him again?*

With an energy born of frustration, she heaved the stool across the patio; it bounced over the bricks in cacophonous rebuke. Before the sound had faded, the kitchen door banged shut behind her, closing all whistlers, feathered or tanned, out of her life.

CHAPTER TWO

Molly stripped to the skin in her laundry room, flung the filthy jeans and shirt into the washer, and stomped upstairs to her bedroom shower. Beneath the steady pulsating stream, she scrubbed her body and hair vigorously in an attempt to send both dumpster dirt and memories of a most unnerving man swirling down the drain.

It worked. She even hummed as she retraced her steps to the laundry room. But the calm was short-lived; as water rose in the washer, she knew it would take more than a shower to clear her head.

Uninvited reminders of the unsettling afternoon popped up without warning, like the chipped nail polish on her index finger when she punched a familiar number on the kitchen phone. Two rings.

"Hello?"

"Hi, Brynn. This is Molly. Are you busy?"

"No, or I should say, not with anything that beats talking to you."

"If it interests you, I will make two significant sandwiches and break out a cold six-pack of diet stuff and tell you a story."

"Molly, it's four o'clock. Which meal is this for you?"

"Well, I'm not sure."

"Ah, which is more significant, the sandwiches or the story?"

"I'm buttering bread as we speak. Time's a-wasting. Are you coming, or do I stop with two slices?"

"Nope, do four. I can promise you one good buddy, namely, Brynn Hilton, sitting in your kitchen in fifteen minutes. I'll be the one with mouth and ears wide open." The dial tone droned an end to the conversation.

Molly whistled as she headed for the refrigerator. This would do it for sure. She and Brynn would laugh the whole thing off and life would resume its predictable, safe pace. Deliberately, she crossed another item off her Saturday list: yard work. *Done. The End. Life now leaves this unplanned, disruptive moment behind and resumes its safe and measured pace.*

Slicing, chopping and spreading filled the minutes until a car door slammed, announcing the arrival of her guest. She rinsed mayonnaise off her fingers and balanced the last slice of bread on a crown of sprouts before racing to the door.

Propping the screen door open, she tapped one foot impatiently while Brynn jogged up the sidewalk. "Are we to expect a visit from the police, if they ever catch up with you?" she teased.

"It's my standard time, fifteen minutes on the dot!"

Molly lifted her wrist with a grimace. "Oh. Well, you can't expect me to know that with no watch. But that's getting ahead of my story."

"I came tearing across town for sandwiches in the middle of the afternoon and a story about your watch? You must be desperate for company. Everything all right?"

"Yes! I'm perfectly fine! I wish everyone would…"

Brynn's eyes widened with a quick flick of concern as she craned her neck to look into the empty kitchen. "We are alone, right? Uh, what's with this 'everyone' stuff?"

Molly grinned ruefully and threw an arm around her friend's shoulders, bringing her into the kitchen. "I'll fill you in on my life soon enough. But first, I'm starving. Let's eat. I'm sure glad you could come on such short notice." She missed Brynn's arched eyebrow as she tightened the lid on the pickle jar and stuck it back in the refrigerator.

Balancing sandwich plates, frosty soft drink cans, and fresh peaches, they maneuvered from the kitchen counter to the oval oak table. Without ceremony, Brynn plopped onto her usual chair and opened her mouth for the first bite.

"Mmmm. As promised, most significant sandwiches. Let the story begin, Bard." Brynn sighed with obvious pleasure as she licked a hint of Mendocino mustard off her lips, and pushed an escaping piece of avocado back under the top slice of bread. "If your story is half as good as all this stuff dripping down my chin, you're not the only one who's glad I came!"

Molly grinned and took her own first bite before she began. "Now that you're here, I feel kind of silly about the whole thing."

"The story, please."

"Okay. Today the major project on my list was the lawn; I accumulated bags and bags of clippings…for the dumpster." She snapped open a can and stared at it, unseeing.

"And?" Brynn prompted.

"Well, at this point it gets a little crazy."

"So soon? I'll be the judge. Keep talking. Skip to the good stuff. I know about dumpsters in alleys." She wrinkled her nose.

"That's what you think! When I took the bags out, my watch fell off into the trash. The clasp must have loosened when I was raking. Anyway, I looked over the edge and couldn't even see it."

"This would be your sixteenth birthday watch, right?"

"Yeah. I've managed to keep track of it for over ten years, and now this." Her shoulders sagged briefly.

"Gee. I'm sorry, Molly. Hey, let's finish our sandwiches and then I'll help. Gum on a broom handle or something ought to do the trick."

"Don't worry. I got it out. And that's really my story."

"There's more?"

"More? Yeah! You call that a story? I haven't even begun. After my watch fell off, all I could think of was getting it back; for once I wasn't even thinking about consequences, which was my first mistake. Even with a step stool, it was too far down to reach. So, I climbed in."

Everything on the table rattled as Brynn jerked upright, hitting the table with her knee. "You did what?" She shuddered. "Molly, there could be rats in there!"

"Lighten up, Goofus! This isn't that kind of neighborhood. Now, quit interrupting. Anyway, whether you approve or not," a penetrating glance paralyzed further comment, "I had just gotten started looking when I heard a whistle."

Brynn dropped her sandwich back on her plate, oblivious to the sprouts that landed in her lap. "Whose whistle? Was it what's-his-name, the old guy next door with the bad toupee?"

"That would be too easy, and actually would have been much better. No, this was another guy; I've never seen him before." She traced shapeless patterns in the wet circle forming around the freshly washed fruit.

"So, tell me about him. Hey, come back to me!" Brynn snapped her fingers under Molly's nose.

"Well, using the standard classification system," Molly paused pensively as she brushed the hair back from her face, "he was beyond a ten; he created a new division: walking advertisement for the human race."

Brynn stared. "You mean to tell me this…whistler-guy was nothing short of exceptional?"

Molly nodded. "Off the charts," she said and took a bite of her sandwich.

"And you're in the dumpster. So! He whistled. Go on." She pushed back from the table and giggled. "I love it!" Her shoes plopped softly to the floor as she hugged her knees to her chest, attentive as a child.

"Naturally, I didn't want to be discovered, so I pulled the cover down and hid inside to wait." She slid her plate to one side and brushed crumbs from the table into one palm.

"You know how much I hate these pauses of yours. Would you just keep talking?"

"He didn't walk past. He was coming closer because he had a load of stuff to dump."

Brynn groaned empathetically and let her head sink back onto her shoulders. "I think I know why I'm eating mid-afternoon sandwiches. Oh, Mol! What did you do?"

"What could I do?" Molly shrugged. "There I was, crouching in a filthy dumpster, when the lid opened and all I could see was a bushel basket full of branches and leaves and stuff, and then two very nice arms..."

"Slow down. Nice? Define nice."

"Strong, muscular, with just the perfect amount of curly hair, tanned, the kind of arms men have who are hired to advertise something where they only show the arms, not the rest of the body. Need I go on?"

Brynn sighed dreamily, "No, I can fantasize the rest."

"He dumped the load of clippings on top of me. And that's when it got real confusing." Her voice stopped abruptly as she bit her lower lip.

Brynn pounded the table once with her fist and sputtered, "When you read for the children's story hour, you do fine, but when you're just plain telling a story, believe me, your style leaves a lot to be desired. Am I going to live long enough to ever hear the end of this one?"

"Hey, it's not like I practiced it! You're hearing the first edition, so shut up," she ordered amiably. "Anyway, we talked some, and then, well..."

"'*We talked some*'? This is hardly the time to start editing the script, Molly Winstead! Details; every little detail. Now."

"I'm not editing. I wasn't memorizing every word, you know! The main problem was that he wanted to help me get out, but I, uh, couldn't with him standing there, because my pants ripped when I climbed in and..." Her voice faded away.

Brynn, good friend that she was, fought nobly to hide a smile; finally, she gave up. The dam monitoring her emotional control broke; she buried her face in her arms which barely muffled her hooting. When she finally lifted her head to speak, tears sprouted from her eyes. "I'm sorry, Mol, really." She wiped her eyes dry with her napkin. "Where was the rip?"

Molly shook her head in disbelief. "I should know better than to expect sympathy from you! Come on, it's past time to put them in the dryer, anyway, so you can see for yourself." They left the table and headed for the laundry room, each step punctuated with Brynn's giggles. Molly pulled the wet jeans out of the washer and shook them out to their full length.

Brynn stared at the jeans, pressed her fist against her lips, and looked at Molly with wide glistening eyes. Both gawked at the jeans and laughter ricocheted off the walls as they clung, weak-kneed, to each other. "Why are you even bothering to wash these, let alone dry them? You'd be arrested if you ever wore them again! They sure don't match the public's image of a librarian. Besides, your personal image pretty much steers clear of ratty jeans. And I do mean ratty!"

"Brynn, I'm sure they weren't this bad when he saw me. Washing them has probably made the rip much worse."

"Well, if they looked even half this, uh, interesting, it would certainly explain why a red-blooded American guy couldn't tear himself away from your alley! Which reminds me, you've got more story to tell." Brynn tossed the still wet jeans on the counter, spun her friend around by the shoulders and half pushed, half led the way back to the table.

"Want anything else to eat, Brynn?"

"Forget hostessing. I know my way around if I need anything. Talk."

Suddenly restless, Molly cleared the table as she continued. "It was a confusing mixture of emotions. Sometimes I wanted to yell at him, several times he made me just want to laugh, and at the end I felt almost sad to see him go. It was like riding an emotional roller coaster. Very bewildering."

"Back up a little, to the yelling part. If he is God's commercial for the male gender, what did you do that…"

"Well, good grief, Brynn," Molly sputtered, "he seemed to think it was all hysterically funny. I think the proper thing to do would have been to go away when I told him to."

"My etiquette book doesn't include dumpster manners, but it seems that when someone finds another person in a mess, and this episode would be indexed under 'Mess, comma, Literal Interpretation', that someone helps the other person out."

"But I didn't want him to see my, uh, posterior, and from the beginning he seemed to think it was all a big joke. He's so…well, what more can I say?"

Brynn rolled her eyes. "Plenty! You could lose a ship in all the holes in your story, woman. How *did* you get out?"

"He finally got around to dropping the step stool inside and then he helped me climb out." Her hands crept up to follow the remembered trail of his hands on her body.

Brynn scrutinized her friend silently for a moment before she said, "Uh, does this story turn R-rated at this point?"

"What?" Molly jerked back to the present. "No, no way. It was just a very unusual experience. When he lifted me over the edge, I was…"

"If you fade out on me anymore, Molly, I swear I'll shake the rest of the story out of you."

"Sorry. He made quite an impression on me, I guess."

"So I see," Brynn said softly. "But you did find your watch?"

"Yeah, Didn't I mention that? Then I climbed out and he went back to trim bushes or whatever."

"And that's that." Brynn peered into Molly's face.

"Yeah." Molly puckered her lips.

"Do I detect a note of sadness?" Brynn teased gently.

"Perhaps. You probably think I'm losing it," she tapped her forehead in the ageless gesture, "but despite everything, he was a pretty decent guy. And I behaved like a miserable, spoiled brat. I didn't even say thanks."

"Hey, don't look so dejected! The dude could have spun on his heels when you told him to go, so don't be too hard on yourself. He must not have minded the whole episode too much."

"Call it pride, I guess, but I hate to think that he's running around town telling everyone about this deranged bimbo he met in an alley."

"Even if he told fifty people, they'd never know who it was. It's not like you handed out business cards!"

"He knows where I live, or at least the general vicinity."

"Pooh. It's not likely to hurt your reputation. In fact, it could help. Busloads will probably come our public library now to get their reference questions answered by a person with such an exciting past. Not only are you a librarian, you have now experienced Trash. This could be big!"

Molly groaned and dropped her head into her hands. "Oh, Brynn, if *anybody* besides you ever says anything about this afternoon, I swear— I'll find that guy and wring his neck!"

"And how would you find him? You don't even know his name."

"Jordan. And he has a blue truck, darker blue than his eyes."

Brynn threw her hands up, addressing the ceiling. "Silly me; here I thought the story was over! You know his name? What's this about blue eyes? And how does the truck fit in?"

Molly waited until Brynn sputtered to a stop and then answered, "At one point he introduced himself. He said his name is Jordan. I wonder what his last name is?"

"Maybe that *is* his last name."

"Ooh, I hadn't thought of that. Anyway, his truck was what kept me from seeing him when I could hear him whistling. It was a blue truck; some kind of pickup. Do you remember that picture of me building a snowman when I was a kid in Minnesota? His eyes are the same color as the sky on that kind of day."

Brynn nodded as her friend lapsed into silence again. "You always have had a thing for blue-eyed men. As long as they don't interfere with The Plan."

"I had better snap out of this 'thing,' right? Thanks, Brynn, for letting me ramble on about nothing. How 'bout some coffee? It's a sad day that's too warm for coffee, as your friend and mine, ole Royce, would say."

Brynn checked the clock on the wall. "Grind decaf beans, and I'm very interested. Anyway, what are friends for, if not to listen? Seems to me we've both taken our turns at rambling and listening over the years. Besides, lots of folks would pay big bucks for this kind of entertainment!" Brynn dodged her friend's feigned punch. "Speaking of Royce. Now there's a man who would love to learn the secret of how to entice you. Maybe I should encourage him to hang out in alleys!"

"Royce? Nah, he's safe. You're the only one of the three of us who refused to accept that he and I aren't destined to date each other. We're too much alike."

"Yeah, both stubborn, both organized to a fault. And worst of all, you're both content to take whatever waking moments you can grab from your busy schedules and spend them *together*, which sure doesn't leave either of you with any time to find anyone else!"

"Pffft! Like there's a line of eligible men who desire me waiting impatiently for me to say 'Next!'"

"Sometimes I cannot believe how dense you can be, Mol. Maybe if your reading tastes ran to something besides mysteries, true crime, and biographies, you'd catch a few signals from time to time. And maybe if you weren't always with good-ole-safety-net Royce, you could see what's going on around you."

"Royce and I enjoy being friends. I'll leave the romance section of the library, and the rest of the male population, for you to pursue. Until I turn thirty, and then I'll join the search party."

Brynn sighed. "I've got to hand it to you, even though I don't agree with the way you plot out your life like an architect. What if these plans backfire, Molly, and you find yourself at age thirty with your education behind you, several years of working at a secure job, living in this fantastic house…and no man looks good then?"

Molly rolled her eyes playfully. "Is that so bad? After all, I'm enjoying life right now. If I find this man you think I need later on, great; if not, that's okay with me, too. I kinda like the days busy with work, the nights quiet with me, myself, and I—unless I choose otherwise."

"But maybe there's a guy out there somewhere who would have enjoyed sharing these years with you?"

"And what part of those years do you think this mythical man is missing the most, the peanut butter sandwiches the week I ordered carpet, or the three years of studying every single weekend?" Ceramic mugs of fresh brewed coffee in hand, the two friends grinned an unspoken truce in their frequent dispute and headed out to the patio.

The vivid hues of late afternoon gave way to the subtle pallet of early evening. "Have you got a full week, Molly?" Brynn asked lazily from her lounge chair.

"Until Wednesday. Thursday morning is pretty open. I work the late shift at the Desk that day. Why? Want to do something?"

"Maybe we can get in a swim or something before you leave on vacation."

"What's your day off this week?"

"Friday."

"Sounds good to me. I'm done at four on Friday, but I work a half-day Saturday. Let me know what and when."

Brynn yawned and pressed her head against the lawn chair, "I wish I could check off the days faster until my vacation. I envy you escaping our world of summer reading clubs and bored tourists. I'm stuck here until August."

"Yeah, I'm looking forward to it; especially the drive. The more I think about it, the happier I am that the enticement of boxloads of old books from my grandmother made me decide to drive back home this time. It will be quiet, no phones, no meetings. For three whole weeks I won't have to answer questions about antique cars, or what gerbils eat, or find a biography of Lincoln that Mrs. Aaronstein hasn't read yet. Yup,

I'm ready for vacation. But I can't let myself think about it too much—there's still one week to go."

"I hear you." Brynn stood and stretched. "Well, kiddo, time for me to hit the road. It's my turn to help the bookmobile driver load up bright and early, so I'm going to make tonight an early one in hopes of being able to read small print at the ungodly hour of 6:00 AM."

"Been there, done that!"

"Hey, I see you have a step stool! How handy that must be for you!"

Molly rolled her eyes and swatted at her friend as they left the shadowed quiet of the backyard and walked slowly to the driveway. "Talk to you later this week about swimming, or maybe an evening bike ride," she said through Brynn's car window.

"Either one." She turned the engine key.

"Hey, thanks, again, for your speedy service as my sounding board."

Brynn nodded and grinned. "Anytime, Molly. Excellent company, always great food, and what a story! Keep me posted, okay?"

"Posted? On what? Storytime is over."

"You never know," Brynn chimed in a sing-song voice.

"You, my friend, are a dreamer! Go home!" Molly grinned as Brynn backed her car out of the driveway.

At the curb, she braked and called back, "Good stories often have sequels; remember that, Madam Librarian!"

Molly groaned, stuck out her tongue, and headed back to the house.

Minutes later, sipping a glass of herbal iced tea, she opened the door to her home office and flicked the light switch. Even after a year of living under the red clay tile roof, she still savored the first moments when light filled the corners of her home.

Magazines fanned across a low oak coffee table between a long couch and the window and formed several stacks under the table, as well. Shaded ceramic lamps cast halos above several easy chairs. Opposite the door, a bay window opened to a screened patio with more inviting chairs and a hammock.

After making quick work of paying a few bills, Molly was soon lost in a crossword puzzle. When she finally noticed the time, street lights were on and the evening had evaporated, as had her concerns over the embarrassment of the afternoon. She watered her pride-and-joy jade plant and headed upstairs to end the night reading in bed.

CHAPTER THREE

When the library doors opened the next morning, it would have appeared that everyone entering had a burning desire for knowledge. If anyone just walked in, met a friend, and sat down to chat, Molly did not see it. All she saw were those making bee-lines for the Reference Desk. Molly was sure she had more than her normal share of inquisitive kids, impatient businessmen, and interesting senior citizens.

Even Summer days brought kids to the library. Maybe it was in response to the television spots—featuring Molly and a few of her peers—that dangled tempting classes on riding scooters or learning about the yo-yo, or the chance to meet local sports heroes.

Whatever the reason they came the first time, kids usually came back to learn more. At the scooter class, they heard about books that could show them how to make a go-cart and they added their names to the request lists for those titles. At the yo-yo sessions, senior citizens promised one-on-one chances to "be the best" if the kids were interested—and interested, they were. It made Molly smile to see white heads bent next to rainbow-hue heads investigating techniques together.

Businessmen dropped in during lunch hours to verify facts they had seen on-line back in the office. Reference books piled up as they invested companies' claims to excellence, or researched stocks. While they used the computers, they still appreciated help from Molly and her crew of librarians to search out the facts. Molly always found it gratifying to see them relax and head back to work more confident and less concerned than when they had arrived. She found it mildly disconcerting that a man she had helped earlier in the summer seemed to seek her out, waiting to one side until she was free, and lingering after the questions were answered. *Did men really flirt with librarians outside of the Music Man movie? Good grief, Molly; quit reading something into an innocent encounter. Just because one guy who roams alleys seemed interested in you, does not mean the world is falling at your feet.*

Senior citizens loved the library. While some had been hesitant to change over from the "real" card catalog to "that confounded computer," many now used the on-line catalog with ease and often helped others less confident to find what they needed. Molly had long ago given up on preguessing what any senior citizen would ask her.

This week she realized that just because a man has only white fringes of hair remaining above his ears does not mean his interests run only to the obituaries. Four times she caught these older gentlemen watching her with interest when she turned back to them with the answers to their questions. *So much for assuming they had been admiring only my mind!*

The range of requests was as varied as their backgrounds—and she loved hearing their stories when they could tell she had time to listen. Whether they were former executives now learning about organic gardening, or retired farmers discovering the world of genealogies, or semi-retired widowers reaching out through teaching English to migrant workers, or elderly housewives leaving their nest to join the legion of library volunteers, Molly loved them all.

Evenings, Molly made the trip to the jewelry store, arranged with neighbors to watch her house, water the lawn, and gather her mail, and fit in a dentist appointment to get her teeth cleaned.

Days, the library kept her at a hectic pace that made the time speed by. Because of noticing frequent requests for information on similar topics, Molly had begun keeping a list of questions and names of people who seemed knowledgeable on specific topics. Her dreams of putting people with similar interests together in the same room was realized when the Library Board had authorized her to recruit citizens interested in providing one-time classes in the Library's Community Room. Not only was there much interest at the beginning, it grew phenomenally.

The opportunities for offering a wide range of events were limited only by the space in the Library available to such groups. Molly brushed aside frequent suggestions—usually from leaders who had found their time in the limelight gratifying—that she should quit her day-job and start up a business in the Valley that could accommodate many more people. She was a Librarian first and foremost. That was plenty of excitement for anyone, in her book.

The task of overseeing the popular events would have been a daunting undertaking for a less organized individual, or as Brynn teased, impossible for anyone with a social life. Molly took the teasing good-naturedly, knowing there was an element of truth but also knowing she loved doing it.

In addition to her Reference Desk duties, Molly kept the community room calendar full, handled requests for new events with the skill of a circus juggler, and kept the public informed of the myriad offerings via the Library's Web site, on-site displays, radio announcements, and television spots. The fact that the camera crews usually arranged for Molly to be in the shoots was lost on her, even though Royce and Brynn often teased her about her alternate life as just another Minnesota girl come to California for the bright lights and glitter.

The week before Molly's vacation had a dozen such events: How to Create and Market a Cookbook; Getting Involved in Adult Literacy Programs; Setting up a Class Reunion; Planning a Wheelchair-Accessible Trip to Europe; Quilting for Charities; How to Start a Current Events Club; Learning about Composting; Collecting Old-Time Toys; Building Your Own Backyard Playground; Clock Repair; Drying Herbs; and How to Get a Patent.

When Molly sent out an e-mail to her colleagues with the list of weekly events, her intention was to give them a heads-up about questions to expect each day. Despite herself, she had to grin when Brynn responded with a return seemingly innocent question, "Will the Learning about Composting group be able to discuss what does and does not go in dumpsters?" Molly hoped no one was reading over Brynn's shoulder when she read her reply: "Oh, shut up!"

As Molly looked over the list, she felt a surge of excitement and a sigh of exhaustion doing battle in her brain. As the date for each event arrived, it required pulling a healthy chunk of appropriate library materials to be made available for check-out, and a final meeting with the leaders to assure them of additional help, if needed, and help them make the event a success. Molly got rave reviews for her working relationships with the event leaders.

When the Cookbook group and the Class Reunion group showed up at the same time for the same room, despite what the original plans and follow-up communication from Molly had confirmed, she was able to work with them to set up an alternate date for the group in error, but she also negotiated a peace treaty that allowed the two groups to join forces. The Class Reunion group decided that selling a cookbook of class members' recipe-favorites was a great idea and the Cookbook group was delighted to help them get the idea off the ground.

It was not on anyone's list of favorite things, but when the sewer backed up overnight and a stench beyond belief greeted the Library Staff, a bookmobile not in use that day was opened for business in the parking lot for the few hours it took to reopen the Library.

Molly quickly arranged to move the How to Compost group to a nearby greenhouse. One television station announcing the change sent a camera crew to cover the event which gave the group so much publicity that the leaders called Molly the next day to book the Library Community Room for a unexpected follow-up meeting.

Every day the book carts filled with returned items and much-used reference materials; every day volunteers reshelved the books, magazines, videos, and newspapers. Each volunteer usually found something in what he or she was fitting back in place that piqued enough interest that additional materials got checked out, or perused over a break, or written down on a wallet-list for future consideration.

Molly grinned each time she saw this happening—she was smitten by the same bug: a little information *is* a dangerous thing because it only made her want to know more.

The Reference Desk staff usually appeared to be all-knowing to their public. They were hard workers, Molly acknowledged as she watched the newest hire tirelessly respond to a woman who did not believe the facts she was being shown. *Unlike some idiots I've run across lately.*

Each person brought individual strengths to the tasks. Molly was careful to staff the Desk wisely. Whenever possible, she scheduled history buffs to work with the mechanically-inclined, she purposefully put the two best financial wizards on opposite shifts to give the best coverage, and she attempted to balance the librarians' personal tastes in fiction whenever possible. If one person behind the Reference Desk didn't know an answer, they could always check the Internet, but usually they relied first on their trusted colleagues. It made work fun, kept the day moving along, and provided the best service.

Several times during the week when her path intersected with Brynn's, her friend hinted at her wild adventures of the last weekend. The comments were just enough to make co-workers curious, and more than enough to prompt paralyzing glares from Molly to her teasing friend. Molly brushed off the resulting questions and prayed for the day when something—anything—more interesting would divert Brynn's attention from focusing on her friend's brief relapse of sanity.

The Library was so politically correct that Molly's relationships with her male co-workers were polite, respectful, and frankly rather dull. These men, fully aware that they were working with a woman whom patrons had been overheard to call "a real looker," would rather have chewed rocks than make overtures that could cost them their jobs. It was a safe place to work, but not a place likely to spawn relationships outside of work.

Any couples that found each other outside work probably had match-making friends who set the wheels in motion. Molly had Brynn who fit that description, but Brynn had given up on trying to interest her friend in anyone from work. Molly viewed them all as friends, and collectively as off-limits. It was enough to give Brynn ulcers.

All in all, each day of Molly's week before vacation was so full of people, questions, computer screens, and scheduled events that she barely remembered to eat lunch. She also found herself wondering where she had parked her car on a day when she had taken the bus; this was a pretty good clue that she was frazzled. Each night, she sank into bed at night with relief and let exhaustion serve as a lullaby.

Before falling asleep one night, she recalled reading that day about life in the factories before vacations were part of the working world. Not only was she glad she did not work under the conditions of earlier centuries, she blessed the advocates of vacations for their perseverance and drifted off with semi-conscious longing for the trip that came closer day-by-day.

Unfortunately, her dreams that night involved a 19th-century mill boss who walked around with a basket tossed over his shoulder. While she could see her watch caught and dangling from the basket, she couldn't catch him to get it back. Ever the librarian, even in her dreams she knew that women working in the mills in the 1800's probably did not own watches. She woke less than refreshed from a night chasing someone in her dreams she hoped never to see again in her life.

Molly welcomed Friday's bike ride with Brynn. A vacation was definitely needed. They pedaled through the quiet tree-lined street, and anticipation dissipated Molly's exhaustion from another under-staffed, over-populated week.

The lingering strands of the past weekend's encounter with the whistling man had disconcertingly intruded into her professional life. Never had so many blue-eyed men come to the library Reference Desk. Seldom had she noticed people's laughter as often as during this week.

Could it be that in pursuing her professional life and living out the fine points and details of The Plan, that laughter had become a stranger to her? Maybe the guy had been right about a frozen sense of humor.

Nah, she enjoyed life. Her life was not only enjoyable, but enviable.

*   *   *

After coming home late from work, Molly was packing on Saturday evening when her cell phone rang from under the stack of ready-to-fold shorts. "Hello?"

"Sorry to be calling so late, Molly. Royce, here."

"Hi!"

"Are you in the middle of anything? I can call you back."

"Just packing. Monday's coming up quickly. Oh," she teased, "have I mentioned I'll be on vacation."

He snorted. "Yeah, a couple of times. Today. Actually, that vacation of yours is what I want to talk to you about. I know it's late tonight, and besides, I would rather talk in person. How about meeting me for lunch tomorrow? My treat."

"Royce Dawson, what is going on? You've never worried about calling late before. And picking up the tab for lunch? All very suspicious!" She let a grin seep into her voice. "Come on, spill it!"

"Mol, I've got a giant favor to ask you. It concerns your vacation. Are you interested in having a passenger on your trip?"

"Not particularly. I enjoy driving alone. And with all the boxes of books I'm bringing back, I won't have room on the return trip for even a goldfish. Oops, sorry, Royce. If the passenger were you, that's different. We could manage. But how can you get away from work on such short notice?"

"I can't; but there's a fellow I play tennis with at the Club who has to get back to Minneapolis and he needs a ride."

"Don't tell me. All planes between the coast and Minnesota are suddenly grounded," she taunted with mild sarcasm.

"Cute. Actually, Beej, for BJ, that's his name, got word from his doctor this week that he's a prime candidate for burn-out if he doesn't slow down. And the doc was pretty persuasive with the 'effective immediately' speech. I'm not surprised. Good grief, the guy is always flying off somewhere, so that's hardly a thrill for him. In fact, it's part of the problem; he must have a permanent case of jet lag. But now he's got to get back to Minneapolis in the next ten days. His doctor okayed the trip as long as he takes it easy; he specifically mentioned a slow, relaxing trip. So I just figured…"

"Slow down. I don't think that…" Molly interrupted, only to be cut off by the usually polite Royce.

"He's a great guy, and I just figured that if you would be willing to have him ride with you, it would accomplish two things."

She didn't say a word. The pair of shorts she was folding would have fit in her back pocket by the time she finished twisting them.

"One, Beej could have that relaxing trip, following his doctor's orders, *and* it would give him time to unwind so he's not pushed into an early retirement. And two, you would have someone along for the boring parts of the trip."

"Royce, there are trains. That's a restful way to travel. I've done the train-thing, myself. But frankly, the 'boring' parts, as you call them, of this trip are exactly what I've been looking forward to."

"He's a very intelligent conversationalist, Molly, and I convinced him that…"

"What? You already told him about me?" Molly squawked.

"Hey, nothing has been set in cement."

"You'd better believe it hasn't."

"I know this sounds like an imposition, but I've thought it through and once you meet him, I know you won't feel so strange about it."

"Just when am I supposed to meet him? I leave in two days! Or were you figuring I could make a snap decision when I see him standing on the curb with his thumb out?"

"Let's have lunch tomorrow, and I'll invite Beej to join us. You can look him over, and if you like what you see, fine. If not, then he can consider the trains, as you said. No pressure, either way."

"Knowing you, you've probably already invited this Beej-person, haven't you? What's he like, anyway?"

She had pushed too far. The normally easygoing Royce snapped, "He's a barracuda, Molly. I've lined you up with a woman-hater who smells like a barnyard, scratches his crotch in public, and picks his nose." Molly sat meekly by on her end of the conversation, unable to conjure up a mental picture of Royce in this mood. "What do you think he's like if I say you'll like him? Trust me, for Pete's sake. He's got a great sense of humor and a terrific personality."

If only he would have quit sooner; Molly's penitence slid away. "That is a deadly thing to say about anyone, 'great sense of humor and terrific personality.' What's really wrong with him?"

"Nothing! You know, you are enough to make me wish I would never have had the idea."

"Bingo."

Silence. Then, "You already said you would ride across the country with me."

"And I would. You're not some unknown entity."

"Exactly. You met me because Brynn knew me, and I turned out to be a pretty good friend, didn't I?" He took Molly's muttering as assent. "This is a similar situation. Beej is not an unknown. I know him, you know me, and therefore, you basically know him."

"Weak logic, Royce, coming from a sensible computer guy like yourself. Besides, when I first met you I didn't immediately make a 2,000 mile trip with you as a way to get acquainted."

"I repeat: lunch will be my treat."

Molly sighed. "You must be serious about this to dangle that bribe twice in one conversation."

"You bet. I figure you can meet each other and see what comes of it. Remember, he may not be interested in riding with you, either!"

"True, but there's more at stake for me. What is he, five feet tall and six feet wide? Does he smoke stinking cigars? Will he insist on telling 'knock, knock' jokes for the whole trip?"

"Lunch, woman."

"Okay! But if I don't like him, it is off." Molly rolled her eyes. "I cannot believe I am doing this. What's his name, again?"

"Beej Kendall. Or, if you feel formal, BJ. Relax! If it doesn't work out for the trip, you'll have met another nice guy like me. You could still be friends, even if you don't give him a ride. Most women seem to find him attractive. When's the last time you met a guy you couldn't forget?"

The answer popped into Molly's mind without warning. *Seven days ago, Buddy, but I know better than to mention that to you.*

She chose to ignore his teasing. "See you. The Club. You pay."

Chapter Four

Lavender did interesting things to her eyes, so Molly debated wearing her favorite blouse with white slacks. After all, this was lunch with a friend she never needed to impress, and a stressed-out, older gentleman she probably would never see again. It really made no difference if her eyes interested the two of them or not.

The sun was bright, the day was meant to enjoy; she hummed along with the last notes of a song on the radio as she pulled her car into one of the few empty spots in the Club's parking lot.

If she knew Royce, he would be at a table as close as possible to the same corner of the room where they usually sat. What even she called ruts, he considered stability. It did not take long to find his familiar head of straight black hair. He had his back to her, but as she got closer to his table, he rose. "I recognized your steps!" He pulled out a chair for her.

"Hi! Isn't it a gorgeous day?"

"It just got gorgeouser!" He bowed low.

"Spare me! Where's what's-his-name?"

Royce frowned sternly at her. "Beej Kendall. BJ. Try to remember, will you?" He shook his head sadly, "Memory is the first thing to go. And so sad to see in a professional woman."

Molly laughed outright. The discovery that they shared the same birthday had resulted in many gibes. Royce gloated; Molly was the elder. "My senility is only two hours more advanced than yours, fella! Royce, thanks for inviting me. Even if this BJ-person and I don't make the trip together, I am glad to spend some time with you. It's been too long since we saw each other."

"That's my line. You're the one who is always too busy. I'm the rebuffed, suffering male."

"You sure play the role convincingly! Even Brynn believes it from time to time! And who's calling who busy?"

"Can I get you anything, Miss?" A lanky teenaged waiter flicked the pen off his ear in preparation for taking an order.

Molly turned, "A cup of coffee while we wait for someone. Thanks."

"You can give me a refill, Bones." Royce tipped his cup.

The long, thin shadow had barely faded from their table before Molly hissed, "*Bones?* That's terrible, Royce! You'll give the guy a complex. He's at such a rough age as it is, and must be new here since I've never seen him before. Don't wreck his new job!"

"That's his nickname, honest! What else could you call a six-foot, four-inch skeleton with skin on?" They ducked their heads in an unsuccessful attempt to muffle their laugher.

"Hey, share the joke, will you?" A voice over their heads halted their merriment. As Molly raised her head in the direction of the sound, she choked. *Oh, good grief, no!* Her mouth dried up quicker than her lawn in midsummer; her pulse pounded wildly in her temples.

"Beej! Sit, my man! Let me introduce my good friend, Molly Winstead. Molly, meet BJ Kendall."

Deja vu. Her hand, unbidden, moved into position for a slow handshake. She looked into wintry gray-blue eyes.

Two voices in unison, each an octave apart, erupted, "You!"

He recovered first, "…are Molly Winstead!"

Those eyes! She swallowed hard, "Is it *Beej* or Jordan?"

"Bartholomew Jordan. Hence, the BJ and also Beej. And sometimes, Jordan."

Royce's voice startled them both. "Hey, I didn't know that. About the Jordan part." He might have been addressing a wall.

"Molly, so nice to meet you. And in such a normal place!" Jordan laughed.

He laughs. She bristled. Her stare and voice were cutting. "Thank you, I'm sure." Sarcasm had no effect at all; she should have remembered that and saved her breath.

Royce stared as BJ threw back his head and howled. "Feisty lady here, Royce. I am going to enjoy this lunch enormously!" He pulled out the chair across from Molly and slid into it.

"Good." Royce stretched the vowels out, releasing the syllable cautiously as he kept one eye on Molly who was visibly nearing her boiling point and the other on Beej, now whistling softly along with the piped-in music.

"What's the special here, today, besides our spit-shined guest?" asked Jordan as he unabashedly contemplated Molly across the top edge of his menu.

Royce reached over and flipped the menu right-side-up. "This would be easier to read if you turn it over."

A look flitted across Jordan's face and was gone almost instantly. "Who wants to spend time reading a stinkin' menu with a lovely vision in lavender near enough to touch?" He reached out and let his hand rest briefly on her arm.

Royce shook his head and released a crooked grin. "Since this is Sunday, the special is prime rib sandwiches, as it has been for probably the last ten years," he said pointedly.

"Sounds good to me," Molly heard herself almost whisper.

"Likewise," Jordan said.

"I'll make it three," Royce said. He caught Bone's attention with a wave, held up three fingers and pointed to the Specials board. "We'll see how long it takes him to figure out my signals and deliver."

Jordan tapped Molly's wrist. "No watch? Looks like I'll have to monitor Bones' time since Molly isn't wearing a watch." He dramatically removed his watch from his wrist and positioned it on the table.

She tensed as her stomach knotted up. "Most gracious of you to offer."

Royce said, "Where's your watch, Molly?"

"I forgot to wear it; I've been without it this week and got out of the habit of wearing it. I just got it fixed at the jewelers; the clasp had broken."

She felt like a babbling fool and tried to regain control. *Stop it, Molly! You're rambling on like late-night radio.*

Jordan nodded and praised, "Important to get that fixed. You could lose your watch anywhere if the clasp broke!"

She stiffened in her chair. *Another word, Buddy, and you're dead meat.* "That's so true, and there's never a gentlemen around to help if I were to lose it," she cooed with a pasted-on smile.

"Sometimes gentlemen are in disguise…just like ladies."

Molly licked her index finger and marked a chicken-scratch on an invisible chalkboard. "That's one for your team."

Royce sighed audibly and wiped the back of his hand across his forehead. "Uh, guys, am I missing something here? Why do I feel like I'm on a plastic air mattress in a shark tank? I wasn't sure what would happen when you two met, but even in my wildest dreams I never imagined a war zone where two strangers…Ah. The light dawns; the problem is that we're missing the 'two strangers,' right?"

Jordan tilted back slightly in his chair. "We're not quite strangers, not exactly friends." His eyebrows performed wildly.

"But you know each other? Where did you meet?" Royce turned accusing eyes on Molly. "If you and BJ know each other, then why all the playing dumb about who he is?"

"Believe me, Royce, I didn't know that the Jordan I had met was the *Beej* you had in mind to drive to Minnesota with me. And if I had…"

"And I had no idea that the Molly you've been raving about since we started playing tennis was the Minnesotan I had met…"

"Met where?" Royce demanded.

Molly spoke quickly, "We met in my neighborhood."

"That we did," Jordan said and slapped imaginary dirt off his hands.

"So here we all are. Two warriors and their sword carrier." Royce had a rode-hard-and-put-away-wet look to him. "What now, do we eat? Or do we push back the tables and duke it out, leaving old Bones with three Specials to consume and blood to wipe off the walls?" Royce asked.

Jordan said calmly, "I vote we eat. And talk about the trip with Miss Lovely-in-Lavender here."

If you think I would even drive out of the parking lot here with you, BJ or Jordan or whoever you are, think again! Molly's thoughts sizzled like meat on the grill in the Club kitchen.

Good breeding won out. Poor Royce, how could he have known? It wasn't as if she had to invite Jordan to ride with her. A week earlier she had chastised herself for not being friendlier to Jordan; now she was glad she hadn't been.

"Sorry, Royce; yes, let's eat." Despite her inner turmoil, Molly bit back an unexpected chuckle. *And Brynn thinks she's heard my best story!*

Royce was obviously relieved. "So, Molly, are you ready for your trip?" He turned to include BJ, "It's a great trip, Beej. You really see the country. I drove back with her two summers ago when I had a computer conference in St. Paul."

With the question of whether she would ever need to see this Bartholomew Jordan Kendall again settled once and for all, Molly turned on the charm. "I'm semi-packed. And fully ready for a vacation."

"I know what you mean," Jordan said. "Royce knows I need some time away when I let him win two out of three tennis games without demanding a rematch!"

Molly shifted uncomfortably in her chair. Royce *had* first suggested this whole fiasco because of the slow pace the trip could force on BJ. She eyed him now, guardedly looking for those signs of strain. "You hide it pretty well; if anything, I would have labeled you as a totally relaxed individual."

"Give me an afternoon of yard work, and I'm a new man. And nothing is more renewing than a good laugh."

Molly flashed a saccharine smile. "How fortunate for you."

Royce laughed nervously and said, "I hope this stress thing isn't catchy. If it is, I'm doomed for sure, sitting here with you two walking time bombs!"

Poor Royce. Shape up, Molly; don't take it out on him.

"Somehow, I don't realize from day to day how busy I've let myself get. And since I live alone, I need reminders to slow down." Molly smiled at Royce. "This guy is good for calling to insist on lunch when I think I don't have time, but really need a break."

"He calls me, too, and convinces me that beating him at tennis will only take minutes from my schedule. When it's all over, I've had my needed time off, although when he beats me it doesn't do much for my stress!" Jordan said.

"But my best idea, sending the two of you across the country together, is my last hope for my sanity! At least I'll know that two great minds have been preserved if you're heading off with no work in sight!"

"Are we guilty of raising your stress level, Royce?" Molly teased.

"Yeah, after I met you guys, my doctor started worrying about me!"

Jordan leaned across the table, squashing the menu that he still held in the process, and looked deep into Molly's eyes, "Molly, I think our course is clear; we simply must save this man's mind. Can we lay aside our petty differences for such a worthy cause?" He batted his eyelashes furiously. *Caramel fudge eyelashes.*

"It does seem so little to do for a dear person who gives of himself so willingly," Molly said, patting Royce on the arm.

"Bless you. My doctor thanks you, my mother thanks you, my cat thanks you…" All three laughed and finally the tension around the table relaxed a bit.

"How did you guys meet?" Jordan asked.

"We were introduced by a mutual friend, Brynn Hilton. Every summer she puts on the barbecue she calls the "Brynn's Annual Picnic for Everyone Who Knows Me Now." It's great fun. We met, whew, it must be five or six years ago now, right, Mol?"

She nodded, "At least. Brynn knows some crazy people, and she's not afraid to mix them up and watch what happens!"

"Amazing, Royce, that you would share this lovely lady with someone else."

Things jerked back into focus. The bantering had gone far enough. She, Molly Winstead, was dangerously close to skating across the thin ice of a long drive with the one person who seemed bent on embarrassing her. Disappointing Royce she could deal with; a trip across the country with a maniac she could not.

"Seriously, I'm really not interested in changing my travel plans at this late date. After all, I leave in the morning. And I really do plan to make it a leisurely trip." She scrutinized him shrewdly; he looked perfectly healthy to her; one more plane trip wouldn't push him over the edge. "BJ's schedule can't possibly be as flexible as mine," she added.

"Don't be too sure of that; time I've got lots of," Jordan said, sending those eyebrows off on an erratic journey again.

"So you said last weekend." *So much for congenial chitchat.*

Royce cleared his throat distinctly.

Jordan twisted his water glass on the table, leaving a wet swirl. "If, just say *if*, we drove to Minnesota together, what are your expectations of me? Am I to navigate by stars, or am I a tire changer, or would I be your rescuer if we'd find ourselves in dire straits?" Except for a tell-tale twitch around those unforgettable lips, the query sounded entirely innocent.

Royce broke in, his head nodding in pathetically visible relief, "Good question." His eyes shot such an obvious appeal for civility to Molly that she felt a twinge of guilt.

She licked her dry lips, "You'd be expected to share expenses and driving time. The return trip wouldn't need to be part of the deal. *If* we decide that you ride with me."

"Sounds fair enough. If, as you say, we agree."

"Three prime rib sandwiches," intoned Bones over their heads.

The next fifteen minutes held little dialogue. Each bite scratched its way down Molly's dry throat to her stomach, but she finished the whole sandwich mostly because eating replaced the need to talk. Royce and BJ bounced conversation back and forth as easily as the tennis balls they shared. Each word, every gesture etched a lasting impression on her memory. They were obviously friends.

Jordan frustrated and fascinated her; Royce smothered and soothed her. A trip to Minnesota with Royce would be restful; with Jordan, that word would never enter the description. She mentally positioned Brynn at the table in the empty chair. *What would Brynn say?* Molly quickly raised her napkin to hide a spontaneous smile. She could hear Brynn's ready answer: *2,000 miles with this man? All abooooard!"*

Jordan interrupted her reverie, "I'm surprised that you aren't interested in having me ride with you."

"Surprised?" Molly's eyes widened in undisguised mystification.

"You've given the impression of someone who courts adventure."

Royce's head nodded again, "Molly's fun, all right."

"Thank you, Royce, for that endorsement," Molly said stiffly. "Perhaps you were misled, Jordan. I really can't think of one good reason to even consider giving you a ride to Minnesota."

Jordan shrugged. "Some might consider it, oh, a humanitarian activity; rather like rescuing someone is distress. Perhaps you have an old favor to cancel that could be settled with a gracious deed." He dipped his sandwich in steak sauce and studied it with great interest.

Royce chimed in, "It really would be a Good Samaritan kind of thing to do, Molly."

"I think Molly is leery, Royce. Which is her right. After all, it *is* taking a chance. She could have a most enjoyable time; but then, again, I could totally ruin her trip."

Royce studied his fork for a moment. "Molly, when you were in college, didn't you ever advertise for a ride home?"

"Sure. Everyone did who didn't have a car. You know, on the big board in every dorm that was always filled with notes about needing rides in every direction."

"Same thing at my alma mater," said Royce. "Tell me, Molly, did you ever get a ride through your advertising?"

"I see where you're heading with this, Royce, and it is not the same. Yes, I did get rides with people I didn't always know. Which was probably foolish. Now I'm older, wiser, richer and free to travel differently."

"And with that freedom, you've lost something, haven't you? We all have. Don't you miss the adventure? But you're right. It is all part of the past. We're all wise adults now." Royce's faint smile pierced her heart.

As the two men scooped up their remaining French fries and those Molly offered them, she made her decision. She *could* trust Royce's judgment. And her life needed something beyond peaceful relationships; something to help her lighten up and enjoy life again.

Besides, what she had against Jordan was something she would rather not discuss with Royce, and he would ask, especially if she turned down his candidate for the trip. Her conscience twitched. *He is interesting, and you are trying to reform that dismal habit of turning off such men.*

No, her decision had nothing to do with pleasing Royce; it had a lot to do with the pull Bartholomew Jordan Kendall had begun to exert on her inner tide a week earlier. As if he had sensed her tumultuous thoughts, he turned his gray-blue eyes toward her and it was like a breaker beating against her already-sodden raft.

She took a long, slow swallow of water before speaking. "If you can be ready by seven tomorrow morning, we're on. But I warn you, you may be the first passenger *ever* on my summer trips who flies home from fifty miles down the road. With the slightest provocation, I'll head to the nearest airport."

Jordan drawled in deep seriousness, "Yes, Ma'am. I'll trust your sense of what's proper."

She glowered. He faked a cringe. Royce stared.

"Where do I pick you up?" Molly asked coolly.

Royce practically squawked, "Just like that? What'd I miss?"

"Jordan has your approval, doesn't he?"

"Yeees…"

"Then I respect your judgment. After all, aren't you the guy who said such a grand speech about how since I know you, and you know BJ, then I practically know him, too?"

"Right." Caution enveloped the single word.

Jordan watched them both curiously. He pulled a napkin from the holder on the table and reached into his pocket for a pen. "I'll give you my phone number in case you change your mind, and sketch a map to my house. Will you pick me up in the front, or in the alley?"

"Don't make me regret this decision so soon, okay?" Molly snapped.

Royce groaned and dropped his head into his hands. "I can see the headlines now: 'California car explodes in Mid-America; cause unknown'. What gives with you two, anyhow?"

Jordan waved the napkin like a white flag as he handed it across the table to Molly. "Truce! You have my word, Royce, that if we actually pull this trip off, I'll treat Molly with all due respect and like the gentleman I am."

"That's a relief. Molly? What about you?"

Molly grinned beatifically, "I'll be a lady to match his gentlemen."

"Fine with me, Minnesota, oops, Molly!"

Royce looked sick. "I could be arrested for unleashing a couple of wild beasts. I'm planning a ten-day hike in the Ventana Wilderness, but when you return, please invite me to lunch so I can see that I haven't been responsible for your horrendous destruction. I swear, my only goal is your preservation."

"You're on," Jordan agreed and Molly nodded slowly. "This trip is the craziest thing I've done in a long time; but Molly, here, lives on the edge of excitement, so I'll probably bore her to death."

Enough.

Molly pushed her chair back and set coffee sloshing in three cups. "Gentlemen, I won't keep you any longer. I'll talk with you tonight, Royce, and unless something changes," she said pointedly to The Adversary, "I'll see you in the morning. Seven sharp. Royce can give you my cell phone number if you have any questions."

Jordan saluted her solemnly.

Molly fled. The car was hot, but she rested her head against the steering wheel for a few minutes before she started the engine. *Brynn Hilton, you are not going to believe this.*

With her uneven mental state, she didn't trust herself to talk on her cell phone even sitting safely in the parking lot. She would probably put the car in gear mid-conversation and roll into a light pole. But once home, she leaned against the refrigerator's cool door, and cradling the kitchen phone's receiver against her shoulder, she told Brynn the latest development.

Predictably, Brynn howled. "Record the conversations you two have on this trip, and retire on the proceeds, Molly! I just wish I could have seen your face when you looked up and saw your alley whistler standing by the table."

Every so often Molly, too, would see the humor; equally often she would panic as she contemplated 2,000 miles of torment. "All I can say is Royce had better decide real soon if this guy is less than what he told me."

Brynn said, "So, what does the Hunk do for a living?"

Molly groaned, "I don't know. Something with jet lag. What ever possessed me to agree to this?" she wailed. "I do not believe I am all set to make a trip halfway across the country with a man I know so little about."

"Royce says he's okay?"

"Yeah."

"Then, don't worry. You'll have lots to talk about on the trip this way!" Brynn's laugh rippled and their call ended.

Molly paced. Each time she contemplated calling Jordan, she remembered that he certainly had been within his limits to tease her at lunch. Who wouldn't have joked after the crazy way they'd met? But, he had not told Royce about the alley experience, at least not in front of her; that showed some unprecedented and encouraging restraint.

Then she would think back to his endless gibes and his blatant enjoyment in watching her stew. He was a walking contradiction. This mix of emotional mood swings was exactly why she did not have time for men in her personal life. Life was convoluted enough without looking for additional complications.

But she made no phone calls to cancel their plans. Royce had called her to say that Beej had been "enchanted" with her.

Right.

Then it was time for bed. She flopped around in a tangled mess of covers unable to enter the quiet world of sleep. Eventually, she gave up the farce and headed out to finish packing the car. The luminous dial on the digital clock clicked 2:00 before she returned to bed and finally drifted off into a restless sleep.

Molly lunged to attack the radio alarm when the peppy announcer's voice slashed the early morning stillness. "All right, already. I'm up." She fell back against the pillows and cringed when her eyelids scraped across dry eyes. Staggering with sleepy drunkenness toward the shower, she forced herself to stand beneath a cold blast. Finally, she was awake. Awake and crabby.

All the way to Jordan's house Molly practiced changing their plans. "Something has come up." *Will he buy that? Not likely.* "I'm sick." *Possibly true, but he'll probably gallantly offer to drive the whole way.*

One last time she checked the well-creased napkin from the Club as she pulled over to the curb. "This is it, so live with it," she commanded herself sternly.

His was a sandy brick house in a respectable neighborhood; old-fashioned lamp poles lined the central boulevard. Several suitcases and an impressive set of golf clubs were waiting on the manicured lawn.

She tossed her head. *Figures; he goes on a business trip and he takes his golf clubs. Must be as serious about business as he is the rest of life. No briefcase, no siree, not for this goof-off.*

She snorted as she followed a cobblestone sidewalk to the house. The front door was ajar; she stuck her head in and called out, "Anybody home? Taxi's waiting…"

"Coming!"

She turned to look back at the peaceful morning street. The door closed behind her; the voice she had heard in the back of her mind for the last week breathed in her ear, "Want to check out my dumpster before we leave? It might have untold treasures in it!"

Cancel everything. Kill Royce.

"Will you give me just one chance to finish…"

He laughed as he took the steps ahead of her. "You'll have hundreds of miles for anything you have to say. Let's get my stuff loaded. Is there room for what's sitting on the curb?"

Molly clenched her fists and muttered a response as she followed him to the car; he did have a briefcase, a soft-as-a-baby's-behind leather number that bumped against his long-legged body as he walked. She opened the trunk and he effortlessly swung the two cases, a suit bag, and a hand-tooled leather golf bag from the curb to the trunk. As she closed the trunk lid, their eyes met. She dropped hers first with a weak smile.

If she had not known before, she knew now without a shadow of a doubt: This was going to be one long trip.

He got in on the passenger side and turned to look in the back seat. A small cooler, a thermos, a canteen, her purse, a box of maps, a paper-back book, a light cotton sweater. He gave it all an approving nod. To fill the silence she explained, "I get thirsty, so I brought lots to drink. The cooler is full of drinks and snacks."

"Good. I'm a thirsty person, too."

"Oh no, in my hurry I forgot…well, never mind. We can stop to get some disposable cups. Don't want you worrying about germs."

"Hey! Who's worrying?" He held the unfastened seat belt in his right hand and leaned across the gear shift. His lips touched hers with a lingering kiss that brought a rousing cheer from a towheaded child roller skating past the car.

Molly crushed the lamb's wool cover on the steering wheel in a sweaty grip. "What gives you the…"

He silenced her with a light finger on her lips. "Just wanted to settle the issue of germs for the rest of the trip." He snapped his seat belt into place.

Fire burned the inside of her eyelids. She swallowed hard, licked her lips and tasted him. She turned the key.

CHAPTER FIVE

The Kiss perched midair between their bucket seats, a jaunty unwanted third passenger in the car.

Molly shifted beneath the seat belt and tensed as beads of perspiration outlined her upper lip. She steeled herself against wiping them away, unwilling to refocus Jordan's attention to where his lips had burned an indelible impression. All the safe, time-worn beginnings for conversation that she had rehearsed last night in preparation for a long trip with a stranger floated out the open window.

Two feet away Jordan was settling in, maddeningly oblivious to her silent fidgeting. The droning of skates outside the car grew louder and then instantly faded into a distant buzz as the child whizzed by on her return trip. "Kiss her again!" the miserable little twerp called to them.

Molly jerked the quiet car away from the curb.

Incredible. Detestable. Uncalled for. Thoughts and emotions tumbled wildly beneath her silent reserve.

Within a few blocks she spotted a convenience store and shot through a break in traffic into the parking lot. Before Molly could open her door, Jordan was in action. "Wait here. I'll take care of it. We only need cups, right?"

Molly nodded and watched as he crossed the parking lot in confident strides; he looked as good in the light-weight warm-up suit as he had in work clothes ten days ago in her alley, or summer slacks yesterday at the Club. She frowned; she didn't want him looking good. She wanted him unappealing, unexciting, sexless.

Crabby would be good, too. She could deal with a cranky guy nearing retirement right about now. She would listen willingly to his good-old-days stories no matter how many time he would repeat himself. But not her. Oh no, she was stuck with Adonis.

Jordan held the store's door open for a leggy redhead in tight shorts who was leaving with a six-pack; her whole body said "Thanks" as she smiled in undisguised appreciation of Jordan's lanky form. Molly's hands tightened on the wheel until her nails pressed half-moons into her palms.

The girl sashayed toward her white convertible, tossed her purchase onto the front seat and arranged her body seductively, facing the store's entrance. The security bell beeped when the door swung shut behind Jordan; he headed straight for Molly, a plastic bag of disposable cups bouncing against his thighs.

With head tipped slightly, the girl's gaze followed his steps; then she slowly shrugged and a pout defined her face as he reached for the Volvo's door. For the first time she noticed Molly.

With rigid self-control Molly bit back a childish temptation to stick out her tongue at her rival, choosing instead to smile expansively at Jordan as she moved the car into the traffic heading to the freeway. She just knew the flirt saw it all and would huff about it for hours.

Jordan's responding smile was only for her. "All right, we are now prepared to keep germs at bay! It's too nice a day to think about little critters." Jordan adjusted the seat's incline, focused the air vents, and dropped his sunglasses from his hair over those unforgettable winter sky eyes.

Molly propped her elbow on the open window ledge and jabbed her left hand through her hair. *He certainly takes it all in stride: The Kiss, that floozy with the wandering eyes; and through it all, he keeps the jokes rolling, never letting a single chance to make a fool of me go unexploited.* Pinpricks of anger sharpened her voice, "Does that happen a lot?"

"Good weather?" he asked, his left eyebrow arched.

"No, getting a come-on like that girl gave you."

"Night and day. Day in, day out. Good thing I stole a 'Do not disturb' sign from a motel to hang on my front door or I would never have any privacy." At least he didn't act like he didn't know which girl she was talking about.

"Jordan," the name out, she paused. The sound of her voice saying his full name, rather than the initials or that ridiculous Beej-business, was strangely unsettling. "I don't know if you can understand this, but it is very difficult for me to make this trip with you mostly because of, because of the way we met."

"Hey, we met," his eyes were now unreadable behind the dark lenses, "and by some fluke, we're together. That's the way it is, despite what either of us may have originally chosen for a trip across the country. I, for one, plan to make the best of it."

His voice, without a tinge of laughter, was foreign to her ear. He glanced at his watch. "We're getting away pretty close to schedule. Do you need to fill up with gas before we leave town?"

"I took care of that already."

"Not afraid of smelly jobs, are you?" he smiled broadly at her.

"BJ." She pounded the steering wheel. "That's one of the things that will…"

"Two minutes ago I was Jordan; what gives?"

"I'm not sure who you are. I can't figure you out," Molly admitted as she slowed for a pickup darting into her lane.

And I'm not real sure I recognize me right now, either.

Jordan sighed dramatically and hefted himself off the seat enough to pull out a leather wallet shaped to the curves of his body. He dangled his driver's license in her range of vision. "See? That's me: Bartholomew Jordan Kendall." He jabbed at the picture and then tapped his chest. "Known as Jordan to avoid confusion with my father, the other Bart in the family." Molly's lips twitched. "Want me to give you the weight, height, and sex since you're driving and really shouldn't take your eyes off the road?"

I'm aware of all three, thanks. Irony tightened her jaw. "I wasn't exactly referring to items of public record. I meant I can't figure you out. Royce hasn't told me anything more about you than that you play tennis together. Not that we spend lots of time talking about his buddies…"

"And I could say the same. We're usually too busy trying to hit the tennis ball to have many in-depth conversations."

"And here we are." Her tight smile hurt all the way back to her ears.

"Royce is probably laughing his head off that he sent the two of us out like this, especially after the sideshow we put on for him at the Club!" Jordan said. The smile they finally shared weighed the same on each face. Molly relaxed.

"I am in desperate need of some coffee. I don't think my coffee maker works before sunrise," Jordan said. He ripped open the bag of cups, reached into the back seat for the thermos, poured, and handed her the first steaming cup. They toasted each other in a silent salute.

The Kiss moved, at last, to the back seat.

Her voice sounded almost normal to her own ears as she said, "You probably were pretty busy this morning, packing on such short notice. Did you eat breakfast?" He waggled his hand in midair in the timeless vague gesture. "I figured as much. Grab a doughnut to eat with this coffee," Molly invited. "On top, inside the cooler."

As Jordan shifted to reach behind his seat, his torso filled the space between them. Unconsciously, Molly drew a deep breath, inhaling his musky maleness. So close up, it was obvious from the moist curls brushing his neck that he had stepped out of the shower just minutes before she had arrived. Jordan in the shower was a image she didn't want to dwell on right now. She hurriedly took a sip of coffee, scalding her tongue in the process.

No sir, I don't need to see a driver's license to verify your sex!

"If you have jelly-filled doughnuts in here, we are best friends!"

"Royce will be relieved. Tell me, how do you feel about ones with custard in the middle?"

"Oh, woman, what you do to me!"

Molly grinned and teased, "What I will do to you is not pretty, if you don't divide them evenly. One jelly each, one custard each."

"Picky, picky! What would you have done if I hadn't liked custard, or even doughnuts, huh?"

She shrugged. "All the more for me."

Jordan devoured his in several bites and then said, licking his fingers as he spoke, "I've got to tell you…"

Her eyes followed his tongue.

"…that it's a relief…"

Her tongue crept out in unconscious mimicry.

"…that you're not one of those…"

She had to pull her eyes away. Or call 911 from her cell phone for roadside respiratory help.

"…perpetual dieters."

"Hey, I'm on vacation. To be honest, if I ate during the rest of the year like I do on these summer trips, I would be one sorry case. I've got a grandmother who acts like edible food is nonexistent beyond the borders of her kitchen!"

The countryside changed from city to rural. "Speaking of food, we need to talk about meal stops, and driving schedules, and meal stops, and other details, like our financial arrangements, and did I mention meals?"

"Not hungry by any chance, are you?" Molly teased.

"I'm always hungry when I travel. Want to trade off driving every two hours or so?"

"Oh, I see right through that plan," Molly said, wagging her finger at her passenger. "Every time we stop to change drivers, we'll just happen to be near food!" Molly reached across and punched his arm playfully before she opened the glove compartment and pointed at a map.

"Grab that and listen to this plan: I drive to the first knuckle," she wiggled the little finger on her right hand in the air as a measurement, "and then we'll change off and you can do the same."

Jordan flipped the map open on his lap. He smoothed out the creases and reached for her hand, opening her fingers to rest on his palm as he shaped her finger along the curving line she had highlighted in green on the map for their route. "Uh, how are you at water navigation? It looks like one of your stretches could include a good-sized lake." Molly laughed and tried to draw her hand away; he pulled it back. "Okay, we'll rethink the route. Some people have no sense of adventure!"

"I do not believe you would accuse me of that!"

Actually, I really can't believe that I am staying on the road with you holding my hand! She felt as if she could laugh and never stop. *Chilly Minnesotans, indeed.*

Jordan stared at her in amazement. "And I do *not* believe what I just heard."

"What?" She frantically hoped her last thoughts had not been vocalized.

"You actually brought up the dumpster."

Molly bit her lip. "No, I did not."

"Did so!"

"Well, only indirectly."

"That's good enough for me! I have been waiting for a chance to interview you about that event in our short history. Ms. Winstead." His hand formed a microphone that he held inches from her mouth.

"Ms. Winstead, may I call you Molly?" A stray doughnut crumb on the wrong way down his throat sent his voice into an even lower range. They laughed together easily; any sputtered attempt at speech for the next minute only made them laugh harder.

Molly recovered first and lowered her voice to imitate his seductive tones. "Yes, you may," she managed before her voice cracked.

"No, no, you really need to be choking to achieve the right effect. Here…" He reached across, broke off a piece of her doughnut and fed it to her.

A vision of a groom, a bride, and wedding cake flashed before her eyes. "I'm driving! Don't mess with the driver, Mr. Kendall!"

"Jordan." Intimacy painted a faint circle around them.

"I thought you had some questions."

He tossed the imaginary microphone at her. "You hold this. My arm's tired. Right you are: Sweet Molly, what were you really doing in the dumpster a week ago Saturday?"

"Looking for my watch."

Sweet Molly.

"That's the truth, the whole truth?"

Sweet Molly?

"…and nuthin' but the truth."

Sweet Molly! Her heart throbbed erratically in her throat.

"At least you're sticking to your story! Ever since I lifted the lid and saw you in there, I've wondered why you put up such a fight. Me, if I were stuck in that mess, I would welcome a helping hand. What gives?"

So! He's been thinking about that afternoon, too. "I didn't want to meet anyone…Being caught in such an embarrassing situation is totally out of keeping with who I am."

"You do realize that you never would have made it out alone, or with your jeans still intact! The ground was too far down for you to reach that step stool from the inside." He chuckled and added, "Assuming you could have gotten out, even radical California has laws about indecent exposure!"

Now is your chance, Molly; don't fly off the handle. "Guess I didn't have to cross that bridge, or dumpster rim, thanks to you. And that's something I want to say: thanks. I did appreciate your help; I'm sorry I was such a brat."

"Shucks, Ma'am, you're welcome. My scout troop leader would be proud of me."

"I've got a question, too. What were you doing in my alley?"

"Helping a friend. You may not have noticed that you gained new neighbors in the place with the low brick wall across the alley. Friends of mine; actually an old girl friend and her husband."

Molly whistled. "That scout leader should be proud! None of my old flames help me with yard work!" She offered a lopsided grin. "Guess I haven't met my new neighbors yet."

"Want me to find out what time of day they take out their garbage?"

"Thanks, but I think I'll try the more conventional way of inviting them over for a barbecue!" The miles slipped by as Molly and Jordan traveled from one topic to another.

"Hey, I don't mean to interrupt this conversation, but pull over when you get a chance. This part of the state is too gorgeous to just drive through. Let's stretch our legs and be tourists for a while in the middle of this picture-postcard scenery."

In answer, Molly signaled and pulled out of traffic. Jordan reached across to open Molly's door and said, "Scouts always open doors, regardless of what may be politically correct these days. I doubt if I could make it around the car fast enough to do it conventionally."

Molly stared at his muscular back as he stretched beside the car. She swung her feet out onto the pavement that had already absorbed a surprising amount of the morning sun's heat. They walked along a path started by other travelers also drawn by the vast beauty spreading across the foothills like a painting on an easel.

Jordan detoured off the path toward an oleander bush in full bloom. He broke off a lush pink flower and turned to Molly. "Now I know why they plant these bushes along the roads in California. For moments like this." She actually trembled inside as he gently undid the clip in her hair, securing the flower over her ear with one click.

"Thanks," she said softly. Jordan matched his stride to hers as they walked again.

"Sorry to say, but if we continue to take such long breaks, we may never reach Minnesota."

Molly stared at her watch. "Good grief, you're right! I lost track of time."

"Want me to drive for a stretch?" he asked when they reached the car.

"Sure." She dropped the keys into his out-stretched hand. He ushered her into the car, and then moved a few things from the floor behind the driver up to the seat.

Seeing a man behind the wheel of her car took some getting used to. He moved the seat back to accommodate his longer legs, tipped the mirrors slightly, and gave attention to driving for the next few minutes. "I haven't driven a Volvo since high school days, and then it was an ancient cast-off when someone's mother got a new one. I like the way yours handles. How old is it?"

"I've had it for seven years."

He laughed.

"What?" she asked, instantly on the defensive.

"Answered just like a woman! Any guy would say, 'It's an '93' or 'This baby's a '79, you know'."

"Well, I'm a woman."

"Yes, you are," Jordan said evenly. He flicked on the turn signal and passed a car that was moving ridiculously slow.

Molly asked about his car, and leaned back to listen to the detailed description of his favorite, a Mercedes, "A '69. My dad bought it new and passed it on to me."

His hands punctuated his words, and his eyes were bright with life as he spoke. "And then there's my truck. Remember, the one in the alley. I use it a lot around town, since I never know when I'll be doing something that would abuse the old Benz." Every line of his body indicated a life of discipline despite his playboy tan. With a flicker of surprise, she realized she liked what she saw.

Suddenly the car was quiet, and she met his gaze as it rose from where the seat belt molded the curves of her breasts beneath her blouse. Her breathing faltered under the summer fabric as he reached to touch the flower in her hair. "Molly, I don't mean to annoy you, but I've got to tell you—you're equally beautiful in coffee grounds or pink freeway bush flowers." His hand dropped to her arm.

"Thanks, I think!" She tried for a light-hearted tone and failed miserably. The tires hummed on the pavement. These emotional swings and surges left her numb. Molly carefully eased back from his touch and rolled the window down a few inches. The cross-draft from his open window created a gentle breeze against her cheeks. "The mountains are beautiful today," she managed eventually.

"They sure are. You must have a terrific view from your house."

"That was the selling feature when I bought the place. If I can't live in Yosemite, give me a view of mountains, anyway!"

"Let's try to have dinner tonight some place with a view of this gorgeous scenery. We'll be leaving it behind soon enough."

Molly nodded, "I usually stop by Mono Lake. Whether I leave home early, like we did, or later, it's become a tradition to eat there. It's a perfect place to end the first day of the trip."

"Sounds good. You mentioned Yosemite; how often do you get up there?"

"At least once a month, year-round. Sometimes for a weekend, sometimes for a day trip."

Laugh lines raced across Jordan's face as he said, "I just thought of something incredible. Do you realize that we've been driving for several hours and still haven't talked about our jobs? I'm sure Royce told me what you do, but I'm drawing a blank."

"I'm a librarian at the Public Library. I work at the main branch. Usually at the Reference Desk."

Jordan's face changed subtly into neutral as he pressed the accelerator and moved forward in traffic. He looked straight ahead and said without emotion, "Very interesting."

"How 'bout you?"

"When I'm home, I work at the Country Club."

"Oh?"

"I play in tournaments, and when I'm not on the road, I teach golf lessons and generally spend lots of time chasing the little white ball."

"And getting lots of exercise."

"Yup. This year I drew the short straw and ended up spending six weeks between tournaments giving lessons to a bunch of Club members' junior high kids."

"Agony!" Molly said with a groan. "I'll vouch for that based on my contacts with the same kids, I would bet, at the library. You deserve a major reward for that!"

"Somedays I think I have one coming. So, how long have you worked at the library?"

"Almost four years."

"Just long enough to get a vacation schedule that allows you to take trips to Yosemite, or Minnesota, whenever you want to."

"Edit that to 'when I can afford it' and you are right on target. Hey, I don't know much about sports, but you must be a pretty good golfer to get hired at the Country Club. What's your secret, or are you just flat-out terrific?"

"I started there as a caddie when I was just a kid. A person can learn a lot from the pros who come through. I'm sure it didn't hurt at all that my dad's name is on the Club Founder's plaque, so folks were a little more receptive to having a kid hang around and ask dumb questions. And I just kept hanging around until I grew up. And loving golf like I do, I guess somewhere along the line I learned a few things about it. Why are you smiling?"

"When you said the word 'caddie,' it reminded me of Scrabble. At our house, whenever there is a possibility of spelling the word, Dad always insists that it be 'caddie' and he quotes righteously from the dictionary: 'Caddie,' also spelled caddy' in what we call his Noah Webster voice. So you're my big chance to prove it, one way or the other. How do golfers spell it, y or ie?"

Jordan rolled down his window and pulled at his shirt as if suddenly choked by it. He took a deep breath before answering, "Never made any difference to me. I was too busy being one to worry about spelling it."

"You've got a point there. The few times I've tried golfing have been miserable failures. All I know is that the hole is either too far away, or it shrinks when it sees me coming."

His familiar laugh wrinkles crept back into place. "Sounds like you need a good teacher."

"Hmm, I wonder where I could find one." Molly craned her neck to look around the car. He grinned in appreciation of her theatrics.

"I'll be happy to check around the Club for you. Better yet, maybe we'll have to find a good golf course along the way and start those lessons soon."

"Time to change subjects! If you knew how embarrassed you would be to have me beside you on a golf course, you would cancel that idea. Tell me about your job. You said you play in tournaments?"

"Yeah. They can be exciting, and exhausting. In professional golf, there are ups and downs like in any job. Basically, I really like my life. No major complaints."

"Professional golf? Like the tournaments on television? Those Tiger Woods events?" Molly asked incredulously.

Jordan grinned guardedly. "Yeah."

Molly whistled softly. "So, if I ever watched that stuff, I would have seen you?"

"Possibly."

"If I had known I was going to have a celebrity riding with me, I would have hung out around 796-point-3, or thereabouts, in the library stacks before I left work."

"Huh?"

"That's the Dewey Decimal classification number for golf."

Jordan nodded vaguely. "Well, if I would known I was going to be riding with a librarian, I guess I would have..." his voice trailed off.

"Dusted off your library card, huh?" Molly teased.

Jordan looked at her quizzically and then smiled thinly as he mumbled, "You bet."

There was something in his voice—or maybe a sudden lack of something—that made Molly steal a side-glance at him and asked, "Would you mind if we pulled over at that rest stop," she pointed at a sign they were just passing, "just for a few minutes."

"Sounds fine to me," in replied in a tone that indicated it would have been equally fine with him to leave her there.

The remaining mile was a quiet one in the car and Molly spent it reviewing every word she could remember between them that could have pushed the day into such a tail-spin. She left the car without a word and took twice as long at every detail in the stop, whether washing her hands, combing her hair, or checking out the displays at the shelter.

Jordan had disappeared instantly. Just when she figured he was a lost cause, she saw him talking to a truck-driver; at last, they shook hands and parted.

She watched quietly as he sauntered a few yards, leaned against a tree, punched buttons on his cell phone, and then spent at least three minutes talking to someone who brought several smiles to his face.

"Probably calling a woman who knows better than to expect him to carry on a conversation," she said and wished she could kick something. Since the only thing close enough was her own car, she settled for thinking dark thoughts. It was a veritable thunderstorm in her mind as she folded herself back into the dent-free car.

CHAPTER SIX

A still-smiling Jordan ambled back to the car and got in. "Ready to roll again?"

Stumped, cranky, and curious—but more interested in letting it go than pursuing it further—Molly nodded and they drove off down the road. *Live on the edge—either he will clam up again, or life will go on. Take a gamble—you could win. But I sure wish I knew who he called!* "So, tell me more about the life of a pro golfer."

Whatever had put Jordan in such a funk was history and he was now willing to talk. "Lots of sun, even more sunscreen; a strange schedule, an even stranger social life. Seriously, I've had unbeatable opportunities rub shoulders with some 'Great Names' in the sport, to travel, and make a good living in the process."

"Sounds terrific to me."

"It is good. But, as with everyone's life, there's a flip side. One bad part is that there's really never a good time to take a vacation, what with committing myself to the Club when I'm not traveling. I took time out for a week-long training session at the beginning of the summer, but otherwise it has been business as usual every day for all too long."

Which is one of Royce's strongest points for Jordan being in this car. Molly shifted guiltily when she thought of how she almost had left the Valley alone. "What seminar was that?"

"A beginner's video photography class."

"We had a poster about that one on the library bulletin board. We were bombarded with questions on photography, especially the video angle and had to rush-order a bunch of new books. You'll have to come in and see them. Do you have a video camera?" Jordan drove and Molly kept the coffee cups filled as they talked. The animation in Jordan's face when he talked fascinated Molly. *You know, maybe I will look into golf lessons when I get home!*

Jordan finally arched in a full-body stretch. "If the clock on your dashboard is right, we should start looking for a place to eat lunch. And after all this coffee, I have a strong interest in locating another special place, too!"

Molly smiled. "That goes double!" He switched lanes and within minutes Molly was reading road signs aloud. "'Grandma's Cooking. Homestyle biscuits.'"

"Look no more; that's the one. How 'bout we fill up the gas tank first, use their facilities, and then we can saunter into Grandma's and give our full attention to food?"

"Hit the blinker. You've sold me."

Jordan offered to fill the tank and Molly insisted he leave the bugs for her to clean off the windshield. That settled, she headed for the familiarly marked door. She raised her eyebrows in surprise as she saw the flushed reflection in the rest room mirror. Ducking, she splashed cool water on her face.

Outside again, she turned the corner and saw that Jordan had locked up the car, and was inside just paying the attendant. His glance at her took in everything from her sandals to the flower, put back in obviously recombed hair. He smiled as she unlocked the car for them.

They pulled up in front of the only cafe they would have found in the small town, even if they hadn't seen the billboard. "Not much of a crowd; wonder if we'll regret this," Jordan murmured as he opened the screen door for her.

Grandma's Cooking was a one-man show. Literally. No Grandma in sight, but it was possibly Grandpa who puffed around from behind the counter to lean on their table. "Special is steak and gravy. Want two of 'em?"

Molly's jaw dropped open, "Uh, that's more what I would eat for dinner."

"We're not open for supper. Just breakfast and lunch. Which do you want?"

"Lunch," Jordan said, studiously avoiding Molly's eyes.

"Lunch is steak and gravy."

Molly marshaled all her self control to ask, "What kind of sandwiches do you have?"

"Sandwiches is Wednesdays, not Mondays."

Jordan cleared his throat pointedly and pressed his foot on Molly's instep. "Two specials, please."

Grandpa's nod indicated the wisdom of this decision as he left them. Molly lodged her fist against her lips. They were alone in the cafe with Grandpa. It would not do to give in to the surge of laughter that threatened to break across the table.

Both customers gave diligent attention to watching Grandpa fill two plates with steaming food. He selected steaks from the covered pan on the back of a huge black stove and added extras in a storm of activity that belied his apparent age. Abruptly, it all stopped.

As he shuffled across the floor to their table, both Molly and Jordan rose to help with the heavy load. He halted in dismay, "Ain't you gonna stay and eat?"

"I was just going to help you," they said in unison.

"Ain't no need to help. Sit."

Sheepishly, they obeyed, staring as he placed before them a feast more appropriate for loggers after a hard day than for two people who had been riding for hours and would continue with more of the same for the remainder of the day.

Thick steaks, rich mushroom gravy, pure white whipped potatoes, a mound of buttered garden-fresh beets, and a biscuit that needed no sign on the side of the road to guarantee that it was homemade. Butter and honey and strawberry jam brimmed over little saucers he placed between them.

"Wow. This is one terrific meal!" Jordan said.

Molly nodded incredulously at the man hugging the now-empty tray to his chest. "There's more, if you want it." Only when they had picked up their forks did he move away from the table.

"Jordan, I can't eat all this food!" Molly whispered.

"I'm thinking we'll never get excused from the table unless we do!" Jordan shot back with a grin. "Don't you want a gold star on your clean-plate chart?"

Grandpa poured himself a cup of coffee and sat at the counter with a newspaper. The rustle of its pages and the tinkle of the silverware against the dishes were pleasant accompaniment to their meal.

Without warning, Grandpa dropped his paper and stared over the top at their table. Molly shifted beneath his scrutiny until she realized that Jordan was the sole focus of his attention. "Young fella, your name wouldn't happen to be BJ Kendall, would it?"

"Yes, sir. That's me."

"How does he know that?" whispered Molly in amazement.

Before Jordan could respond, Grandpa rattled on, "Says here beneath this picture," he jabbed the newspaper, "you're playing in the tournament in Minnesota."

"That's where I'm headed. You a golfer?"

"Used to hit a few balls. Arthritis. Now I only follow it in the papers and on TV. Saw you play in Florida last year. And then Georgia. Son, that was golf at its finest."

"Thank you, sir."

Grandpa, having said his piece on golf, resumed reading, and left his guests to finish their meal. Molly gave up first. She stared, astonished, as Jordan continued to work at winning his gold star. "Do you have a hollow leg, or merely a tapeworm?"

He licked his lips and said, "Neither, but an extensive diet of airline food balanced against my miserable cooking sure makes this go down

easy! Don't tell my mother, but I have never tasted garlic mashed potatoes to beat these."

"I had been meaning to ask you why you fly so much, but he," she
nodded her head in the direction of the counter, "answered that one for
me. I presume it's the tournaments that keep you on airline food?"

"Yeah," his shrug was nonchalant, "I play all over the place."

"And this time it's in Minneapolis?"

"Yup. It a charity event. Kids' Wishes Anonymous." Jordan chased the
last drops of gravy with his spoon.

Molly wished she had ten minutes to head for the library reference
shelves she knew so well and read up on this mysterious man and his
career. She could visualize the very books she would consult, and her
fingers itched to open their covers. Instead, her mind filed away
newly gleaned details of Jordan's face, physique, and personality for
future reference.

Grandpa shifted on his stool. "Ready for pie? Apple or peach." His
only answer was a united groan as Molly and Jordan leaned back in
their chairs signaling an end to the meal.

"Sir, that was an awesome meal," Jordan said. "If I had room, you'd have
to cut pieces of both pies for me. Tell Grandma she is a dynamite cook."

"There ain't no Grandma. Just me."

"But the sign...?" Molly protested.

He shrugged. "Seemed like a good name."

They grinned and left a big tip.

Molly slid into the driver's seat and blew air out of pursed lips. "I am
one full puppy."

Jordan groaned. "I know. Don't feel that you have to stop for dinner
tonight on my account. I'll admire the view as we drive through. My
next meal is the last thing from my mind right now."

"You sure impressed that man, Jordan."

"Well, he made a pretty good impression on me, too. Wish he could
cook for some tournaments. My buddies would not believe the spread

he puts on the table. He could retire just on the proceeds if he bottled that gravy."

They had driven along making companionable small talk for almost half an hour when Jordan said, "Say, I was just thinking, have you made motel reservations for tonight, or were you just going to drive until you got tired?"

Reservations! "Yes, I made them over two months ago." Her heart beat with a wild staccato.

"Fine." His head jerked toward her. "Ah, the same thing just dawned on both of us, didn't it? They were reservations for one, am I right?"

"Right." She tossed her cell phone into his lap and said, "What kind of reception is it getting here?"

"Not great."

"That figures. Oh, well, I can use my phone card." she glanced frantically in the rear view mirror and signaled a turn off the highway. She fumbled for her purse on the seat behind her and grabbed a small notebook, "At the next service station, I'll call, no," she tossed the notebook in his lap, "you call, so you can make your own choices and give him your credit card number. Check under Reno for where I have my reservation."

Jordan thumbed quickly through the book and closed it. "Don't worry, I'll make it perfectly clear we want separate rooms. All very proper." The laugh wrinkles around his eyes tightened and his cheek twitched. He drummed his fingers on the dashboard.

"There's a phone booth," she said and heaved a sigh of relief.

"Pull up so it's on your side and you read me the number; that will be easier. I don't want to drop your address book. It looks like all those loose papers are pretty important." He handed the book back to her as she braked in front of the booth.

Jordan waved aside her proffered phone card, pulled out his own wallet. Within seconds of her calling out the numbers for the motel, he gave her a thumbs-up signal just as traffic noise blocked out his first words. He pulled the door shut; she watched his lips move in soundless conversation.

Molly chewed her bottom lip as she waited. *What a doof you are, Mol. How did you forget a major thing like sleeping arrangements? It's all Royce's fault; until he came up with this crazy plan, my plans were fine.*

"Mission accomplished. No sweat. It's all taken care of. Let's roll."

She released pent-up air as quietly as possible. "We'll call ahead tonight to fix up the rest of the trip. I'm sorry that I didn't…well, I'm so used to having the reservations made way ahead of time that I didn't give it another thought. Obviously, I needed to."

Something about the open stretches of highway helped conversation flow. Jordan was surprised to learn she hadn't grown up in the Valley. "You really aren't a Californian."

"Nope, not this kid. I was born and raised in Minnesota. Mom and Dad live in Duluth, and I've got a sister, Mara, in Rochester."

"So how did you end up leaving the state where I'm told the mos-quito is the official state bird?"

"You've been there before! I should be insulted, but you're pretty close to the truth. To answer your question, Dad took a sabbatical one year in the Valley. He's a college professor. When we lived in California, I was at the very impressionable age of ten and fell in love with the place. Especially after I realized that I could pick my own fruit. I swore I would live there someday, and here I am."

"I've never lived any place but the Valley. Well, I take that back; if you collected all the months I've spent on the road into one count, I've had a few years away over the past 34, but it's the only place I've every called home."

Hmmm. 34. Just seven years difference in ages. She snapped back to attention. "No wonder they let you wear that shirt!"

"This shirt?" he stared at his chest and then met her smiling eyes as he remembered. "Oh, my *Welcome to California* shirt!"

"Yeah, but don't slide over the rest of the message: *Now Go Home*! That's brutal, Jordan!"

Their laughter hung in the air. "Don't take it personally!" Suddenly, he slapped his forehead. "Oh, no, is that why you're going back to Minnesota?"

"You better believe it! I can take a hint."

Jordan reached over and enclosed her hand in his. "I feel just terrible about this. What can I do to change your mind?" He pulled her hand against his chest in a mock-earnest entreaty.

Molly shook her head and said, "Too late. My bags are packed." Their playfulness continued throughout the afternoon.

After they stopped for gas, the day gradually gave way to evening as they drove. The lights of Reno brightened the sky.

"Tired, Molly?" His voice was soft and caring.

"Yeah, I didn't sleep much last night. Too busy packing."

Liar!

"I know what you mean. Does this motel have a swimming pool? A couple of laps would be the best way to relax that I can imagine."

"It sounds wonderful. I'm still full from Grandpa's so-called lunch! To answer your question, their pool is great."

"Let's get checked in, have a swim, and then we can see if we're hungry."

"You're on." She pulled up next to the motel office. They stood side-by-side at the desk; the clerk squinted at them beneath bright lights. "Yes?"

Jordan spoke. "We have reservations. Molly Winstead. Jordan Kendall."

"Oh, yes. You're the one who called. Two singles, wasn't it?"

"That's right," they chorused.

"Sign these, please." The man slid forms across the desk and slapped two keys down on the counter. "I've given you Rooms 120 and 220, both around the corner, one downstairs, one upstairs. Nothing closer together, sorry. We're pretty full tonight."

"No problem," Jordan said. He offered to move the car closer to their rooms, and Molly walked the short distance, glad to stretch her legs.

"What do you need out of the car for tonight?" Jordan called out softly as he dropped one of his cases on the ground.

"Just the smallest one."

Jordan lifted it out and held it in place with his foot when she bent to pick it up. "Let me carry it to your room for you, Miss."

"You just want a tip! I know your type."

"Hey, just for that remark, I get first pick on the rooms. I choose the upstairs one. Last one to the pool buys breakfast!" He picked up both suitcases and ran, looking like an old-time movie jammed on the wrong speed. He dropped her bag outside her door without losing his gait; she collapsed against the door frame, weak with muffled laughter that had erupted from an untapped source, while he took the stairs two at a time.

At the top of the landing he leaned across the railing and called down in a stage whisper, "Be warned, Minnesota, I eat a big breakfast!"

Jordan was floating on his back beneath an early moon when Molly opened the gate and walked to the edge of the pool. "I believe I'll have steak, hashbrowns, eggs, bacon, pancakes, and a gallon of ice cold orange juice..." he gloated.

She dove in and came up under him, catching him off guard. Their tussle ended with Jordan trapping Molly briefly against his rock-hard, athletic body as he looked into her sparkling wet face. She kicked against the softness of the water and the power of the man with beads of water glistening on his eyelashes who held her his prisoner.

"The desk clerk thinks we're married and had a spat on the way here," he said with a chuckle.

She stopped struggling and stared at him in genuine horror, "He thinks *what*? How did you come up with that fable?"

"I heard him talking to his replacement when I went in to ask about getting pool towels. To buy a little more eavesdropping time, I bought soft drinks from the machine in the Office." He nodded toward a low table between two chaise lounge chairs where Molly could see two cans and a heap of towels.

"Did you set him straight?"

"And let him know I had been snooping? No way!"

"But we have different last names."

"So? You look like a liberated woman!" Molly dove under water and circled the pool until she split the surface, gasping for air. Jordan was intent on laps and she joined him. Their splashes echoed in rhythm around the fenced-in pool.

After almost twenty minutes dedicated to intense swimming, they climbed the ladder and padded across the still-warm tiles. Jordan spread one of the towels and stretched out on his back, staring up at the stars just emerging from their cloudy haven.

Molly bent at the waist to wring the water out of her hair. Not a word had been spoken since Jordan's announcement until she handed him a slippery can, "Thanks."

She nodded and spread her towel beside him. "You're welcome; thanks for thinking of getting them. I owe you one."

They talked softly, conscious that their voices could carry to nearby rooms, but partly because they were caught in the web of the evening. Their wet suits drying in the evening air were a natural air conditioning; Molly shivered. "You okay, Minnesota?"

"I'm fine. I had better get to bed soon, though, before I fade away on you."

He helped her to her feet, and they walked beneath the moon's shadows to Molly's room. As she put the key in the lock, his warm hand on her bare back turned her around to face him. "Sleep well, Ms. Winstead. See you for breakfast in the coffee shop?"

Molly nodded, more aware of his arms than his question. "How does 8 o'clock sound?"

"Awful, but you're on." He cupped her face in his hands like leaves around a flower and drew the honey from her soul with a lingering kiss. "Pool germs. Dreadful things," he said softly as the shadows swallowed all but his footsteps.

Molly closed the door slowly behind her and leaned limply against it for several moments before turning on the light. One simple kiss began her day, another ended her day; both wrecked havoc on her heartbeat, her will-power, and those unpredictable feminine instincts that seemed to have taken on a vitality of their own lately. For the first time, age thirty seemed an eternity away in her carefully detailed life.

She went through the mechanical motions of getting ready for bed. Such romantic encounters wrecked havoc with The Plan. *From now on, once this dreadful trip is over, Molly, you will stay far away from men who insist on kissing; they are far too dangerous.*

She had been in bed, with fingers laced behind her head, for several hours before the footsteps in Room 220 overhead finally stopped circling. Fringes of dawn patterned the drapes when Sleep finally made two captives.

CHAPTER SEVEN

The moonlight swim, a comfortable bed after a long day of traveling, and distant night-muffled noises had all failed; Molly had not slept well. The first official rays of morning sun teased night from the motel room as she snuggled deeper into the covers. Sleep stubbornly refused to return.

Molly moaned, threw back the blanket and reached for her watch. Her jaw-cracking yawn echoed in the room; she squinted to check the time; 6:30 the clock on the night stand informed her. *Some vacation.* It was small comfort that her paying passenger had probably not slept any better, if his nocturnal pacings were any indication. She glared at the ceiling where all was now calm.

Coffee. This was motivation enough to spur her into activity. Thirty minutes later the creaking coffee shop door bugled her arrival. Two truck drivers hunched over the counter, coffee cups suspended mid-air, as they unabashedly stared at Molly.

The morning paper hid one lone body in a booth along the wall. As the door inched shut behind her, an unseen bell clanged harshly. More heads turned her way and the paper lowered to disclose Jordan in the booth. "Over here, Minnesota! Good morning!"

Interested eyes followed her long legs as she headed toward the only familiar face. But she forgot everyone else as she slid along the cool seat across from Jordan and caught his admiring glance as he appraised her, head to foot. "This is your big breakfast?" she teased, nodding at the nearly empty coffee cup on the table.

"A gentleman waits for the lady who will be buying breakfast!"

Molly opened her mouth in playful protest.

Jordan held up a cautionary finger. "Remember? You were the last one in the pool; you buy. Unless, of course, you'd like to have a rematch and try to drown me again."

Molly retorted, "You held your own pretty well, I would say."

Jordan looked quizzically at her, "Yes, I would say so."

Molly flushed in memory of his arms around her in the cool, moonlit pool. He grinned as if hearing her protest, *That's not what I meant!*

She turned her cup upright on the saucer to signal a segue to a safer topic. Jordan quickly lifted the pot on the table. "Do you always get up this early?" she asked and stifled a yawn behind tight lips until tears blurred her vision. "I was sure I would beat you by an hour."

"Hard to sleep late in a strange place, I guess." He ran his hand through his curls forming ridges that quickly filled in the path left by his fingers.

"Let's eat. What was it you said you were going to have? Hash browns, steak, eggs, a gallon of orange juice…" She stared impishly into space, ticking the items off on her fingers.

He poked her with the folded newspaper, "Maybe I'll get both pancakes and waffles! Actually, their breakfast special smells good. I've gotten several good whiffs when the waitresses go by the table."

"Specials! After Grandpa's dining extravaganza yesterday, I cannot imagine you would suggest that again." She scanned the list on the plastic card on the table. "Maybe we can take a side order of toast along to tide you over between now and morning coffee break!"

They clowned around until the waitress arrived to take their order. Then Molly inhaled the fragrant coffee and asked, "Can I share your paper? What's new in the world this morning?"

Jordan shifted his shoulders beneath his shirt, turning the motion into a full-fledged shrug. "New? Everything, and nothing. Pick any section you'd like. I'm only interested in the sports section." He disappeared behind the full expanse of newsprint.

"Pkooo."

The paper lowered. "Pkooo? What's pkooo?"

"The sound of me hitting the wall you just put up."

Silence. Then, "There's no wall." The paper lifted again.

A frown creased Molly's forehead. White knuckles clutched his section of the paper.

He lowered the barrier to ask, "Aren't you going to read?"

"Sure." She picked up the section that topped the pile and stared at a page until their food arrived. *Men! And they think women are moody!*

Between bites Jordan said, "It's a good thing we both showed up ahead of schedule. We'll get an earlier start this way and from what I heard those truck drivers saying," he tipped his head toward two men polishing off pancakes at the counter, "it's supposed to get pretty hot by midday." He yawned and looked sheepishly at Molly. "How did you sleep?"

It was as if the wall had been a mirage. "Good. Great."

"Me, too."

Liar-liar-pants-on-fire, both of us! Molly grinned and picked up their ticket, waving off his proffered money. If the Sexy Whistler could not even own up to being the Midnight Pacer, she could let him keep his secret.

Jordan waited at the door for her. They squinted in the early morning sunshine. "Yup, today could be a sizzler. Good thing we're both dressed for it." He eyed her flowered gauze blouse over a lavender halter top approvingly. His eyes followed the lines of her body to the fern green shorts. "You look like heather in a meadow."

"I suppose you're allergic to heather. Great. You'll be a basket case by tonight after a long day trapped with me!"

Jordan stopped short and faked a body-wrenching sneeze and, dodging her attack, ran ahead. "I'll get my luggage and be right down." He took the steps three at a time. Molly opened the trunk where she had already put her bags and waited, grinning long after he had disappeared into his motel room.

"Where do we spend tonight?" Jordan asked as he positioned his suitcase between the others in the trunk.

Molly slid into the driver's seat. "Salt Lake City. We've got to get gas, so we can call the motel then before we hit the desert."

"Before I forget, thanks for breakfast."

"You bet." They grinned at each other like old friends. Two old friends, one of whom could send a lifetime of plans right out the window with an innocent kiss. Molly felt like a frog on the edge of a kettle of boiling water, wary but increasingly unable to maintain her footing.

The road was clear and they settled into an easiness that had not been born before. "Do you mind?" Jordan asked, pointing at the radio.

"Not at all. Listen to anything you want. There are cassette tapes, too, if you prefer them to the radio."

Jordan twisted the dial until he found an FM station playing rousing marches. Sitting ramrod straight, he directed an unseen band. "Dum dum de dum de de dum de dum de da dum."

His brows were knit in concentration. His voice was deep and full-bodied, and Molly's laugh faded as she nodded in approval. When the song ended, he sighed and leaned back against the head rest. "These early morning rehearsals are always so invigorating!"

Molly anchored the steering wheel securely with her knee to applaud. "I'm impressed, Maestro."

An instrumental song began; Jordan tapped her arm and said, "Sing with me."

"This song doesn't have words," she protested.

"So? Make 'em up! What do you think I'm doing?" he retorted. Without waiting, he picked up the melody. "What a beautiful day…"

She rolled her eyes and obliged him with a hummed harmony.

"…together…ah, yes, we're together…"

She felt a blush creep up from her neck and quickly reached to fiddle with the air vents hoping to divert his glance from her now-pink cheeks. The song ended and Molly's bottom lip puckered into a teasing pout when a commercial followed instead of another song.

Jordan reached for the thermos of coffee in the back seat. "Do you figure this is still hot?"

Molly grimaced. "We should have gotten it refilled this morning at the coffee shop. But, try it; it should still be hot enough to hit the spot. It's a good thermos."

He poured a cup for each of them. "There will be plenty of stops. The day is but a pup, as my grandpa would say. Hey, we sounded pretty good together."

"Yeah." Her soft assent arched between them like a wispy rainbow. "We weren't bad."

Both jumped when an eighteen-wheeler roared past the car, shaking them in its back wind. "Where did he come from?" Jordan's laugh was the needed bridge between dreaming and reality.

"Just crept up on us, I guess. Man, my mouth feels like a dirty old sock. I should have brushed my teeth after breakfast. Will you get an apple or something out of the cooler for me? We're about an hour and a half from Winnemucca. That's a good place to stop and then I'll brush them for real."

"Wow, what choices. Red, green, or golden?"

"Green."

He pulled out two, cold and dripping from the melting ice. Their first bites snapped in unison and they smiled. "You have a beautiful smile, Molly."

The compliment caught her off guard; she mumbled her thanks before veering away from the personal with "Tell me all about your house. I love your neighborhood." His nod said her question pleased him.

"It's a great old house; been in the family for years. One of these days, when chasing the white ball gets to me, I would like to revamp the down-stairs into a studio for my new career," he grinned slyly at her, "in professional video photography services. I've had a class, you know! But, I'm not sure how living and working under the same roof would work."

"It works out fine for lots of people. My tax accountant has her office at home, and so does a friend of mine who is a painting contractor." Molly rolled down her window and sent the apple core spinning.

At her request, he gave a verbal floor plan for his house and she was astonished at the magnitude of the old mansion, and also impressed with his ability to describe wallpaper, wainscoting, and the unique features in the structure. "You must be very happy to be living with so many memories. Is there anything written about the house's history that you know of? Lots of old places…"

"No." A trace of a frown brushed his lips as he cut her off abruptly. There was a long silence. "I would hate to ever have to give it up. My parents were glad to turn it over to me since they need smaller quarters with less responsibility at this stage in their lives, and I love the place so it's working out well. But enough about me. How do you manage to live in such luxury?" His smile kept offense from his question.

"Ah, yes, sweet luxury! Good clean livin' will do it every time. Seriously, I've worked hard and I'm a natural hoarder, and I was able to keep my school loans low, thanks to my grandfather's estate settlement. I chose to put my money into a home. It's all part of my goals. Since my parent's home has such pleasant memories for me, I wanted to create one for myself."

Jordan asked, "Just for you?" offhandedly.

So, we've come to this point. "Just for me," she replied, equally casual, but with her heart in her throat.

"How does Royce fit into all this?"

"Royce? Oh, we're just friends…" Once again, since meeting Jordan, scheduling love to strike at age thirty sounded far too regimented. Maybe Brynn was right. "I mean, I've worked hard to get my degrees, find a good job, get settled in my house…there will be plenty of time to fall in love later."

"But what about some guy who might be unaware of this plan-deal and falls in love with you off-schedule. Does he stand a chance?" he asked nonchalantly. Before she needed to respond, he flipped back to their earlier conversation, "Living where you do, most everyone in the Valley envies you. It's a dream spot."

"Thanks. I love it," she answered quickly, grateful for the reprieve.

"Tell me some more about your family. You have parents and a sister. Is that it?"

She nodded. "Just four of us. Dad has taught at the college level for years. English Literature. My favorite memories from growing up include all of us in the den studying or reading at night. For years I thought that when my friends studied, their parents studied, too!" She laughed and relaxed against the seat.

"Sounds like what was that TV program, Little House on the Prairie?" he muttered, his quiet sarcasm lost on Molly.

"Dad would read to us from his stacks of freshmen themes if he thought they were especially well written, and Mom let Mara and me help her correct spelling papers when we got done with our homework. Or Dad might read something from the day's newspaper and we'd get a good debate going. Usually, it was pretty heady stuff for young kids, but we grew into it."

"Good grief. Your mother's a teacher, too?"

"She has taught first grade ever since I can remember. I guess we were latchkey kids before they had a name for us. But Dad was able to be home when we got home from school at least a couple of days per week, so it wasn't bad; for a long time my grandparents lived close by and we'd stop by their place on our way home."

"Quite an intellectual group, your family." Almost imperceptibly his voice had taken on a sharpness.

Molly looked quickly in his direction. Was that smile wooden or was she imagining things? "There's even more! My sister is a special education teacher in Rochester and her husband owns a bookstore!" She laughed and pushed her sunglasses up into her hair. "It's not surprising my sister and I are in book-related occupations. Mom was always so worried about the kids in her class who couldn't get the hang of reading. I guess it rubbed off on us."

"That's just great." The words were appropriate, but with just three words, the air between them had frozen. Instantly she sensed that if she went chop-chop-chop with her hands, the letters would form icicles that would shatter everywhere as they fell around their feet in chilly piles.

What has gone wrong? The unspoken question left her frantic. Her words tumbled out, "I think you'd enjoy my family. You should see the den in our house! Three of the four walls are floor-to-ceiling bookcases. And almost every room has at least one bookcase—even the bathrooms have baskets of books!"

"Did your family ever do anything besides read and study?" This was not a friendly question; each word was darkened by scorn. *Scorn?* No one had ever viewed her family with anything but respect before this sports-crazed jerk entered the scene and destroyed her tranquil existence.

"Well, sure. We played games…"

He interrupted, "Oh, right, Scrabble, probably."

This is my life we're talking about here, buddy! "Or Chinese Checkers, or Monopoly or a host of other games!" Molly retorted, responding in kind to his taunting.

"All guaranteed to produce brighter children, no doubt." His smile did nothing to soften the words or his tone of voice.

"I guess I've made it sound like my parents pushed us to succeed. The picture I've painted of my family isn't appealing to you." The brightness in her eyes dimmed.

"With your upbringing you probably don't believe this, but there's a lot more to life than reading, you know. Personally, I would rather experience life than just read about it." Board by board, a fence was rising between them. She could see the splinters in the rough boards just waiting to lodge themselves in her hands if she tried to climb it.

Any resolve to keep the peace was forgotten in the intensity of the moment, "So you think my family and I haven't experienced life? Good

Lord! I can't think of a family that does more living than we do. The best part of every vacation we ever took was preparing for it by all of us reading up on the place."

"You read about places you were going on vacation?" Jordan asked with disdain underscoring each word.

"Yeah, and we'd talk about it every night at dinner for weeks ahead of the trip," Molly said, ignoring his jibe. "We had the liveliest dinner conversations you can imagine."

He stared at her, sapping her enthusiasm with each steely blink of his eyes. "Well, in my family, we went out and did things and talked about them afterward. We didn't need books to make a good time better. My folks own and operate one of the largest catering businesses in the whole Valley."

"So?" she challenged rudely. "What's that prove?"

"They've been involved in every major political or social function on the Valley calendar for almost half a century. And let me tell you, they don't sit around and read about cooking. We have made some great trips to Europe and New York and met countless famous chefs, but we didn't sit around the dinner table and talk about cookbooks, for crying out loud."

"But…" Molly paused long enough to collect ammunition before she barreled on, "Take Alcatraz! We ferried out to the Island on one summer vacation, but for months before, Dad told stories about famous prisoners on The Rock," she took a deep breath and kept on firing, "and Mom told us about the exciting dramas that have taken place there over the years. Without that kind of preparation, what kid is going to understand Alcatraz? Answer that, Mr. Hoity-Toity 'We-Met-All-The-Great-Chefs'."

"*Hoity-toity*? What the deuce does that mean? Oh, I get it. Must be a word from one of your family's wall-to-wall books."

"'Hoity-toity' is a perfectly good, totally wholesome, all-together non-bookish word. Look it up sometime. It means 'haughty and patronizing' and that certainly describes you accurately."

His shoulders sagged. "Let's not resort to name-calling. We are two adults, with different opinions about something that really doesn't matter."

"Reading doesn't matter? *Doesn't matter!*" Her voice rose shrilly. "It matters very much. Reading is one of the freedoms we enjoy in…"

Jordan cut in, "And so is *not* reading."

Molly filled her lungs and huffed, "True. If you choose to live like someone who doesn't have the freedom to read, that is certainly your business. But let me say this, if you knew the rest of my family, you'd regret your words."

"I could say the same thing about my family." The car was oppressively silent. "Maybe we should drop the subject. Neither of us is going to change our mind, and we're just hurting each other. Truce?"

Molly's heart thumped wildly. *Whatever happened to our beautiful day?* She nodded in answer to his plea. "Truce. I'm sorry." But her voice did not have a convincing ring, even to her ears. Each word had been loaded with too much pain.

"And I'm sorry I said such harsh things about your family and their ways. Let's take some time out from each other over lunch and that will give us a chance to cool down." A cold skeleton of a smile shaped his lips.

She chose a roadside cafe without consulting him. He headed for the door without waiting while she grabbed her paperback book from the back seat and locked the car.

The waitress's ponytail swung wildly as she looked from one to the other of her newest customers and in a split second decision headed after Jordan to the table he selected. Molly chose a seat as far away from Jordan as the room allowed. Laughter from his table soon floated across the room and Molly ducked behind the menu.

Laugh all you want, Toots; you haven't been trapped in a car with that opinionated, bullheaded boor.

The waitress eventually remembered Molly and nonchalantly strolled across the room, each step designed to add a man-pleasing swing to the shapely hips curving beneath her skin-tight uniform. She tripped over the leg of a chair; Molly stifled a snort.

"Soup's chicken noodle. And there's 'nana cream pie," she rattled off between chomps on her bubble gum. She was clearly bored with Molly and kept glancing over her shoulder at Jordan until Molly wanted to shake her.

"I'll have a salad with Bleu cheese dressing, a bowl of the soup, and coffee. Where are the rest rooms, please?" The girl tipped her head, indicating some vague direction beyond, as she finished scribbling Molly's order. She chose a route to the order window that would take her back by Jordan's table again.

Molly strode past the two of them, her purse swinging wildly from her shoulder. When her meal finally came, she dug into the food with a passion born more of frustration than hunger. She forced each mouthful down; it could have been wood chips floating in rain water for all her taste buds knew. *Royce, come get your buddy before we push each other over the edge of whatever sanity and civility we have left.*

Jordan finished first. The waitress almost laid rubber with her smoking tennis shoes as she headed for the cash register. Molly obstinately sipped the last of her coffee rather than join him any time soon at the counter. When he had finally finished chatting with his newest conquest, Jordan went to the men's room and Molly hurried to pay her bill before the waitress could disappear.

Since the girl could not tear her eyes away from the door through which Jordan would reappear. Molly pulled out a traveler's check and waited to sign it until the cashier would be able to verify that it was signed in her presence. This proper procedure was wasted for the most part since Molly caught her flat-out looking back at the still-closed door twice during the 13 letters of her signature.

Molly handed the check to the girl who suddenly took an interest and read it with the care of someone who regularly caught forgers. "Say now, this is the second one of these weird things we've had today. Never saw one before, and today I see two. Yup," she plucked another traveler's check out of the drawer and waved it at Molly. "Look here. This one was from that guy sitting over there." She smoothed invisible wrinkles out of the check with a gentle touch. "His name is BJ Kendall. Wonder what the 'B' stand for?" She gazed blissfully at the empty table.

You won't be hearing it from me, Chickypoo. "Could I have my change, please?" she snapped.

"I could just die, he's so good looking. And I think he likes me." She dropped wrinkled bills into Molly's hand, breathing like someone in dire need of medical attention.

"Just spend a morning with him and your tune will change," Molly muttered.

"Huh?" A bubble fizzled to a sticky mess below the girl's confused eyes, but she retrieved her gum with a practiced tongue.

"Never mind." Molly stuffed the money into her purse.

Jordan crossed the room. "Ready to go?" The waitress stared after them with a limp lower jaw.

Molly handed Jordan the keys. "I believe you wanted to drive after lunch?"

"Yes, if that's okay with you." Politeness personified, he opened her door, waited, and closed it ever so gently. He played with the keychain dangling below the ignition for a few seconds before he spoke. "Molly." How different her name sounded when the smile was gone from his voice. "I apologize for the hurtful things I said to you. Will you forgive me?" His eyes were navy-blue pools of deep sadness.

She swallowed hard. "Yes, I will. And I am truly sorry, too. Will you please forgive me for calling you hoity-toity." Ghostly smiles traced their lips. "I'm sure we both wish the morning had never happened."

He reached out and traced a lavender flower on her sleeve with one finger. "Not all of it," he said softly.

"Yeah; we may not always be singing the same song, but we can harmonize, if we try."

"Getting to know you, Minnesota," he said with a weak smile, "is certainly an escape from the ordinary."

Apologies had thrown water on the fire, but the coals were still hot; she flared, but managed to keep her thoughts to herself. *You have made that clear ever since we met in my alley, Jordan.*

CHAPTER EIGHT

A tape recording of their chitchat for the next few hours would have been judged the genteel talk of two strangers. Each made a conscious effort to avoid controversial subjects, commenting on scenery ad nauseam. Molly read aloud from numerous road signs, bumper stickers, personalized license plates, or billboards.

For his part, Jordan pointed out features on every car that passed, or noted interestingly painted water towers, or directed her attention to multitudinous cloud formations. Nothing unusual or ordinary escaped their comment or attention.

They expressed opinions on such hotly-debatable topics as "I think it's warmer this afternoon." (Jordan's opinion; Molly agreed wholeheartedly and repeatedly) and "This iced tea sure hits the spot." (Molly voted yes; Jordan cast the deciding ballot.)

Jordan remarked that he had really not seen many of the small towns that make up so much of the United States. Itineraries can change, Molly decided and suggested, "There's no reason at all why we couldn't take a little detour off this freeway and remedy that." The next exit ramp's signs indicated that there was, indeed, one of those fine parts of Americana just a few miles to the North. They set out. Two pilgrims on a mission. Americans discovering all that is America.

The desert heat was intense outside the air-conditioned car when they noticed the first signs of trouble. The car hiccuped, coughed, sputtered, and died. Jordan steered it off the road as it rolled to a stop. They looked at each other in accusing silence.

Jordan spoke first, "I imagine you had the car serviced before you ever started the trip?"

"Yes." She clipped the word clean. "Even though my father is a hopeless bookworm, he taught me that machines require faithful maintenance."

"This is your car. Do you have the foggiest idea what the problem could be?" His eyes bored holes into her.

"No, in fact, I don't. It's a reliable car, so this isn't an everyday occurrence, you know. I don't know what's wrong, but I'm getting the message, loud and clear, that I had jolly well better figure it out, and quick, right?"

"Well, let's sit and think for a minute."

"Sitting and thinking won't start the car," Molly snapped. "Get the manual from under the driver's seat and see if it gives any clues." Hot desert air slapped her in the face as she slammed the door on Jordan in his air-conditioned comfort. Her bare feet stung on the pavement and she leaned against the car to shift her weight and yelped.

Opening the car door, she grabbed her sandals without a look at Jordan. She dropped them to the ground and slid into them, each step moving her toward the back of the car.

She kept on walking around to the driver's side and knocked sharply on the window. Jordan rolled it down just enough to let his words out, "What's wrong?"

"I need the keys to open the trunk."

"I thought the trunk was open if the car doors were unlocked?"

"Not when someone, who shall remain nameless, locks the trunk purposely." She spoke slowly, distinctly, as if to accommodate the feeble-minded. Jordan rolled the window down a little more to drop the keys into her hand. Their cool metal warmed instantly.

The raised trunk lid hid Molly from Jordan's sight in the rear view mirror as she finished zipping up the coveralls she kept for emergencies. The heat had already fired her face a brilliant red, and she squirmed as rivulets of perspiration ran down her spine.

He was staring at the unopened car manual; she tapped on the window to get his attention. "Release the hood, please. The lever is on the left under the dash." She kept walking to the hood.

The car door slammed behind Jordan as he joined her to stare at the hot engine. Fury rose in her throat as she heard an unmistakable chuckle erupt into a spasm of laughter; he leaned against the fender and hooted. "I don't see what's so infernally funny. Maybe if this were your...your golf cart you'd be more concerned about helping to get it fixed."

She stood back, left hand on her hip, and watched in disbelief as her tirade prompted a further gale of laughter. "Move," she ordered as she slammed the hood back into place and marched to the passenger door. She flopped back in the seat, blowing damp hair out of her face with a long, vexed breath as Jordan rejoined her.

"If you find this so blasted humorous, Jordan, I suggest that you go back out there in that furnace and see how long it takes to get over your hysterics. I see nothing funny about a *gentleman* sending me," she thumped her fist loudly against her chest, "out there," her wild gesture took in the whole world, "while he stands by like some hyena. I don't care if it is my car. I obviously didn't sabotage it. Don't you know anything about cars?" Her outburst ended on a plaintive tone.

Jordan listened in subdued seriousness for a moment, "Very little. At least about Volvos. I putter around with my truck, but I let the experts work on the Benz. And by the way, I don't use a golf cart during a tournament! Let's call for help."

They reached simultaneously for their cell phones and groaned in unison. "I have had this happen in Mendocino—a worthless cell phone. We must be in another dead zone."

Jordan stared at his own phone with a frown, and then looked out the window. "I suppose, but this looks like a place that could sure justify putting up a few towers. Man, what a desolate place!"

"So, back to square one. What do we do?"

He looked back at her and sputtered again for a second despite her frosty gaze. "I'm sorry; I'm not laughing about our situation. But you look so...where did you get that..." He laughed like a man possessed.

"Oh, I get it. This is one of those moments when, if I had a sense of humor, I should be laughing. Ha. Ha. Ha. See? I have a healthy sense of humor. Satisfied?"

"No, no!" He plucked at her sleeve.

"If you are hysterical over my Ernie outfit, I see nothing funny about a woman trying to keep from looking like a mechanic's rag." She pulled her leg up close to her chest and adjusted the rolled-up cuff of the midnight-blue coverall.

"'Ernie outfit'?" He watched as she dramatically pulled at the folds that half hid the orange embroidered name over the left breast pocket. "Who's Ernie?"

She sighed eloquently, "I don't know, Jordan. It came from a thrift shop; I would imagine Ernie is the fellow who owned the coverall first. I think it fits my needs very well, especially when I travel with men who aren't in any hurry to assist."

Jordan bypassed her sarcasm. "You're quite a character, Molly. Most women only have designer jeans, but you have a special Ernie outfit!" At his first chuckle, Molly threw her door open and stormed around to the other side, flinging open his door. "Get out."

"What? What do you plan to do, Molly? The car is dead. I doubt if our walking around it and poking under the hood can change that."

"May I sit in the driver's seat, please? I believe this is my car, as you pointed out earlier." She flashed a terrific drop-dead smile.

Jordan swung his long legs out and walked to the back of the car. He stood looking out over the desert. The freeway was beyond his range of vision or hearing. Molly crawled into the driver's seat and felt the unwelcome warmth of his body there. She stared at the dashboard.

Suddenly, she stuck the key back in the ignition, turned it to the first click, and watched the fuel gauge. Nothing. She looked out over the empty road. No one. Miles and miles of no one. Just that infuriating male standing back there like some Olympic hero.

Where is everyone? Why did we need to leave the freeway just to show Jordan a small town here and now? This reaffirms precisely why following a plan makes life so much simpler. She pressed her forehead against the steering wheel and clenched her fists into two tight balls.

Jordan didn't even turn when she slammed the car door; Molly strode to his side and tapped him on the arm. "I figured out what the problem is. No gas. Didn't you notice that it was getting low when you started out after lunch?"

"No; neither did you before lunch, right?"

They could have been two statues erected beside the highway. Two living monuments to Machines' Victory Over Man. Desert stillness and stiffling heat menaced until finally Molly moaned, "Regardless. No working phones, and we are out of gas. Dry as a bone. It's much too hot to stand out here, and besides, I…"

He looked quizzically at her, "What?"

"Nothing. Never mind," she snapped, glad he could not read her thoughts. *Just because we're traveling together doesn't mean I'll go to the bathroom in front of you.* She traced a senseless pattern on the dusty ground with her shoe. Since the desert did not offer much privacy, other options were limited.

"Do you have an idea about getting help?"

"No! Forget it, okay?"

Jordan shrugged and wiped his forearm across his face. "Okay. Come on, let's get back inside while we wait for help. Someone will come by soon. I don't want you passing out on me."

"I'm not the fainting type of female, sorry. I have no secret desire to faint into your arms," she snapped.

"We're both testy because it's hot, and nobody likes car trouble." She nodded in self-rebuke and they returned to the fast-fading coolness of the car. "Let's have something cold and wet from our stash in the cooler. I'm dry as a bone, just like the car."

"No, thank you. Help yourself."

"Did you say, 'No, thank you'?" His mouth stayed open after the sound stopped. "You're the one who is always thirsty and travels with lots to drink."

"I said, 'No, thank you' as in 'I'm not thirsty'."

"I don't believe you. I don't know what you're trying to pull, but I don't believe that for one minute." She stared as he popped open an icy can and consumed an enormous gulp. "You at least ought to have some water, or something, you know. You could get dehydrated." She jerked her head toward the window, listening as half the can's contents disappeared, each swallow punctuated by a satisfied sigh.

"I don't see what you gain by being so ticked off that you deny yourself a cool drink," Jordan said.

"I'm not mad at you. We're being friends, remember? No more mean thoughts, no more arguing. Friends."

Jordan was silent for a long minute. He crushed the empty can with one hand. "You wouldn't by any chance have turned down a drink you desperately want because you have to go to the bathroom, would you?"

"Would you quit worrying about me not having a drink?" Molly's flush renewed itself without assistance from any desert heat. "Talk about having a mind like a steel trap."

"I'm right, huh?"

"I can wait."

"Molly, why couldn't you tell me that? It's something humans are supposed to do. I use the bathroom, too, you know, beast that I am."

Molly glared at the road stretching ahead of them. "Where is everybody? Doesn't anybody ever leave that stupid little town?" The emptiness was as oppressive as the heat.

"Someone will be along, you'll see. It just seems longer to us because we're frustrated." Jordan dropped his hand, still cool from holding the pop can, to her arm. "Here's my offer, Minnesota, I'll walk up the road to that billboard and check things out over the hill ahead. You know, see if anyone's coming. You just open the door, like a shield. You'll hear anyone coming from behind the car before they drive into sight. And while you're at it, take off the Ernie outfit and you'll be able to drop ten degrees from your body temperature."

Molly smiled faintly at him. He opened his door and set out toward the sign.

When he returned a few minutes later, she was drinking deeply from a cup of water. "Thanks, Jordan. Sorry I'm such a…"

"Hey, I'm not winning any good behavior awards today, either, so no apology necessary. The good news is, I think I see someone coming, unless the desert is playing tricks. They're driving pretty slow. Do you have a gas can, just in case?"

"Yeah, in the trunk." She was already pulling on her sandals. "Let's get out there and wave them down."

They stood by the car and waited. Time dragged its feet.

A station wagon crested the hill, brimming over with people. As it rolled to a stop, an unbelievable number of kids peered out at the living drama, Travelers In Distress Beside The Road.

The father held them back, much as if Molly and Jordan were desperate fugitives whose faces he had seen recently on the Post Office bulletin board. The mother sat stoically in the front seat, completely disinterested in the proceedings. "Gotta problem?" the man asked cautiously, eyeing their California license.

"We've run out of gas. Can you help us out?" Jordan asked.

The man chewed his toothpick and spit a piece of it, expertly missing his shoe. "We're heading home. Place is just up the road a piece, other side of the second hill." He wagged his head, indicating no specific direction. "I reckon we could sell you a couple of gallons. Cash," he added, still suspicious.

Molly and Jordan heaved sighs of relief and Jordan said, "Cash is no problem. That would be wonderful. I'll come with you." He looked questioningly at Molly; she nodded.

"Move over, kids. Make room for the man back there with you." Molly bit back a giggle as Jordan dove into the mass of arms, legs, and bodies in the back seat. The man perched, one foot in, one foot out, and turned to Molly. "We'll have your hubby back to you in no time, little lady." His wife showed her first sign of life and waved limply as they pulled away.

Molly watched until they were out of sight. *Hubby, indeed.* This trip was proving over and over just how right she was to have a plan. How on earth would she have achieved all she had with the distractions and frustrations a man created in her life? Today, thirty seemed far too early to change her lifestyle. Forty was looking enticing before she introduced chaos into the mix.

She opened the trunk to find paper towels. After she refolded the Ernie outfit and stashed it in a corner of the trunk, she slid back into the car to wait.

Despite the sapping heat, smiles brushed her lips as memories of Jordan came to mind; he had looked like a figurine packed for mailing with all the kids piled around him like Styrofoam bubbles! She carefully poured some drinking water on a paper towel and wiped her face and arms.

Then she rolled the seat back to a comfortable reclining position and waited. "What a trip," she said to a bird that landed on the hood of the car and stared at her curiously. Two cars whizzed by, neither so much as slowing down. "Good thing we weren't counting on any of you turkeys for help!" she shouted into the dust they raised.

With horn honking and seemingly dozens of arms flapping out the windows, the car returned to the scene, pulling up ahead of the stalled Volvo. It took Jordan almost as long to free himself from the back seat as it did for the man to get the gas can untied from the rack on top.

All the kids piled out to watch the next exciting episode of the newest roadside drama, Pouring Gas Through A Funnel. When the job was completed, Jordan shook hands with the man, thanked him for his assistance, and aimed a polite salute at the wife.

"No problem, Mister." The man smiled broadly at Molly who had joined the roadside parade. "You have a real nice trip now, Missus. Come on, kids."

All but one small girl obeyed. She inched her way next to Molly and lisped, "You're very bootiful, even when you sweat," and then fled to the safety of her family. Like bees swarming around a hive, all were soon contained and the car rolled away. The wife outdid herself with a wave and a smile this time.

Jordan must have really wowed the socks off her.

"The fellow said there's a truck stop just three miles beyond the exit we took from the freeway. We'll make it there fine with the gas they sold us." Jordan looked tired and Molly felt guilty.

"I appreciate you doing all this for me."

"For us. I did it for us. I wasn't crazy about sitting on the desert all night, either, Missus! The kid's right. You do, somehow, manage to look bootiful."

Molly jutted her chin and tossed curls off her neck. "Thanks for omitting the sweaty part of her compliment! Jordan, let me drive until we get to Salt Lake City. I'm rested up."

"What say we skip the small town today, okay?"

"No argument here."

They were silent as they headed back to the main road. Molly pulled in at the promised truck stop. She filled the tank and washed off the windows while Jordan headed for the men's room. "Grab some cheese and crackers or something from the cooler. We'll get a good dinner in Salt Lake City," Molly suggested as they left the station.

"Thanks, I think I will. It felt good to wash that miserable desert dirt off, didn't it? And I think I might have even ended up with some of baby Pete's peanut butter on my neck during that adventure back there!"

Peace reigned as Molly accepted pieces of cheese from the tip of the knife Jordan extended to her and said, "Oh, by the way, I think my cell phone is a goner, even when we get out of the dead zone. One of the kids snitched it off my belt when I was crammed in that car with them, and then he dropped it when his brother chased him, and then he tossed it to another kid who missed, and like I said, I'm afraid we'll be down to one phone."

"Bummer. I'm sorry. Maybe it will survive. If not, when will you be able to get it fixed or replaced?"

He shrugged. "I'll probably wait until I get home, even though my manager won't like not being able to reach me." They rode in silence for almost half a mile.

"How 'bout some 'wash all our troubles away' music?" Molly asked. "Pick a tape." Rich music filled the car. Molly felt the tensions fall away; she wasn't surprised to see that Jordan relaxed to the point of dozing off.

Perhaps the day isn't beyond retrieval. An orchestrated down-time for both of us as we drive along, then a nice dinner, perhaps a swim. Our fledgling friendship will survive.

She smiled; he slept on.

Salt Lake City rose out of the desert in all its famed splendor. Dinnertime was long past, but Jordan had shown no signs of awakening, so she had let him rest undisturbed. He had every reason to be tired, she knew. He had still been pacing in the room above her when she had fallen asleep last night; he was first to the coffee shop this morning; and then he had their afternoon adventure to round it all out. *Let the man sleep!*

Molly found the motel where she had reservations but could not find a parking space in the front lot or along the curb.

What's going on? Her body was frazzled, unable to deal with any crisis, large or small. She glanced at Jordan; even stopping the car had not fazed him. She got out of the car and watched through the window as she quietly eased the door shut. Still no movement. She shrugged, clicked the lock and turned to go into the motel office.

Molly had tried three other motels and was coming out of the fourth when she saw Jordan was awake and waiting for her. Her body's response to his sleepy desirability unnerved her.

It's been a long day, kiddo, she warned herself.

"Whew, I feel like a truck ran over me. I've really been out, haven't I?"

"You bet. Like the proverbial light. You missed all the excitement." She looked at him, dreading to drop the bomb. "I hate to hit you with this, but we're without a room in Salt Lake City."

He groaned. "We never called ahead, did we? We talked about it, and never did it. Man, this could get old real quick." He shook his tousled head and Molly's breathing faltered. "Minnesota, we've got to get our act together. Two nights in a row we've blown it. I thought you had reservations?"

"Confirmed ones up to 6:00 o'clock. After that, they put me out to pasture. There's a big convention in town and when I didn't arrive in time, I lost out."

"That's the perfect end to an absolutely prize day, Molly." For a moment his eyes blazed; he had been far more appealing to her as a sleepyhead than he was now as a spitfire. "Let's try another motel," he sighed, his emotions sapped.

"We did. You slept through numbers one through four. And this last clerk called around to seven other motels for me." The flashing no-vacancy sign streaked Jordan's face eerily. "I even checked out campgrounds. The closest one is 22 miles away, but that's our only choice."

"Campgrounds? You plan on camping out tonight? Where do you propose to sleep? Under the stars? I should tell you that even when I go to Yosemite, I get a room."

This from a man who preaches 'experiencing life'? "They rent tents and stuff at the campgrounds. It won't be so bad. Hey, when I go to Yosemite I get a room, too."

Jordan stared at her in unreadable silence.

So much for the good times. "Well," she continued resolutely, "we don't have much choice. The motel clerk drew me a map; he said it's a breeze to find. I called the campgrounds and the guy said to come on out, so let's just do it."

"Priceless advice at the end of a jewel of a day."

They drove off, leaving the throngs of conventioneers to their comfortable rooms. Jordan said nothing for 22 miles.

"I can't understand it. That fellow back at the motel said that finding the road where we turn was a snap." Molly peered at shadows in the darkening night.

"You talked to the guy. You should have asked for better directions. Why don't you call him again and let him talk us in?" There was no defense against such unimpeachable logic except for the fact that Molly remembered writing all the details like name of the campground and phone number for the campground on the very piece of paper she held in her hand with her wad of gum firmly wrapped in it. She knew better than to mention this detail.

The sun had almost completely set when they pulled up in front of the campgrounds' office. The sign on a post still promised *Vacancy* and Molly stifled an insane desire to throw her arms around it. She signed the register for their space; Jordan wandered restlessly around the small combination office and camp store.

"Only one tent left and one sleeping bag," said the manager. "It's been a busy night."

"We'll take 'em," Jordan answered grimly and slapped the money on the counter.

They drove to their assigned space. On one side the ominous shapes of four motorcycles loomed beside the drivers sacked out on the ground in sleeping bags. Across the roadway, six Recreational Vehicles were parked like the spokes of a wheel. No one was awake anywhere. The closest light, behind the RV fortress, allowed only a fringe of light to reach their space. Even the moon played an eerie game of tag with the clouds.

Jordan loosened the ropes that held the tent pieces together. Support poles clattered to the ground and an unseen dog growled and rattled his chain.

"Shhhhh! We'll wake everyone up!"

"Frankly, my dear, I don't..." The predictable end to his sentiments was muffled as he dropped to the ground to grope for the lost and vital rods. "I will get this tent set up for me while you clear out the back seat for yourself. Do you want the sleeping bag, or do you have something in the car you could use?"

"There's a stadium blanket in the trunk," Molly said. "Are you sure you don't mind sleeping in the tent?"

"Oh, sure; no problem. There probably aren't very many bears left in Utah. Mind? How could I? It's every American boy's dream, isn't it? Rattlesnakes, field mice...Sorry, Molly, I'm just sick of it all."

"Let me fix up the back seat and then I'll come help you," Molly said, handing him a rod that had rolled near her feet.

"All right. To be honest with you, after being cooped up in the car, the tent will give me a welcome chance to stretch out. Are you as hungry as I am? We didn't eat dinner, you know."

"How about if I go see if the geezer at the office sells anything that resembles food? At this point the cookies we have left in our stash don't sound very appealing."

"No argument here. I'll figure out this tent while you're gone. Here, take a flashlight with you, and be careful, okay?" His warning almost sounded as if he cared, but then again, maybe he was worried about a possible attack from unfriendly neighbors.

Molly stumbled over a rock and yelped as she caught herself. "Molly?" Jordan called in a stage whisper.

"I'm okay," she answered.

As expected, a voice yelled from the darkness around the motorcycles, "Quiet down, will ya? Jerks!"

She tensed, gingerly pushing herself up off the ground. She made a wide circle around the motorcycles.

Jordan was lying on his back, holding the tent in the air with both feet, legs spread eagle, when Molly returned. "'Bout time you came back. Get this confounded thing off me and let's eat." He rolled over; the tent fell. He thrashed his way free of it while Molly grabbed futilely at the slippery material.

"All he had was beans. And doughnuts."

"Nothing shocks me anymore. Do we have a can opener?" He stood up, glaring at the mess on the ground that was supposed to provide him with shelter for the night.

"Yeah, just a sec." Molly headed for the car and grabbed a bottle opener out of emergency pack in the open trunk. "Well, we've got this." He stared at it and mumbled something she was glad she missed. Jordan poked several holes around the edge of one can, but couldn't budge the top. He thrust it into her hand and attacked the other can. He finally tipped his head back and shook beans through the holes into his mouth.

As he wiped the juice off his chin with the back of his hand, he motioned to the can she held and said, "Eat. You can always wash off the bean juice."

She jumped up, "I just remembered; we should have some milk in the cooler. That will help wash the beans down." She returned and handed the carton to Jordan. "Help yourself."

He drank deeply from it and with a sudden, violent jolt of his body, spit the milk out on the ground and glared at her. "Did it occur to you that in this heat, even in a cooler, milk might go sour? Put that on your list for next year: throw out milk when the ice melts." His sarcasm punctured her exhausted mind; she closed her eyes against his anger. She moved away from him, letting the darkness divide them even more.

The tent was finally assembled, the sleeping bag unrolled, and Jordan grabbed his shaving kit. "Let's find the rest rooms before we hit the hay. Here, give me your hand so you don't trip and get those brutes next to us mad again." His grip numbed her hand as she trotted along beside him, trying to match his gait.

When she came out from the women's side, Jordan was waiting, leaning up against the light pole and swatting bugs. They walked in chilly silence through the darkness back to their campsite.

Jordan stood by the trunk waiting for Molly to turn the key that would unlock all the car doors. She groaned and dropped her head into her hands, fighting back tears. "What?" Jordan was by her side in an instant.

"When we left the car, I locked the driver's door from the back seat. See my purse between the front seats? The car keys are in it. So is my phone."

Silence.

"Looks like you get the tent, and I get the sleeping bag."

"At least I grabbed the blanket out when we were talking about it." She pointed to the plaid shadow on the hood of the car.

"Well, one good thing. Hurray for Molly." Seven sarcastic words served only to deepen the menacing chasm between them.

It seemed they had nothing left to say to each other. She crawled inside the tent, held up the sleeping bag before Jordan zipped the tent shut around her. She turned inside the small space, spreading out the blanket and taking off her shoes. She shifted, experimenting to find a bumpless spot. Suddenly, she jumped. Outside the tent loomed a massive form.

You goose! Calm down.

She held her breath as the shadow bent in two, rose again, and moved along the length of the tent. "Jordan, is that you?" she hissed.

"Yes."

"What are you doing?"

"Spreading out the sleeping bag."

"Why are you so close to the tent?"

"What difference does it make?" he asked testily. "It's the only flat spot on this whole site. You wouldn't believe the rocks and gopher holes and…"

An irate voice cut through the black night, "Will you two idiots shut up over there?"

A cricket sang.

"Never fear, Molly, I promise not to rape and plunder during the night. I'm on the outside, you recall," he hissed, his face pressed against the tent's fabric.

She pulled the blanket up around her neck and watched his movements outside the tent, sitting on the sleeping bag, lifting the sleeping bag to form a pillow of his shoes, zipping the covering, pausing stiffly for several minutes.

Molly listened and waited; he sighed and burrowed into position. All was still. She swallowed hard. In the faint light from the pole beyond the campers she could see the long range of humps and lumps that was Jordan.

He was close. Really close.

She caught her breath as the unmistakable thumping of a private drum announced the intensity of her unsettling interest in Jordan's masculine presence.

A scratching. Once. And again. Jordan whispered, "Good night, Minnesota."

"Good night, Jordan."

She could hear his steady, gentle breathing change as he slid into sleep's embrace. His three words dropped a bridge into her heart for an unexplored passion to walk across.

It was an unstable bridge; each gentle touch had placed a board, but each angry word had ripped out the nails. A smile crept across her lips in the darkness. Outside, the night noises broke into her musing.

This is classic. I'm spending the night with a gentleman of his word. Someone unworried about appearing macho, whose self-confidence isn't tumbled by apologies, who admits he's no outdoors man. Somehow, I wasn't expecting all that from him.

She shifted carefully to keep the blanket in place and turned in the darkness to face Jordan. Lightly, she touched the tent, feeling closer to him with the gesture. With most other men she knew, the sleeping bag would have been inside the tent, whether she liked it or not.

The rangy body lying motionless outside her tent breathed heavily now. Sleep had won. Tonight it was Molly who was awake, pacing the boundaries of her heart.

CHAPTER NINE

The whistling man lifted the breathless lady out of the giant hole. She clung to him, and covered his face with kisses. He pulled away, jumping into a pool. She followed him and they swam, creating huge waves that either pushed them apart or flung them together.

Then, abruptly, he left the pool without a backward glance. And to her horror, as he walked away, he was...shot by rapid-fire guns! "Oh, dear God, no! He's dead!" Molly thrashed wildly, but something bound her legs and kept her from escaping.

"Shhshhshhshh." The voice was soothing, kind. Molly instinctively reached toward it in the early-morning dawn. "It's okay; you were dreaming," she heard.

Jordan pulled his feet into the tent and let the tent opening fall back into place. Molly stared sleepily at him and pulled the blanket that had restricted her legs up around her shoulders. "What are you doing in here?"

"From out there, it sounded like you needed a little comfort."

Molly grimaced and pulled away from his touch. "Did you hear a gunshot, or was that only in my dream?"

Gently, he smoothed her hair back from her face. "It was the motorcycles backfiring; it scared me, too. I've been awake for a while. Those guys tried to get even with us for last night. If you're as scared as I was, it seems they effectively got revenge on us for daring to set up camp next to them."

Molly found it very difficult to concentrate on his words rather than his early-morning stubble. *Such an intimate thing, morning whiskers. He was so very close…so sleep-tousled…and undeniably, enticingly…bare-chested.*

She sighed. "Well, I'm wide awake now. Shall we hit the road early, or do you want to sleep a little longer? Oh, that's right. We're stuck here until someone can come out and open the car." She frowned. "I don't even have a quarter for the call. I wonder if the guy in the office will let us use his phone."

Jordan patted his front hip pocket and coins jingled. "That's why God gave men pockets. For emergency phone calls. Let's break up camp. By then, someone should be up and willing to drive 22 miles to help us out. I think we should try for a professional, rather than a coat hanger. Aren't Volvos pretty hard to break in to?"

"Yeah; usually that's good news," she said woefully.

"Come on, cheer up. It will all work out." He pushed himself out of the tent, pausing to say, "I didn't have any problem getting the tent to fall down last night, so dismantling shouldn't take long this morning! Get out carefully, unless you crave another dramatic rescue!"

He's certainly in a better mood this morning, Molly told herself in relief and hurriedly checked the clothes she had spent the night in. She wrinkled her nose; after having smelled the morning dew outside, the tent was oppressively musty.

She scooted over to hook open the tent flap and let in the freshness of the new day. Jordan was nowhere in sight. She pushed her shoulders out into the world and pulled the blanket out behind her.

Stretching to her full height, she released a wide yawn and glanced lazily around the awakening campground. A man sneezed as he poked at a campfire; two small boys picked up branches, dropping many, keeping few; a woman pulled towels off a rope stretched between trees. Stray fingers of sunlight reached through the leafy shrouds and brightened each vignette.

"Do you believe this: the showers can be used only after sundown, and we missed out last night. It seems they are rationing water due to a drought." Molly jumped. "Sorry, I didn't mean to scare you." Jordan touched her shoulder lightly and reached for the blanket she still held.

"That's okay; I was just daydreaming. What did you say? I can't take a shower?" She groaned at his answering nod. "I'm positively ripe."

"I know the feeling. But we don't have any towels, anyway, do we?"

"Paper towels, locked in the trunk. Well, the rest room ought to have some, too. I wonder if they'd mind if we used a couple hundred to dry off?"

"Since we're restricted to sink water, we can probably limit it to two dozen!" He bent to retrieve his shaving kit and her make-up bag from inside the tent. "Luckily, we didn't get a chance to stow this stuff back in the trunk before we got locked out last night."

Gone was the blame-placing of the previous evening. *We,* he said. Molly stared at him in wonder. Around the edges of her carefully organized world, a tiny fringe of tenderness loosened and fluttered in the breeze. *I hope I find someone like Jordan when I'm thirty, I mean forty...well, someone with the good parts of him.*

Jordan finished first. When Molly returned to the campsite, he had already taken down the tent and spread it out to roll it around the poles. While he tied it together in a neat packet, she stared at the two flattened spaces where her tent and his sleeping bag had been.

So close.

No matter where they were, she was intensely conscious of his nearness, and yet last night they had been just inches apart in the darkness, separated only by the tent. *Talk about an interesting subject for a study on personal space!* Jordan turned just then.

"Hey, you didn't just brush your teeth; you look magnificent! Amazing! A woman who doesn't take all day to get spiffed up." He struck his forehead in mock disbelief.

Clenching her fists, Molly danced toward him with a boxer's fancy footwork, growling, "Put yer dukes up, Buddy—them's fightin' words!"

Jordan cowered, sprawling on the ground at her feet where he lay grinning up at her. "Grab the sleeping bag and let's go make a phone call."

"Don't try to divert me from the fight!" He rolled over and nipped at her ankles. She grabbed his shoulder and he brought her down beside him. "Uncle!" she conceded, pushing herself up off the ground, panting, to offer a peace-making smile to him.

The manager let them use his phone and offered them coffee while they waited for the truck to arrive. The half hour went by quickly. They sat on a bench outside the office and sipped fresh coffee as they squinted in the early morning sunshine.

Within ten minutes of his arrival, the locksmith had the car open. After Molly paid for his services, he said, "Have a good trip now, Winsteads!"

Jordan found this very amusing.

While Molly cleaned out the cooler, reloaded it with fresh ice from the machine outside the office, and replenished their supplies, Jordan carefully cleaned out the car, tossing out papers and cans accumulated during the trip. Each time he passed Molly he would say, "How's it going, Mrs. Kendall?" or "Need any help, Mrs. Winstead?" or "I'm almost done, how about you, Ms. Winstead-Kendall?"

She responded each time with a good-natured, "Pffff."

They had just come back to the car after changing clothes when they heard another voice. A man in suspendered pants crossed over from the nearest RV.

"Those motorcycles woke you up, too?" They nodded, but the man needed no encouragement to continue. "They wasn't married, you know." He spat a brown, disgusting circle onto the ground. "Nope. Four guys, two gals. None was married to the other. Like I says to the Missus last night, I says, 'What's this world coming to,' I says, 'people who isn't married, sleeping together right out in public like it was something they is proud of.' That's what I says." Two bright red suspenders twanged against his plaid shirt in emphasis.

Jordan made an indiscernible noise and reached for Molly's hand. The man's voice droned on, "You folks came into camp pretty late to have to pitch a tent and all. And then you had the trouble with the lock this morning. Holy moly, listen to me flapping my gums and no proper introduction. Boyd Hardy, here." He wiped his hands on a bandana and offered a husky paw to Jordan.

The men shook hands firmly, a smile flitting across Jordan's face. "We're the Kendall-Winsteads. I'm Jordan and this is Molly." Mr. Hardy turned to Molly and pumped her arm hard enough to produce water had she been a long-dry cistern.

"Kensteads, eh?" He glanced at their license plate as his thumbs reinserted themselves beneath the suspenders, ready for action. "California. You wouldn't happen to know Lou Hardy, down in San Diego, would you now?"

"No, sorry. Name doesn't ring a bell," Jordan responded after a moment of thoughtfulness. "Well, it's nice to meet you. We've got to be shoving off now." Jordan and Molly nodded together as if in a rehearsed scene.

"Which way you folks heading? Maybe we'll run across each other somewheres along the trail." Another shot of brown juice flew through the air and landed expertly on the grass behind him. Molly twitched with restrained mirth. Jordan grabbed her hand again. She looked at him just as his lips signaled glee about to erupt.

"No," Jordan's voice rang with assurance, "we don't plan to do any more camping on this trip, do we, Sweetheart?" He gave Molly a husbandly smile and pulled her close in a warm hip-to-hip embrace. Boyd Hardy, the great champion of married love, beamed on them.

"So good to see young couples like yourselves enjoying the simple things of married life. A marriage ain't only beer and roses, like I tells my Missus." Twang! The flash of red was mesmerizing. "Well, mighty nice to have met you." He shook their hands again. "Jordy, Little Missus…"

Jordan's arm slipped around Molly's shoulders; they silently watched Mr. Hardy's retreat.

Sweetheart, huh?

To prevent the echo from playing again in her memory, Molly teased, "Pretty quick on the draw there, Old Shoe, even if you did give us a ridiculously complicated name'!" She pumped his hand and faked a spit over her shoulder.

Jordan pulled her flat against his chest and whispered in her ear, "Careful! They obviously spend lots of time looking out their windows; we're probably still under scrutiny!" They rocked in muffled laughter.

"What's this 'Old Shoe' business?" Jordan asked in her ear. Molly broke away from him; something caught in her throat as she tried to swallow. "Huh? Oh it's just a…it just popped out."

Her thoughts made her blush. *It's the love name Mom and Dad call each other; they've been married thirty years, and you called him 'Old Shoe' like he was…*She caught a flash of blue velvet eyes as Jordan looked quizzically into her face.

She ran her fingers through her hair and moved toward the car. "Do you suppose Mrs. Boyd Hardy is a smiler and a waver like the lady in the car yesterday?" she asked to divert him.

"I *knew* you were thinking about that guy yesterday when this fellow spit! I wonder what the odds are of meeting two men in two days who both turn out to be spitters?"

"Probably the same odds of two people meeting the way we did and ever becoming friends."

Jordan raised an eyebrow over a gentle smile. He opened the passenger door and bowed low, ushering her into her seat. "Madam, your carriage awaits."

As they pulled away from the campsite with two flat spots in the grass, the door to the Hardy's RV opened and the Missus stood in the doorway and waved a farewell, smiling brightly.

Good vibrations reverberated throughout the car rolling away from the campgrounds.

They stopped at the office long enough to refill the thermos with hot coffee and buy two cups to go. Heading East, Jordan said, "Feast or famine, huh?" Molly raised a questioning eyebrow and he explained, "Not the coffee. The fun. It's back. Yesterday I was afraid we'd never laugh again. Today looks a lot better."

"That's positive thinking in action! A rude awakening, no showers, no breakfast yet. I'm glad you can call this better."

Jordan studied the open road as he spoke, "I guess relationships are more important to me than circumstances, I just don't always remember it. If I acted on the golf course the way I've been behaving these past couple of days, I would still be a caddie," he smiled ruefully, "however you spell it. By the way, I didn't mean to embarrass you with Mr. What's-His-Name this morning."

"Boyd Hardy." Molly blew needlessly across her coffee cup. "After his tirade on morals, I figured you'd rather let him assume we're married than subject ourselves to an unwarranted personalized lecture."

"Yeah, thanks. He must have assumed we slept together in the tent."

"He probably thinks we made wild, passionate love all night." His voice was steady, but it knocked the props right out from Molly's reserve.

The coffee sloshed in her cup. "I want to say thanks for not, uh, taking advantage of the situation last night. Some guys would have figured it was a perfect chance."

"It had not exactly been a day to inspire romance, had it?"

Molly ran a finger around the rim of the Styrofoam coffee cup and shook her head vaguely. She recalled her body's response to his nearness outside her tent and pushed the memory aside with the first words she could summon, "I wish you could have seen how you looked in the back seat with all those kids yesterday!"

"Too bad you missed the thrill of being pinned under all those bodies in that heat!" He slumped dramatically behind the wheel.

"And that lady! She only showed signs of life twice. Each time they drove away, she waved. Well, she's probably in shock, living with that tribe!" Her words seemed to wipe all levity from Jordan's face. "What's wrong?"

"The reason she wasn't any livelier was that she was reading."

Molly whistled. "Now that's what I call concentration."

Jordan's voice grew harder with each word he clipped off, "She was the perfect illustration of my point, even though I don't mean to start up again with our disagreement. The most exciting thing that's probably happened on a family drive in the last ten years is going on in living color right outside their car, but does she see it? No; she has her nose buried in a book."

"Well, good for her. She deserves a break from her life."

"Molly, the woman was a zombie and you know it. She didn't relate to the real world. Life goes on around her, but she lives in a make-believe world of black letters on a white page."

"Stop. Right. There." Her eyes torched the space between them. "You can't walk into that woman's sphere and apply your misguided rules and ideas..." Her tirade skid to a halt. "Why are you so antagonistic against reading, anyway?"

The question caught him off guard; he answered defensively, "Some people put reading up on a pedestal, like it was the most important thing in the world. They have no tolerance for anyone who doesn't worship the printed word."

"And some people are the same with sports, perhaps golf, for instance," she challenged.

"Life just isn't found between the covers of a book. Life's not like books make it seem."

"And isn't that the saddest thing you've ever heard?"

"Look, I think we've pretty much established that I'm not much for reading, and it's your whole life. In fact, it's your whole family's history, it seems. Where I'm coming from, that's a pretty wide ditch to cross." He twisted his collar with one finger and leaned forward in the seat to yank his shirt away from his back as if suddenly choked by it. "Let's not talk about it, okay?"

"Is that your way of handling conflict, Jordan, not talking about it?"

Jordan's lips formed a hard line. Molly twisted her shoulder free of the seat belt and faced him. "So you're not interested in reading. Lots of people aren't until one day they get intrigued by something and discover that between the covers of a books lies a wealth of information or excitement."

"Pffff." He stared stonily at the road ahead.

"Even if your whole life is golf, what a shame not to read about the sport, and famous golfers, or some fabulously exciting tournaments that are history now."

"I would rather not continue this discussion."

She snorted, most unbecomingly, "Fine." As she looked out the window, she remembered her threat at the Club to deposit her passenger at an airport if the trip went sour. If she saw an airport anytime soon, that was exactly what she would do. She would gladly pay for his ticket just to get this guy out of her life right now.

Chapter Ten

The piercing whine of an ambulance interrupted her plans. Jordan pulled over to let the vehicle pass. They had reached the fringe of a town without having seen much of the intervening miles.

Jordan reached for Molly's hand and ran it flat against his palm; his thumb bumped across each pink-tipped finger. "Molly, I like you. A lot. But being with you frustrates me no-end. Well, it's not *being* with you that…oh, I don't know." He tightened his fingers around her hand and lifted it to his lips. "There are some things that won't change," he said and softly kissed each polished tip.

Talk about disarming? Not only did every thought of airports disappear, but those angry wishes were instantly replaced by nearly unquenchable longing to sooth the tight lines on his jaw. "Maybe so."

He nodded and shifted their hands to her lap. "We might just have to agree to disagree agreeably. We've said some things that are hard to hear, but no blood has been drawn." He offered a wistful smile like a peace pipe and steered the Volvo back into traffic.

"I guess we get gold stars on our behavior charts for that," she said. The Kiss, that haunting third passenger, flitted by and once again held them suspended in time.

Bugles played in Molly's mind. *He likes me.* A red flag waved over that thought. *But I frustrate him.* Unaccountable sadness welled up inside her chest. *Well, I could say the same about him!*

"Are you starved, or would you be open to a suggestion?"

"Let's hear it, Old-timer; I can eat anytime, or I can wait. I doubt you'll be able to hold out, though!"

"Old-timer?"

She resolutely banished sadness. "Didn't I tell you? When Royce called about you needing a ride, I had you pegged for some old fellow, close to retirement, who would be so deaf that I would have to spend the trip yelling everything I said!"

Jordan raised his voice to an aged, reedy pitch, "Fella back at the stage coach stop said there's one of them newfangled health clubs in the town up ahead. How 'bout it, little darlin'? We stretch these old bones and then enjoy a wholesome breakfast of prunes and oat bran."

Molly rolled the window down for fresh air and answered with a grin that felt good as it unfurled taut muscles, "Forward, Gramps."

"Eh? Can't hear ya with the wind blowing through the buggy."

Molly tapped Jordan on the shoulder. He swiveled his head, looking for her. "Over here. Read my lips." She enunciated distinctly, "Your idea is the best one since sliced bread."

"So? They're slicing bread now, eh? Swell!"

"Goofus!" Molly said and let her fingers rest on his arm. "Hey, slow down! That could be the health club right there." She ducked and read aloud, "Fitness. Swimming. Visitors Welcome. That ought to be it."

After they signed the register for towels and the use of the facilities, the young attendant asked, "You've been here before, right?"

Jordan answered casually, "No, I don't think so. Nice place you've got here."

The young man stared at Jordan, "You look so familiar. Well, you ought to know where you have been, or not. Oh, the pool is co-ed this morning, if that interests you."

"It sure does," Jordan said and turned to Molly. "A quick swim will sure give these old bones a thrill."

"Anything to postpone the prunes!"

He shook his head and turned to confide in the attendant, "The younger generation's misconceptions."

Molly was suddenly solicitous, "Are you sure the pool won't be too strenuous?" She turned to the youth listening wide-eyed to their whole exchange, "Maybe you have a whirlpool?" Jordan hooted before the fellow could do more than nod. Molly asked Jordan, "Can you find the locker room? If not, perhaps this young man could be of some assistance."

"Get out of here, you young upstart!" Molly grabbed a towel and sashayed backwards toward the exit marked *Women's Dressing Room*, pausing to teasingly wave before it closed on Jordan's laughter and the confused attendant's blank stare.

Minutes later, Molly floated on her back in the pool, watching Jordan poise and spring into a faultless dive. Diving beneath the surface, she found him; their hands met in the private underwater world until they burst through the surface gasping for air.

"You must swim a lot." Jordan matched Molly's stroke.

"Yeah. And I do water exercises, too. See?" She propelled herself across the width of the pool with jumping jacks from a back float position.

He tried to imitate her, but could hardly keep above water. He finally gave up, shook the water from his ears and said, "Not fair! You women have an advantage in your shape for floating. Bet you can't do this, though." He dove into a handstand on the bottom of the pool.

Molly took a deep breath and kicked her feet into position. "Nope, I just float back up. Unfair!" she sputtered after three unsuccessful attempts.

"I rest my case. Males are natural sinkers; females, natural floaters!" He flopped back, flailing the water. "Help! Sinking man needs rescue!"

She splashed her way to his side and flipped him on his back. "Don't drown! Life is worth living!" She grasped his chin and towed him to the edge of the pool with several powerful strokes and lots of heavy breathing. They splashed each other as they tread water, giving Molly time to rest. "I saved your life!"

"You know, in China that means I'm your slave for life." He paddled in circles around her; she patted his head and sighed, "I suppose that means you'll be dogging my footsteps from now on!" She rolled her eyes and pushed off toward the diving board.

Jordan swam along behind, dog-paddling, woofing, grabbing at her ankles.

"Hey," she called back to him, "this is like riding a tandem bike!" He gave a forceful kick and they shot ahead with his hands clasping her ankles. "You pump, I'll steer!" she said.

They must have swallowed gallons of water goofing around. "Enough! I can't take any more on an empty stomach." Jordan moaned at last. He hoisted himself up and out and helped Molly up beside him. She lay back on the tiles long enough to flick a water bubble off his back.

"I'm starved, too," she said, wringing water out of her hair. "Let's hit the showers. See you in the lobby in half an hour." Her footsteps left sloppy wet puddles behind her. Jordan headed for the men's locker room whistling.

As she stood beneath the shower's spray, or while she combed out her hair, or when she quickly ran a razor over her legs, images of Jordan wove their way through her thoughts.

The feel of his hands on her ankles.

The smell of the freeway bush's flower.

The way he pulled at his shirt when he was frustrated.

How the skin by his eyes crinkled just before a smile hit his lips.

A teenager around the corner in the dressing room laughed to her friend, "I've got to throw out these old shoes one of these days." Color instantly rose on Molly's cheeks. "I can't believe I called him Mom and Dad's special love name!" she muttered.

"Were you talking to me?"

Molly turned, startled, to face a hefty woman in shorts and a perspiration-streaked shirt.

"Sorry, I was just talking to myself. Bad habit. I didn't know anyone was around."

The woman leaned against the wall and wiped her forehead with a towel. "I heard you humming and talking. Well, you know what they say, as long as you don't get answers…"

Molly smiled politely and turned to the mirror. Undaunted by the disinterest of her captive audience, the woman continued, "I used to be like you. Skinny, good looker. I exercise a couple of days each week, but it's kind of like locking the barn after the horse is stolen, as they say."

She slapped her thigh in enjoyment of her joke, setting rolls of skin of motion. Molly sensed no reply was necessary. "Nice outfit," the woman wheezed when she stopped laughing.

"Thanks," Molly said and tucked the tails of a raglan-sleeved blouse into white slacks, threading a braided rope that matched the blue piping on the blouse through the belt loops.

"I bet he loves it." She nodded approvingly as Molly added dangling earrings to complete the outfit.

Molly almost jabbed a new hole in her ear. "Who?"

The woman shrugged. "Whoever he is you're dressing up for."

Molly stared at her reflection in the mirror.

"I mean it. Don't change a thing. He'll love ya."

Molly felt the blood rush to her face as she murmured a quick thanks and stuffed her belongings into the case. She forced a weak smile and fled to the lobby. The attendant was talking on the phone, his back to her, "I tell you, man, he's here! BJ Kendall, the pro golfer! I saw him and talked to him! He gave me his autograph. I know there's no tournament in town. He's on his way to the one in Minneapolis. And he's married to this babe who is…"

Molly cleared her throat distinctly. A fiery blush inflamed each pore from the young man's collar to his hairline. He took her wet towels and locker key and squeaked, "Your husband said to tell you he'll be right back, Ma'am."

So we're back to the married routine again. Resignedly, she looked quickly at the registration clipboard and found that Jordan had hyphenated her signature; according to the record, the Winstead-Kendall's had used the facilities today. She grinned in spite of herself and headed for the door.

Her car was gone. *Well, maybe Jordan had needed to run and buy deodorant or something.*

She dropped into a chair by the window to wait. The attendant kept eyeing her. She controlled an urge to wink at him. *So I'm a babe, am I?* After overhearing as much of his phone conversation as she had, she understood why Jordan had resorted to borrowing her name. *The guy is genuinely famous, it seems. What a life. Not to be able to sit in a restaurant or sign in at a health club without creating a scene...I wonder if it's worth it to him? So, where is the show-stopping dude?*

She fidgeted for a few minutes, keeping one eye trained on the entrance until at last she saw him. Striding confidently, he came up the sidewalk. His beyond-a-doubt-male body filled his short-sleeved white knit shirt and crisp white slacks with the blue and tan belt at his waist.

He swung the door open and wiggled his eyebrows. "Would you look at us? Both dressed in white, like the angels we are!" His eyes ran the length of her body in evident approval.

He'll love you, he'll love you. She jumped to her feet to silence the inner echo of these unsettling unsolicited words from the locker room.

"Nice duds, Mr. Winstead-Kendall." He tipped his head toward the desk and muttered, "I had hoped it would help, but it didn't. Thanks for the loan of your good name. For now, come with me. I've got a surprise for you." He picked up her suitcase and ceremoniously bowed her out the door.

The car was closer to the building than where they had first parked it. "Jordan! You washed it! How did you manage that so fast?"

"Zoom. That's me. Lightning. I ended up with the car keys, so when I was putting my case in the trunk, I noticed a car wash across the street, and went with my impulses."

"Well, it looks terrific. Thanks." She stepped off the curb on the driver's side.

"Wait. You've got to cover your eyes."

"Two surprises?" She obediently covered her eyes with one hand and rested the other on Jordan's proffered arm.

"Careful, now. Step carefully, that's right. Oops, watch it. I won't let you fall. Okay, turn around, sit. There. You can look now."

"Jordan! Where did you get these gorgeous flowers?" Molly buried her face in tissue paper wrapped around a rainbow of colors and scents. "You found time to wash the car, buy flowers *and* take a shower? I admire your organizational abilities!"

"It's easy. Just choose a carwash stall next to a florist's truck."

"Hmmm, thanks."

"You're welcome. Now, let's eat. The kid at the desk told me about a good place."

Their waitress leaned over to inhale the bouquet on the chair beside Molly. "Happy birthday?" she guessed.

"Uh, thank you."

"Lies, lies, lies!" Jordan scolded in a whisper when they were alone at the table.

"Pardon me, Mr. Winstead-Kendall or Kendall-Winstead, or what ever alias you're currently using!"

"I think Kendall-Winstead has a nice ring to it, don't you. It flows better than Winstead-Kendall."

Molly shook her head in mock dismay and said, "Pffff. At least no one will suspect that we're married. Aren't husbands notoriously negligent about bringing flowers to their wives?"

"I would hope anyone married to you would never forget." His voice was oddly quiet; she broke the stem off a red carnation and clipped it over one ear. He leaned back in his chair, watching the whole procedure. Finished, she looked into eyes reminiscent of summer skies above Minnesota's 10,000 lakes.

The heady fragrance of the flowers surrounded them like a veil that set the mood for their light-hearted conversation. Back on the road, with Jordan at the wheel, signs for the next town were popping up regularly when he asked, "Any interest in an ice cream cone?"

Molly flung her hands in the air in mock horror. "In the middle of the morning? Are you trying to corrupt me?"

"Absolutely. You're on vacation, remember?"

Off the main road, he pulled over to the curb and whistled to a small boy riding by on his bike. "Hey, son, catch!" Gravel flew as the child hit his brakes and rose off the bike seat to catch the quarter Jordan tossed in the air. "I'll match that one if you lead the way to the nearest ice cream store." The boy was lost in a moving cloud of dust.

Jordan paid the promised quarter and, to their young guide's ecstasy, told the counter boy dip the boy's choice of a double dip cone, too. Jordan then turned to Molly and asked, "Decided yet?"

"Nope. I've been too busy watching you make that kid's day." She peered into the glassed freezer cases. "I always have the worst time deciding."

"Okay, then I'll pick for you and you pick for me."

"And there will be a contest to see if we know what we're eating!"

"No sweat. Pick two dips for me. I'm making up for the supper I missed last night."

Molly pointed out the flavors she wanted for Jordan and left the cone in the wire rack as Jordan did the same for her. Molly waited outside on the steps with the small boy who was contentedly licking his diminishing cone. "Your husband sure is a nice man." A chocolate-coated tongue darted around to catch a potential drip.

"We're not married." It felt good to set the record straight with someone.

"Well, your boyfriend, then." His disgusted look indicated that relationships were low on his priority list right then.

The door swung open and Jordan held out Molly's mystery cone. "Quick, or these white pants of ours will suffer!" His tongue made a wide swipe around the top dip of his cone. "Mmmmm. Let's see…could this be, uh, mmmmmm…" His words were lost in another lick.

Molly savored her first taste. "Wow. This is great. I could get used to this life of midmorning decadence!"

"Thank you, Mister. For the ice cream and the quarters." The boy patted his pocket and licked his lips.

"You're welcome. You showed us to the perfect store." With a quick shove away from the curb, the chocolate-mustachioed boy and his bicycle disappeared.

"Yes, thank you. How much do I owe? I was rushed out of the store by a man in white before I could pay!"

Jordan nodded and kept on licking. "Guys dying for ice cream can be downright rude, so they should be required to pay." He shifted on the step beside her. "Turn around a little. I need a backrest." He wiggled up close until their backs were touching. "Lean back and we'll bask in the sunshine and enjoy the moment."

The strength of his body against hers lassoed all her thoughts. She leaned against him with enough pressure to keep them balanced. It was a special moment. Warm sensations. Cold ice cream.

Hilary spoke between licks. "So, let the contest begin. Hmm, the bottom dip is very pink; almost red. The top dip is a definite berry. Okay, here's my vote: The bottom is cherry something-or-other and the top is," lick, lick, "raspberry. Right?"

"You're close. The fellow said they call the bottom flavor 'Cherry spasms' for some unknown reason, and the top one is Berry Delightful, which could be raspberry. I picked them to match the flowers you've worn in your hair."

"Good show. Always coordinate food with outfits, in case of spills," she said in mock seriousness. "Your turn. Name those flavors."

"Easy. Blueberry and Maple Nut. I love 'em both, but why the interesting combination?"

"To match your blueberry eyes and maple nut hair." With the words in the air, Molly blushed like a teenager, glad he could not see her.

Before they left town, Jordan pulled into a gas station and said, "Not that I'm against having fun today, but let's start with a full tank and vary our entertainment!" Molly applauded.

She took the wheel when they started up again. "Story time!" Jordan announced, settling back in the passenger's seat. "The topic is 'When I Was a Kid.' Your choice of variations on the theme."

"Miss Gebhart, Miss Rinehart, Miss Klug, Mrs. Simmons, Miss Peters, and Mrs...." Molly chewed a fingernail absentmindedly. "What was her name? She was the prettiest of all."

"Incredible. Is this a demonstration of a librarian's mind at work? Who are those people, your grade school teachers?"

Molly nodded, "Yup. Or, as Miss Peters insisted, 'Yes'. I'm two short because I didn't go to kindergarten and because I can't remember the one for sixth grade."

"Oh, you missed a good time in kindergarten. How ever did you learn how to take naps on a hard floor, or to share your toys?"

Molly slapped the steering wheel. "So that's my trouble! No wonder I've flunked Naps on a Hard Floor all these years. And no wonder you did so well on the hard ground outside the tent!"

The morning sun coming through the sunroof breathed life into their early years as they captured stories and uncovered long-forgotten events for the retelling.

Jordan gave a special flourish to his stories of learning to ride his bike, skipping school the day the barber cut his hair too short, and the time he was sent to bed without supper for throwing the neighbor girl's doll in the back of a passing garbage truck. "If it had been you, instead of Missy, the doll would have had a dramatic rescue by its 'mother'!"

Her wilting look ended with an untamed chuckle.

Then he plied her with questions on each person or place she mentioned as she mentally turned pages. She had nearly forgotten about painting extra flowers on the wallpaper in her bedroom, or cutting her most-expensive doll's hair, or sprinkling five pounds of special imported candy as she and Mara had acted out the story of Hansel and Gretel on their way around the block.

"I thought it was bread crumbs in the story."

"It was, but we thought pretty foil-wrapped candy would be more fun to follow than plain bread crumbs. Mom was furious! It was her anniversary present from Dad!"

In telling a highly amused Jordan about the day she had been treed by the "wild" collie next door, and the episode of exploring the empty— if you don't count the owl in the rafters—garage on the lot next door, she enjoyed again the best of that magical time called childhood.

"Great stories! If you had been a little girl in California, or if I would have lived in your neighborhood, I would have played with you. You were a fun kid, Minnesota!"

"And you're not too shabby a storyteller, yourself! And it's nice to have an appreciative audience."

"Don't mean to disenchant you, but that's not applause you've been hearing for the last half hour, it's my stomach rumbling! Our ice cream cones were a long time ago."

"No argument here. Check the map and see what's ahead in the next half hour."

He spread the map open on his knees. "I haven't got a clue where we are; I've been listening and talking instead of navigating. Guess that's what happens when a person flies too much. We tend to forget to pay attention to where we are." He refolded the map and looked out the window. "Doesn't this feel like hamburger country?"

"Sure does. Big ones, guaranteed to drip down to your elbows. I'm game on one condition."

"Anything for a lady with wilting flowers. Here, let's douse their wrapping with a little more water." He reached for the water jug. "What's your deal?"

"Pizza tonight. We should be in Cheyenne by then."

"Where are we scheduled to stay?"

They groaned in unison and looked at each other sheepishly.

Molly said, "We are getting worse, instead of better. You would think that after last night, we would have called ahead. But did we call? No!" She pounded the car horn in frustration which scared a flock of crows out of the ditch. "My brain cells are dying like flies." She pulled her cell phone from her purse. "This will remind me to call when we stop."

"We'll call. I will remind you, I promise, when we stop for drippy hamburgers." Jordan stuck out his hand and they shook solemnly to seal the deal.

"It shouldn't be hard to get you a room."

He groaned. "Don't say that. It brings to mind putting up tents in the dark!" He slapped imaginary mosquitoes on his neck.

They drove past an inviting park in a quiet little town and parked the car under a spreading oak tree. They walked several blocks to a hamburger stand and asked for take-out service. "Whew, the smell from this bag is driving me wild! Walk faster or I'll devour everything before we get back to the park!" he warned.

They spread the stadium blanket on the grass beneath a tree. Sitting cross-legged, they faced each other as they drank lemonade to wash down the hamburgers that did threaten, with each bite, to drip down to their elbows.

When they were putting the blanket back in the trunk, Molly caressed the leather golf bag and asked, "Shouldn't you practice, or something, occasionally?"

Jordan grinned, "Are you worried about me?"

"Well, not worried, but if you're heading back to some big important tournament, it seems to me that you'll be a little rusty if you don't practice."

Jordan threw his arm casually around Molly's waist and guided her along the walking path circling the park. "What's the worst thing that could happen? I would lose." He shrugged. "Then someone else would win. Nobody wins every single time. Well, unless you're Tiger Woods, and that position has already been filled. Maybe if you toss a good-luck penny in that wishing well this will be my turn."

The fountain sparkled in the sunlight directly across the park from where they stood. Molly headed left on the sidewalk toward it as Jordan followed it to the right. They collided head-on. "Sorry, I forgot to signal that turn," Molly grinned, extremely conscious of Jordan's hands on her elbows.

He cupped her face in his hand and tilted it until their eyes met. "Just you watch it, Lady," he growled. "We don't put up with no anti-signalers in this here town. Got that?"

A delicious shiver ran through her body and she shut her eyes. "Sorry, so sorry. I'm not exactly anti-signaling, you know."

His lips brushed across her cheeks to her lips as he murmured, "Best lie-detector in town is these lips of mine…" The Kiss was undemanding and lingered briefly, holding the fragile moment between them. "Liars are easy to spot…I'll need to verify my findings on this case, though."

The second kiss pulled on an invisible string that ran from Molly's trembling lips straight through her body to her toes, releasing a wave of passion behind it. The heat in the core of her body rivaled the mid-day sun in its intensity.

"Am I guilty?" She was so close she could see his whiskers getting an early start on their afternoon shadow.

"Maybe not guilty of…what was the charge? I forgot. Oh, was it that you didn't share your Berry Delicious? Give me just a taste. Mmmm, very good, thank you."

"I just got my first taste of…whatever."

Jordan looked around like a kid under the watchful eye of a teacher and muttered out the side of his mouth, "Pssst. Eyes, hair," pointing to each.

Molly nodded, "Eyes, hair. Oh, blueberry, maple. Well, you weren't exactly generous, yourself, with sample tastes."

"Guilty as charged. We'll have to hang on matching gallows. The whole town will remember the day when two criminals in white swung from the ropes at dusk. Would you be willing to settle out of court and forego the gallows?"

"You're forgiven. Case closed." Molly murmured as her head just naturally rested against his shoulder.

Jordan sighed in mock relief and pulled her closer. For the seeming frivolity of their words, there was nothing superficial about what was changing between them. Molly felt out of control, as foreign an idea to her ordered world as any could be.

As he rubbed his chin on her hair Jordan said softly, "Want to know what I found out when I called about tonight's reservation?" She nodded and waited, forgetting to breathe.

"While you ordered hamburgers, I talked with an obliging motel manager. The good news is, your reservation is intact. The rest of the news is that," Molly pulled back and watched his eyebrows lift above a hesitating smile, "there's no other room empty."

"We'll just try another motel, or drive farther…"

He cut in gently, "I told him that we'll take it. It's a suite, so it's actually two rooms. All very proper. You have got to admit that's more space than we had last night within the circle around the space we occupied when we slept."

So, we both noticed. Molly's pulse pounded with the thought.

He drew her back into his embrace. "I promised you pizza and I do not want to spend the whole night looking for a room."

They walked slowly back to the car. He opened her door and then came around to climb behind the wheel. As they drove away from the quietness of the park, the rhythm of the tires sang in Molly's ears: *one room.*

CHAPTER ELEVEN

The scent from the surprise bouquet was overpowering for Molly. She rolled the car window down a few inches and leaned into the breeze. Jordan had said nothing for several miles, as if he, too, were sorting the rush of emotions.

"Talk to me about how you feel." His low voice released a response first from the center of her being and then from her lips.

"I feel like I'm a kid, swinging." The words sounded to Molly like they were coming from a cave inside her head.

"You mean like I'm pushing you?" A tinge of concern shaded the question.

"No. Like I'm sailing through…good times, and I don't want to…well, I don't want bad memories or things we've said or I've imagined or whatever, to get in the way of my enjoying the good times." Her eyes mirrored her turbulent soul, despite her calm tone. Words she couldn't say tumbled around in her thoughts.

What does this man do to me? What's happening to the Molly I know? She had no answer to the unsettling questions.

He leaned forward in the seat, twisting so that he looked her straight in the eyes for a moment. A playful smile tugged at his lips, "Does a librarian have a soft spot in her heart for an old golfer like me?"

"A dumpster diver can't exactly reject an old ball-whacker!" Their banter lightened the moment. Molly hesitated briefly and then reached over and touched Jordan's arm. His hand covered hers, keeping it in place.

"Just so you know, I plan to keep the door shut between the two rooms," he said softly.

"Thank you." She let relief race through her, glad that she would not need to spend the rest of the day wondering how to say whatever it was she would have needed to say if he had not ventured first into the void.

"Want to talk?" Jordan asked softly, breaking the comfortable silence that had embraced them.

"That's one thing long trips are good for, lots of talking."

"Pick a topic," Jordan challenged.

"Any topic?"

"Well, how about telling me what you were thinking just now?"

Molly bit her bottom lip pensively. "Maybe you are right, to some degree, about books." Jordan raised a quizzical eyebrow, even as his cheek muscles tensed.

She hurried on, "Nothing in all the books I've read prepared me for knowing how to respond to you. I've read psychology books, even some romances that my friend, Bryn, insists are the best thing out there, and then there are the biographies of supposedly famous lovers, and the continuing best-seller 'men and women' type books." She shrugged. "No help from any of them."

"Sounds like a lot of reading about relationships, am I right? I gather that's what you mean."

"To use a phrase I detest, I've always thought I'm a people person, but in meeting you, I have come to realize that I really do not come close. I am perceived as aloof by people who wonder why I am not more, uh, open." She took a quick breath and plunged into the deep waters. "I have not been in love since I left college. I am a single, 27-year-old professional woman who thinks, from time to time, about who, if anyone, I would marry. Meanwhile, I am too busy, too structured to allow for the unpredictable world of male-female relationships." Her voice had grown progressively softer until the last words were but a whisper.

"Describe the person to me who lives in your dreams," Jordan leaned toward her to catch her response.

Molly's saliva dried up instantly. "I really do not have a physical description in mind. It is more of a…well, the man I marry would have to share my interests, but I do not necessarily mean doing everything together." She stared, unseeing, at a car passing them. "I know that I am a strong personality; I overpower anyone who is not equally strong."

"And you have a hidden sense of adventure. On the outside you look like a reserved, sedate…" He waved his hand as if to conjure up the right word.

"Librarian?" she teased.

"Maybe, but you are no stereotyped librarian, Minnesota!" His deep laugh rumbled through the car. "When I opened the dumpster and saw you…" he silenced her sputtering with a cautionary finger, "if I had been asked to pick ten possible occupations for the person looking up at me from that mess, librarian would not have even been on the list!"

"Would you believe I know librarians who are sky divers, helicopter pilots, and rodeo riders?"

"And now your name enters as an exciting addition to the list of Librarians With Daring Hobbies!"

Molly stared coolly at him. He mimicked her until a smile melted a path from her lips to her eyes.

"Point Two in my case that you love adventure: you are taking a trip with a total stranger."

"Wrong on both counts. The watch I had lost in the dumpster was my grandmother's gift on my sixteenth birthday; the sentimental value outweighed any fears I had about climbing in there."

"No big, mean dude gave it to you?"

"Nope."

"Hmmm, that makes you a sentimental adventurer. Okay, what about this trip?"

"That is purely a matter of trust, and a big heart, I guess."

"Explain."

"Royce has been my friend for a long time. Not a romantic friend, just a friend. If he says you are okay, then I trust him. Like I would a brother. Remember, I figured you for an eighty-twelve-year old!"

"And when I wasn't?"

"What can I say? I am a wonderful human being. But it was all balanced with trust in what Royce had to say."

"I still think you are an adventurer."

Molly responded with a jutting chin. "I would peg you as impulsive."

"Impulsive? *I* was *outside* the dumpster!" Jordan pounded the steering wheel with glee, honking the horn in the process. Two passing cars responded and he waved at them, setting off a series of wondering stares at the Volvo's occupants.

"Good! Now seven more people realize that I am trapped in this vehicle with a maniac!"

"Nah, they see the California plates and just figure that we are both a little goofy!"

Molly called out the car window to the scenery racing by, "Royce! Come get your buddy! I cannot take it anymore!"

Jordan's laughter rumbled. "Let's hope there's no one within ten miles named Royce! They would have to handcuff me to get me to leave you now. I am having too much fun!"

"Tell me, do you usually kiss women within the first three hours you have known them?"

Jordan grinned lopsidedly. "Whoa, now that is an abrupt change of topics! Nope, can't say I have."

"So, why the kiss before we even left your curb?"

"All the rules changed when I met you, Minnesota."

Molly bobbed her head, "Impulsive, I knew it."

"No, responsive."

"Responsive to what? I wasn't asking for it!"

He ignored her bait. "Did it upset you, when I kissed you?"

"Let's say it surprised me. If I had been upset, I would have spoken up. After all, it has been drilled into me since I was a kid that I am in charge of my personal space."

"Actually, it surprised me, too."

"Why?"

"Because it seemed the most natural thing in the world to do. When I went into the store to get the cups, I gave myself a pretty good talking to."

So, that's why the flirt in the convertible didn't even get a side glance! Molly brushed back a wandering strand of hair, studying the passing scenery until she could be sure her feelings were under control again. "It sure was one interesting way to start this trip!" she said with a crooked grin.

Signs heralding the approaching town sprouted along the route and Jordan cut the conversational thread gently. "Since our room reservation is solid, why don't we find that pizza before we go to the motel? Once we hit our room, I would like to shower and not get back into this car again until tomorrow."

Our room! Intimate, and intimidating. She was awed by the power of life that surged through her, resurrecting responses she had thought long dormant. *Okay, breathe normally, Molly. In and out, in and out.*

Aloud, she offered, "I agree. This car has lost its intrigue for today."

They decided a jammed parking lot was recommendation enough for a pizza parlor and they joined the noisy crowd. Molly handed a huge, plastic covered menu to Jordan, but he waved it away and let his body relax on his side of the booth. "Your choice. I must have left my reading glasses in my suitcase."

"I didn't know you wore glasses. Amazing," she teased, "that even after riding this far across the country with you, I still don't know these little details."

"Oh, I still have lots of secrets." He shrugged and shifted beneath his shirt, the tension in the gesture in sharp contrast to his casual tone of voice.

"Well, do you want what they call Colossal, or shall we just settle for a smaller version, 'Family-sized, feeds six'? Wait! That's not all the choices. Do you want six vegetables, seven meats, and four 'assorted' things?"

"Is there an 'everything'?" he asked. She nodded. "That's my vote. As for size, let's be a family."

"I can only be two hungry people; you'll have to be four."

While they waited for their order, they relaxed. Jordan said, "See the couple directly across the room from us? The guy with a beard."

"Yeah."

"Married, or dating? Which would you guess?"

She shifted slightly to allow for unobtrusive peek. "I would say married, but not happily."

"Yeah. What a pity."

"How about the two at the little table in the middle of the room? They're eating salads now."

"Definitely dating. And obviously thinking ahead to when they get out of here!" His eyebrows rose over a playful leer.

"Jordan! Just because they're playing footsies and holding hands across the table!"

"I rest my case!"

"It could be anything. My mom and dad hold hands a lot. It used to embarrass Mara and me when we were teenagers, but looking back, I realize it gave us a great sense of security."

"How so?"

"Subconsciously, I guess, we felt that since Mom and Dad's marriage was strong, our little world was stable. They are two of the world's great romantics! I wish you could meet them."

Now why did I say that? There's no way, and no reason, that they'll ever meet.

"I would like to. My folks aren't very demonstrative, but I know what you mean about feeling stable. When I was young, my room was above the kitchen. I used to listen to them at night, and hear them teasing each other and laughing. I always knew they loved each other. They could have long, heated discussions about meat prices, or menu changes, but I never felt unsafe."

They were quiet for a moment, then Molly said, "Maybe that is what has kept me from falling in love. I just keep waiting for the spark to be there that I have seen between Mom and Dad all these years, and I have never sensed it in any relationship I have had over the years."

"It is worth waiting for. Oh, good, our pizza, at last!" The next few minutes were spent dishing up.

"For having been cooped up in the car all day," Molly said between bites,

"...we are both pretty hungry," Jordan finished, catching a long cheese strand expertly with his tongue.

"Jordan, I had a really good time with you today."

"Same here. You are really easy to talk to, Molly. You know, I think I have learned more about you on this trip than I've known about some of my so-called 'serious relationships' that seem so important in anything written up about me."

"For instance?" Molly asked, despite her longing to hear about those relationships.

"Your first bicycle was blue, you collect shells, your parents are *not* pushing you to get married, you keep your games on the shelf in your coat closet, lima beans make you gag but you crave popcorn, you are naturally blonde, and your favorite spot in your house is a big corduroy recliner chair," he rattled off the list, his smile growing with each item.

"Wow, deep, dark secrets, huh? Okay, wise guy, where was I born?"

"St. Paul, Minnesota. Only because your parents were down in the Twin Cities for something or other."

"Not bad. So, what is my pet peeve?"

Jordan squinted, deep in thought, "People who laugh at you when you are hiding in places you will not admit to being found? Nah, I guess we did not cover that yet."

"It does not surprise me that you would guess that, the way I get all riled up when you bring up the dumpster, but an even bigger gripe is people who are not up-front with me. What gets you?"

A shadow flitted across his face. "Uhhh, I guess I have never given it much thought." He wiped invisible crumbs off his face with his napkin. "About ready to go?"

So, end of conversation. Now what happened? She forced herself to stay calm, refusing to worry about something she might have merely conjured up. She pushed an almost empty glass away and groaned, "Yeah. I should run around the parking lot, or stumble behind the car all the way to the motel."

"If it is exercise you are after, it can be arranged!" Jordan teased, the cloud, real or imagined, having lifted. "I will meet you at the car." Molly handed him the money for her share and headed out into the evening air while Jordan chatted with the man at the cash register.

"Have I got a surprise for you!"

"Tell me!"

"Patience, Minnesota!" He swung the car around and left the parking lot with a sense of purpose.

Molly opened her mouth to question, but after a look from Jordan, opted for silence. They rounded a corner and her jaw fell open, "Miniature golf?"

"Aren't you the one who wanted me to practice?"

"Oh, sure; like your big tournament is on this scale! Jordan, I am no good at this golfing stuff."

"Not to worry. Just have fun, breathe the fresh air instead of exhaust, and stretch your legs."

After they had paid and selected balls and clubs, Molly said, "I have not played miniature golf for years, you realize, and I am supposed to pretend this will be a fair game?"

Jordan shrugged and balanced his club on the tip of his finger in midair. "It's not a typical course for me, you know. I do not usually face a moving windmill at the fourth or fifth hole!"

Molly swung at his club but he caught it easily. "I get to tee off first, so there will be one hole I won't be self-conscious about!" she said defensively.

"Hey, for a non-golfer, you really know the language. I am impressed!"

She positioned herself and swung carefully at the vivid orange ball that had a mind of its own; it rolled nowhere near where she had envisioned. Jordan pushed his lips in and out silently. "Do not say one word, Jordan. Remember, this was your idea, not mine."

He stared in wide-eyed innocence. "My lips are sealed."

Molly snorted and moved aside for his first swing. The bright green ball responded to his gentle tap like a trained seal. Molly jabbed her hair behind her ears and bent over the obnoxious orange ball.

She swung.

And missed.

Jordan carefully examined a tree growing along the sidewalk. "Why don't you take another shot at it?"

"I do not need any special favors from you," she retorted.

"Nothing special. I just figured you were taking a practice swing. Golfers do that a lot."

"Oh. Right." She walked back and focused her attention on the vivid enemy. She swung and the ball slowly meandered toward the hole.

He nodded his approval. "I would like something cold to drink before we get too far from the machines. Want anything?"

"Something diet and brown sounds good." In his absence, Molly used up two shots to get her ball into the hole.

"Here you go," Jordan said, handing her a slippery can. "Hey, good! Next hole."

"Mark me down for four on number one," Molly confessed.

"Gotcha," Jordan said as he studiously marked the card. He made the next two holes under par. She smiled weak praise at him.

As they were finishing the fourth hole, they noticed a young boy trailing along behind them. He moved in closer and stared up at Jordan intently. "You're BJ Kendall, aren't you?"

"That's right."

"Wow, this is my lucky day!" He took his eyes off Jordan long enough to call, "Mom! It's him! Really!" A young woman, unmistakably his mother, nodded from several yards away and smiled.

"What's your name?" Jordan asked.

"Benji. Benji Jamison. So my initials are BJ, too. That's what all the kids call me now, since we started playing golf in gym class." Fear passed over his face. "That's okay, isn't it? You don't mind if I borrow your name, do you?"

"No, borrowing names is something other people have been known to do, too." Jordan winked at Molly. "Well, BJ, my man. Maybe someday we'll have a game between the young BJ and the old BJ."

"Yeah! I practice almost every day. And I watch you every time you're on TV, too. You can just put that ball anywhere you want to," he said worshipfully.

"It may look that way, but there is always a challenge. Hey, it's terrific that you play golf. Try to get a job as a caddie at a club. That's what I did when I was about your age and it helped my game to follow better golfers around the course every day."

Head bobbing, the boy beamed. "Thanks, BJ. Next summer I'll be old enough. Hey, can I have your autograph? Otherwise no one will believe I saw you today."

"We cannot have that! What do you want me to sign?"

"My scorecard?"

"Sure thing." Jordan scrawled his name. "Wait here for a second. Since you are practically my namesake, I have something extra for you." He loped across the course toward the gate and Molly watched as he spoke briefly to the attendant before he headed for the car.

Benji tugged on Molly's arm, too excited to stand still. "Who are you?" He squinted up at her. "Are you famous, too?"

"I am afraid not. Just traveling with Jordan, er, BJ."

The boy sighed deeply, "I would give anything to travel with him."

Molly sighed, too, as Jordan came back. He handed a rolled up shirt to Benji. "Here you go, kid. This is the shirt I wore for my last big tournament. Sorry it's not new. Would you like to have it?"

Benji stared in disbelief at the object that would propel him into golfing folklore in his neighborhood. He tore his eyes away from the shirt and stammered, "Would I ever! Thanks, BJ. You're…" Suddenly speechless, he awkwardly shook hands with Jordan and stumbled off to show his mother.

"Well," said Jordan turning to Molly, "back to our game."

She could only nod. The child's mother called over to them, "Thanks. You have made my son one happy boy."

Jordan tipped a salute in her direction and moved toward their next hole. Inevitably, they made it to the dreaded windmill. "How about if you go first on this one, and I will watch your tricks?" Molly suggested.

"No tricks. Just timing. Watch." He came around behind her and slid his hands down her arms until they rested on top of her hands. His chin brushed her hair and she could feel his breath on her cheek. She shivered. "Imagine the ball moving along, and count how many seconds you think it would take."

Molly couldn't have counted her toes accurately at that point. Jordan leaned against her, moved her arms into position and carefully guided her stroke. The orange ball rolled perfectly through the windmill and headed straight into the hole.

A couple playing ahead of them cheered, and Molly moved quickly away from Jordan's embrace. "How did you do that? I thought you said there were not any tricks?"

He grinned and bent to position his ball. Beneath his swing the ball hit the moving windmill arm and rolled aside. Molly looked up quickly, "Sorry!" Her sincerity was evident.

"You are my opponent; opponents are not supposed to be sorry!" He swung again, and both watched as the ball obstinately stopped just short of the swinging blade.

A man from a nearby bench called out, "Seems to me like you did better when you had her in your arms!" Scattered clapping and cheers brought a grin to Jordan's face and a flush to Molly's. "Well, it *is* worth a try! Come here, Molly!"

In answer, she stuck out her tongue at him.

Jordan took a deep breath and two more strokes, one to get the ball through the windmill, one to sink it. He dropped a casual arm around her shoulders as they walked to the next hole. They stood, hips touching, surveying the next challenge.

The water was deep and peppered with water lilies. "Yikes. Look at all those balls in there."

He spoke calmly, "They probably toss them in there to psych us out."

"Well, mission accomplished. I am thoroughly psyched out."

"Nah, you will do fine. Just hit the ball beyond the sloping part and you are home free."

Molly stared at him in amazement. "You act as though I had some control of this ball."

He grinned wickedly, "Hit it, Minnesota!"

She hit it. Within seconds it had reverberated off the far wall and crossed the water for a second time to roll back to her feet. "What is it, a boomerang?"

"How nice. You get a second chance to tempt the water!"

She glowered at him and took her sweet time positioning the orange ball. When she hit it the second time, it cleared the water and came to a stop on the far side of the slope, close enough to the hole for hope to rise in her heart. She crowed with delight. "I think I like this game!"

He winked at her and poised his lanky body over the green ball only for a second, lifted the club and moved his ball gracefully across the water, hitting her ball squarely and moving it far from the range of an easy hit.

"Jordan! You did that on purpose!"

"No, Molly, I did not. I swear."

"Pffft. Even what's-his-name, Benji, said you can put the ball any- where you want."

"Molly, I did not hit your ball on purpose. I was just trying to get it across the water, like you."

"Yeah, like that poses some real challenge for a hot-shot golfer."

"Do you want me to forfeit a play?"

"No, just forget it."

"Just a game, Molly, just a game. We are out here just having fun and getting some exercise."

Her shoulders slumped dejectedly. "Sorry. I don't mean to be a bad sport, it's just that I am so self-conscious playing with you. I feel like cameras are going to pop up out of the bushes. I do not like being out of control."

"So I have noticed. Quit thinking about playing the *BJ* who looms so large in your mind. Just play *Jordan* who is right here, okay?"

She stared at him. He stood three feet away from her and wiggled his eyebrows beneath her gaze. She rolled her eyes and grinned, tugging his shirt sleeve. "Come on, *Jordan*, let's play."

She swung and the ball rolled downhill before her club came near it. They laughed as Jordan had the same problem. "This hole could be the challenge of the evening," Jordan said as they missed again. "Shall we cheat?"

"We can do that?"

"Here." He handed her the green ball. "Maybe if *you* hit it, it will behave!"

She solemnly took her place above his bright green ball. It moved toward the hole like a paper clip toward a magnet. Without a word she handed him the orange ball. In one stroke it was in the hole. "So that has been our trouble. We have each had the wrong ball all along!"

"Do I get the score for the green ball up to this point of the game?" Molly teased.

He pondered her request in mock seriousness, "Sounds fair."

Molly strutted to the next hole, twirling her club like a baton. The remainder of the game was punctuated by their teasing. When they turned in their clubs, it seemed the most natural thing in the world to link arms as they walked beneath the first stars of the evening to the car which would take them to the motel where they would share a room.

CHAPTER TWELVE

The man behind the motel desk looked down at the register. "Okay, that should about answer all our questions for you folks. You've got Room 214." He peered over the top of smudged glasses. "We call it our Honeymoon Suite. 214. February 14. Get it?" A throaty chuckle erupted. "Any chance you are honeymooners?"

With her back turned as she selected a soft drink from the machine in the corner of the lobby, Molly grinned, letting Jordan field the question, "I guess that depends on a person's definition of a honeymoon! It is a suite, right?"

"Right. A real nice suite. There is one thing to say for Room 214, if people aren't honeymooners when they go in, that room works its magic before they leave. Maybe we ought to raise our prices. It works faster than most of those high-priced marriage counselors!" His grin threatened to split his face wide open as Jordan turned from the counter.

Molly pressed the can against her warms cheeks. When Jordan looked at her questioningly, she said quickly, "I neglected to get you anything to drink. Do you want something?"

"No, newlyweds should share!" He held the door open for her and they went out into the night air.

"Who are we this time?"

"Tonight, we are the Kendalls. It always looks better if the name on the form matches the one on the credit card! Actually, it is better than using cash just to be Mr. and Mrs. Smith. Motel managers get real tired of that half-baked lie."

Molly's mind was only half on their conversation. Thoughts of what waited behind the door of Room 214 created havoc with her emotions. "I would like to walk from here if you want to drive the car around," she offered. "The breeze feels great."

Molly watched Jordan as he walked toward the car. Thoughts tumbled over each other in her mind. *What if he had been old enough to be my grandpa? Or, he could have been impossible to talk to. The trip's bad moments are being outweighed by his devastating and overwhelming effect on my emotions. His touch. His voice. His laugh. Molly, knock it off!*

"Where do you want your roses, Lady?" Jordan called softly out the car window. Molly stepped off the curb and held out her arms as Jordan gave her the drooping, but still fragrant, flowers. "Let me grab our bags and we'll head for the Valentine's Day Room. Is that a Coke you bought?"

Molly nodded and shifted the bouquet to hand it to him, "Was that a subtle hint? Help yourself. I've had enough."

Jordan tipped his head back for a long swallow and gave her back the can, "One swallow is all I need. Thanks." They walked slowly toward the door with the numbers 214 glowing from the light over the arch.

He put the bags down to fit the key into the lock. As the door swung open, Molly reached down for the bag closest to her. The movement shifted her purse off her shoulder and jerked her hand. Coke sloshed over her hand and down her legs.

"Oh, no!" she wailed. "All over my favorite white slacks!" She pushed past Jordan, moved toward the sink in the bathroom, tossing the flowers on the dresser she passed on her way. Wetting a washrag, she sponged the sticky trail going down both legs.

The stain already seemed permanently set. Frustrated, Molly unbuckled the belt, unzipped the pants, stepped out of them and held them under running water in the sink.

A sharp intake of breath behind her pulled her eyes up to the mirror where Jordan was reflected, standing in the doorway, still holding one bag. His Adam's apple the size of a walnut, he stared into her startled eyes in the mirror. "Anything I can do to help?" His voice had jumped an octave.

"Yes, go away."

His face was now a study in control. He dropped the bag on his foot and stared down as if both the suitcase and the foot were foreign to him. He seemed to have an inordinate amount of saliva.

"Would you please leave?" Molly's voice lurked close to hysteria. "I'm sorry to yell, but this is not my finest moment."

"I think I had better go make sure the car is locked. That's where I'm going. To make sure the car is locked." The words tumbled from his mouth. "Will you be all right?" She nodded. He fled. For a man who had seemed set in cement just moments before, he moved like greased lightning now.

As the door closed behind him, Molly shook water from her hands, dropped the troublesome slacks into the sink, and navigated from the bathroom to the bed. With her blouse doing it's pathetic best to cover her derrière, she flopped backwards on the spread and hid her eyes with her forearm.

"Way to go, Winstead. The prescription for a perfect evening: take an already tense situation and magnify it ten times by coming up with the stupidest, most embarrassing activity—basically stripping for a man who has never even tried anything with you." Her voice echoed in the room. "Except for a kiss or two…"

She lay perfectly still, waiting for the pounding of her heart to subside. She would have given anything to be back home in her easy chair, reading the paper. She jerked when she heard a noise in the hallway.

Diving across the room to where she had flung her suitcase, she fumbled with the latch, and finally pulled out her robe. Just as she knotted it around her waist, the key turned in the door. "Molly?" Jordan asked from the doorway.

"Come on in. I'm decent again."

"Did you get the spot out?" The door closed softly.

She stared at him in amazement. *Is this guy for real? He actually sounds as if he cares. No lewd remarks, just a concerned question.*

Aloud she said, "I don't know. I'm letting it soak."

"I think I would like to take a shower first, if that's okay with you." He dropped a brown bag beside the door.

"That's fine. I can bring my slacks out here and work on them in the wet-bar so they can drip dry overnight."

Listen to us; here I just performed an unrehearsed striptease for a person I have known for less than a week, and we stand like two neighbors discussing the weather.

She escaped into the bathroom and quickly pulled the sink's plug. As the water gurgled down the drain, she looked at herself in the mirror. With a conscious effort, she commandeered a pseudo-relaxed smile to replace the tension that had built up. Wrapping a towel around the dripping slacks, she headed for the sink beside the little refrigerator in the wetbar.

Jordan picked up his suitcase and disappeared, whistling softly, into the bathroom.

Molly blew a curl out of her eyes and stared across the room at the closed door between them. *What a gentleman. It is quite the stuffy word, but there is nothing puritanical about the effect he is having on me!*

As she hugged herself, a shiver ran through her. She moved to a chair by the window as if putting distance between herself and the man in the shower would muffle her throbbing signal.

From her corner, she scanned Room 214, the famed Honeymoon Suite, for the first time. In her rush to the bathroom, she had missed most of the room. A round table with four chairs formed a barrier between the wetbar and the chair where she sat. The small refrigerator and counter-top microwave gleamed next to the sink where her slacks soaked. An inviting, pillow-laden sofa sat next to an over-stuffed chair and coffee table. Across the room, the door that led to…*wait a second.*

She jumped out of her chair and, in three galloping steps was across the room. *A closet. Not another room—a closet.* Now it was her turn to gulp saliva. She turned back to scan the room. *At least it has a sleeper-couch.* She could hear Jordan whistling in the shower. Three cushions hit the floor. She pulled open the bed.

No sheets. No pillows. No blankets.

She spun around and made a frantic search of drawers, closet shelves. Nothing. Just a neatly lettered sign saying, "For extra bedding, please contact the Office."

With her hand on the phone, she paused. She could hear the guffaws in the Office now, "Hey, Charlie, guess what! The honeymooners in 214 wants sheets for the hide-a-bed! Love must be rocky for the Kendalls, huh?"

Through the bedroom, behind the bathroom door was the one and only Bartholomew Jordan Kendall. Perched on a hide-a-bed without sheets in the sitting room, was the evening's usurper of the name.

Heading for the wet-bar, she automatically rinsed out the slacks. She weighed the reflection in the mirrored tiles that covered the walls behind the sink as if seeing it through Jordan's eyes.

Slender waist. Worry wrinkles. These deepened further with her frown while she rolled the slacks in the towel to soak up excess water.

The pipes shuddered as Jordan turned off the shower. Her hands grew still as her mind became active. *He must be drying off now. Lean physique. Hair curling around his neck.*

The door swung open and he moved across the bedroom towards the sitting room. She blushed as if caught peeking in the keyhole. Maple-colored hair patterned his chest and legs. "Next! You will love the shower." He was splendor personified, even fully ensconced in the over-sized towel. "It has a real good pulse."

So do I, Buster! So do I. "Great. I can just leave these miserable things wrapped in this towel and hang them up in the shower when I am done." Her heartbeat throbbed in her neck.

"Please pardon this towel—my robe's in my other bag. Out in the car. I'm pretty tired, so I didn't want to get dressed again."

Tell me he doesn't sleep in the nude. Please.

"No problem. I am ready for my shower now. See you in the morning," she said, fleeing for the privacy of the small porcelain world behind the locked door, forgetting for the moment that the man sharing the honeymoon suite had no linens.

You ninny! He's behaving like a gentleman and you're acting the part of an adolescent.

She turned on the shower full blast and stepped into the steamy cloud. Turning the dial, she let the pulsating beat of the water on her skin match the pounding of her heart. Her thoughts went on their own trip.

Mountains to valleys.

Dawn to nightfall.

Storm clouds to sunshine.

She toweled herself dry as memories of Jordan's touch, gentle yet firm, etched themselves on the page that would always be remembered as Today.

As her negligee's folds fell around her body, her hands followed the soft lines. She, too, had not expected to share a room when she had packed her carry-in bag for the trip. The filmy gown hid little of the curving lines—for that she turned to her robe, which helped only enough to give her courage to leave the bathroom.

Jordan sat in the easy chair, thumbing through a newspaper, still wearing his towel. Long hair-shadowed legs stretched to rest on an opposite chair. The cushions she had left in a heap on the floor piled neatly in place. It was deceptively peaceful.

Her damp hair fell in tendrils around her shoulders, leaving circles where the tips dripped their last memories from the shower. Nervously, she shifted her body inside the satiny safety of her robe.

She moved into the circle of light formed by the lamp beside the easy chair, her bare toes curling into the soft fibers of the carpet. She was drawn to him like an evening moth to light. "I see you discovered there are no sheets for this bed," he said.

"Right. I should have said something, but…"…*your near-nakedness blasted reasonable through from my mind!* She smiled weakly and marshaled her thoughts enough to say, "there's just a note saying that we have to call the desk to get extra linens." She nodded at the card on the table.

"Oh. I guess I didn't see that." His face darkened briefly. "Well, do you want to call, or should I?"

"They think we're Mr. and Mrs. Kendall." He could barely hear her whisper.

"I suppose we could pull a blanket off the bed and if you will share a pillow, I'll be just fine out here."

"I'll even go you one better and give you a sheet." She spun on her heel toward the bedroom. "Or," she called back to him, "I could sleep out there and you could have the…" Her words faded as she looked at the bed.

Rose petals. Scattered across the sheets and pillowcase of the turned-down bed. She turned toward the door, sensing Jordan's presence in the room with her.

He said softly, "There were a few flowers that hadn't survived the heat too well. Rather than throw them out, I thought maybe it would help you remember roses, instead of Coke, when you think of this day."

Molly sank onto the bed, crushing several petals. Their scent permeated the room.

"Have you made plans for the evening, Minnesota?"

"Hmmm?" she breathed, looking up at him with glazed eyes.

"When I checked the car, I stopped by the office and got some quarters." He walked to the night stand and tapped a small box beneath the lamp. "This handy bed shaker could shake, rattle, and roll all your troubles away. I will drop a couple quarters in the slot, and you can relax. Crawl in, and I'll head off to my bed."

The coin-operated box gleamed on the table.

"You make a good salesman."

"You tell me nothing I don't know, my lady!" He bowed slightly and Molly sucked her breath in slowly as his actions shifted his towel until it opened across one thigh.

Whew. He's got underwear on beneath that towel! She giggled.

"The lady laughs?"

There was no way she was going to let on that she had figured his scanty attire for anything other than his waiting for her to come out of the bathroom! She had been so caught up in the trauma and drama of her own life that she had totally missed seeing his clothes hanging there. She plumped up the pillows, snuggled down in a nest of rose-petals, and smiled at the ceiling.

"Well, I haven't thought about ruined slacks for ten minutes, how about you?" Jordan asked.

"Can't say I have."

"Ready for the evening's entertainment? With these shiny quarters I will summon the gentle, vibrating motion guaranteed to send your troubles down the river."

"Let the good times roll."

Jordan dropped three quarters into the slot and dropped a couple more on the bed. "Sweet dreams."

"Thanks, Jordan," she murmured to his retreating back.

As the door closed softly behind him, she finally realized that she was not in motion. No vibrations, nothing. She leaned over and turned the knob firmly to the right. Something happened; the bed lurched into motion. She reached for the controls and pounded, shook, and examined the box that held the quarters. "I feel like a little kid on one of those merry-go-round rides outside a grocery store," she grinned to herself. "Well, stay on the horse! You don't want to waste any of this pulsating rhythm, paid for by your famous passenger!" Her whisper warbled as if someone were pounding on her chest and this made her giggle even more.

After trying unsuccessfully to turn the knob back and forth several times, she swung her feet off the bed. "I've got to get off before I get seasick." She came around to the other side of the bed and bent over the box. "I would say the bed vibrates quite well! How long does a quarter last, anyway? Oh, good! Ten minutes, so three quarters is one massive dose of stress reduction!"

She grabbed up a pillow to smother her laughter. "After half an hour on there, I would probably have numb buns for the rest of this trip!"

She moved away and dropped into one of the easy chairs facing the bed and watched the drama in bedsheets. The bed rattled and moaned. A knock so quiet it was amazing she heard it was followed by Jordan's soft voice, "Molly? Are you awake in there? Everything okay?"

Laughing, she crossed the room and opened the door to a hastily clothed Jordan.

"You're not in bed?" No sooner were the words out of his mouth than he saw the reason why and rubbed his chin. "Well, I guess I see why!"

"What time is it?"

He looked at his watch twice, "Five minutes after the quarters should have run out. It must be broken. I'll unplug the thing."

"Can you? I thought of trying, but didn't want to set off any alarms. Don't they rig it, like the television, to prevent theft?"

"Nah, I don't think so." He dropped to the floor beside the bed. His head was soon lost from sight as he stretched his arm beneath the bed. "I can almost, but not quite, reach the plug."

"Don't get electrocuted."

Strange muffled noises came from under the bed. "You're right. They've got the thing rigged so you can't unplug it. So we'll just call the front desk and let them solve the problem. I'm coming out."

Molly watched as his legs went through the right motions, but no head or shoulders emerged. "Jordan?"

"Huh?"

"Anything wrong?"

"I'm stuck."

"Stuck? What got stuck?"

"My hair is caught on a bedspring or something. We're going to have to get help because every jerk of this bed is pulling on my hair and it hurts incredibly."

"Yow." Visions of laughing ambulance drivers rolling on the motel room floor flashed through Molly's mind. "Let me try to help you first." She dropped to her knees and peered under the bed. It was very dark. "I'll put the lamp on the floor so I can see better." She scooted across the bed, only to hear yelps from under the bed.

A yelp rose. "Are you trying to kill me? I'm under the bed you're on, you know!"

"Sorry, Jordan," she said meekly as she unscrewed the lamp shade and moved the well-secured lamp from the stand to the floor, which was the best she could do. Chastened, she circled the bed on her way back to Jordan. The lamplight allowed her to confirm that he was indeed firmly caught, by a healthy lock of hair, to a bed spring that had pushed its way down through the fabric.

She held her hair in place with one hand as she cautiously squirmed along beside him to try to reach his head. The carpet burned her legs as each movement pushed her robe aside. No sooner did she get positioned where she could touch Jordan's head than the bed shuddered to a stop.

"About time this infernal bed quit shaking. Good, you can reach me. Can you get me loose?"

In answer, Molly ran her fingers across his hair, thinking as she did so that this was something women the world over probably would give their eyeteeth to do. And here she was, the envy of unseen millions. She swallowed hard and gently pried a few hairs free of the spring. Her next efforts pulled a few free of his head. "Whoops, sorry."

"Ouch! You're turning me into a bald man, and all you can say is 'Whoops, sorry'?"

"You won't be bald. It was just a few hairs." she retorted.

"That's how you get bald. A few hairs at a time," he said testily.

Molly poked and pulled and made no progress. "Don't be so cranky. The rest is really lodged in there, Jordan. I'm afraid I'll have to cut you loose."

"Oh, no, you don't! You're not coming near my head with scissors."

"You're safe, then. I only have a nail clipper with me."

"Oh, swell. Just let me try again before you start in on me." He struggled to move his arm up to reach his head; there wasn't enough room beneath the bed for his shoulders to move. She stared at him in the close quarters.

"I'll have to come at you from the other side," Molly said as she pushed herself back from under the bed. She shook the contents of her purse out on the bed and sorted through them until she found the nail clipper. Dropping to the floor beside the lamp, she crept in as close as she could get to Jordan.

"Please be careful, Molly," he pleaded. "My hair won't grow out before the tournament in Minneapolis."

"Quit worrying. You'll be fine, you'll see. Ouch!"

"What's *your* problem? I'm the one who's stuck."

"I just backed into the light bulb on the lamp. So we each have our own little corner on pain, don't we?" she snapped.

Silence.

Slowly, Molly began clipping him free of the bedsprings, hair by hair. The only sound beneath the now motionless bed was the breathing of tonight's two occupants of Room 214, the Honeymoon Suite.

Molly giggled.

"You find this humorous?"

"I was just thinking, if the maids in this motel really clean, they're going to wonder about this hair under the bed!"

"You will understand, I hope, why I cannot join in the merriment of the moment."

Molly dropped her hands to the floor. "Okay, you're free. Back out carefully."

He lowered his head to the carpet and slid out, rubbing his cheek along the floor. They stood up at the same time, facing each other across the bed. The carpet had burned a dull red mark on his cheek. Wisps of dust from under the bed were caught in the buttons on his shirt. Molly's stare, however, focused several inches above his right ear.

He reached up, running his hand across the bristles which rose from his scalp. Tiny maple-brown soldiers standing at attention. Tucking his shirt around his waist, he raced to the mirror over the dresser.

"You've sheared me!"

"I did not! Manicure scissors are hardly the tool to…well, it just looks, uh, it was, uh, pulled funny for so long. Just wet it down and it will be fine."

He included her and the bed in his glare as he marched angrily into the bathroom and slammed the door behind him. She paced the room, snapping the nail clipper nervously with each stride. She was opposite the bathroom when the door opened.

He loomed in the door frame. A giant with a stony, paralyzing gaze. "I thought I wasn't going to be bald?" He turned sideways and she gasped at the jagged clearing in the dense forest of hair. "That's the response I'm sure I'll receive when I show up on the golf course, a gasp that will echo through the country."

"Maybe if you just comb it differently, it will…"

"There are limits to the creative ways I can train my hair in the next few days. I've been combing my hair for the last five minutes. This is the best I could come up with."

The fire died in him, and he wilted before Molly's eyes.

"Let's get some sleep," she suggested, crossing the room to him, withdrawing her hand from his arm when he stiffened beneath her light touch.

"I'm not sure I can sleep right now."

"We ought to try. Tomorrow's coming up pretty quick."

He took quick look at the clock and sighed. "You're right. Thanks for your help. I mean it. I'm sorry for getting so mad at you."

"Ditto, in reverse."

"Beg your pardon?"

"I'm sorry, too. 'Ditto, in reverse' originated when Mara, my sister, was dating Matt, the guy she eventually married."

"Ah, a new story! Maybe we don't have to toss in bed quite yet!"

She grinned and motioned toward the chairs, "Can I offer you some tap water in sanitary glasses?"

"What a hostess you are. Now, what's the story behind 'ditto'?"

Pulling two glasses out of their cellophane wrappers, she filled them and came back to the chair she had vacated earlier. "It started as a Mara and Matt thing. Mom and Dad would pace the hallway to signal that she had spent long enough on the phone and if she missed the hint, they would linger. Well, it complicated things if Matt was telling her how much he loved her and she had her parents standing ten feet away!"

"Naturally."

"So, when Matt said, 'I love you,' or some such mushy stuff, Mara would answer, 'Ditto, in reverse.'"

Jordan nodded, "Very clever."

"It didn't take my parents long to figure out this code, and now it's a family joke."

"Your family sounds great."

"They are. We have lots of good memories, like most families. It sure would be fun if we could meet each other's tribes, after all the stories we've told during this trip. I would love to taste those fresh sesame rolls your Dad makes, or that special vegetable sauce of your Mom's, or see your Dad deal with the delivery guy who hits the loading dock everyday!"

"You've probably attended some dinner they have catered and just not known it."

"Very possible. I'll pay closer attention from now on." She tried unsuccessfully to swallow a yawn and knew Jordan had caught her. She picked up her water glass and tilted it in a toast, "Here's to a miracle growth of hair."

He smiled weakly. "Yeah. Thanks, Minnesota. For getting me out. Consider your dumpster debt settled."

"Sorry about the bad haircut."

"I'm sure you had no alternatives. I'm just glad we didn't have to call anyone for help."

"Do you believe this night?"

"Do you believe this week? Are your trips to the Midwest always this exciting?"

She shook her head. "Wouldn't Royce be happy to know that I've done such a terrific job of reducing your stress level?"

"And wouldn't he be overjoyed to know that I've been such good company for you?"

"You have, you know."

"Ditto, in reverse."

"Hey, a quick learner!"

"Yeah." Even in the semi-darkness, she could see his face darken, After an almost imperceptible moment of silence, he continued, "at least the range of stress-inducing situations has been broadened."

"I guess that's a compliment."

"It was. I've never met anyone like you before," he said as he stood up.

"And that's a relief, huh?"

He shrugged. "Do you realize that I have never ridden in an elevator with you, or picked up Chinese take-out and swung by your house on a

Saturday night, or waited for you after work, or any of the things that help people feel like they have known each other for their whole life?"

She smiled. Peace reigned, at last. It was a quiet moment; Molly fingered a rose petal that has escaped its wild ride on the bed and landed on the floor. "Room 214 probably hasn't this kind of excitement in years."

"Ain't that the truth?" he grinned.

"Well, friend, I'm bushed."

"Me, too."

"Pleasant dreams," she said.

"I'm sure they will be."

She was in bed within seconds. In the darkness, she listened to the creaking of his sofa-bed as he settled in.

The night noises filtered through the air. A distant car's horn honked. The breeze carried a dog's bark. In Room 214 there was an unnatural silence.

"Good night, Molly."

"Good night, Jordan." She could not have been more conscious of Jordan in the next room if she were nestled in his arms.

"Hey, Minnesota?"

"Hmmmm?"

"I just wanted you to know that just because you're sleeping in there, and I'm sleeping out here, doesn't mean that I'm made of stone. Given a little more time to get to know each other, we couldn't put ourselves in this kind of situation without seriously discussing our…can you hear me?"

"Yes."

"You're a very desirable woman. I hope you know that."

"Thanks, Jordan," she said so softly it was unlikely he heard it.

Out of sight, out of mind.

She breathed in the fragrance of the remaining rose petals beneath her.

Right. Out of sight, out of mind.

CHAPTER THIRTEEN

Molly woke when her bed shook. She opened one eye just enough to see a bare foot that was none-too-gently rocking the foot of her mattress.

Jordan. Right here.

"Awake?"

"Umhmuhhmm," she muttered, burying her face in the pillow.

"Good! I've been awake for hours," he said as he flung open the drapes.

"That's probably because I didn't keep you awake with my snoring," she said and pulled the covers over her head to block out the light.

"What? I don't snore."

"You did last night."

The bed rocked again.

"Did not."

"Did so."

"So you didn't sleep well?"

"Once I got to sleep, I slept great."

"Good. Then let's get going."

"I hate morning people," she said, snatching the sheet off her face to shoot a glare in his direction.

"Ooh, I sense some early morning hostility."

"You betcha." She stretched. "Do you want the bathroom first?"

"Ha! I can see through that one! You want me in the bathroom where I won't bother you while you catch a few more zzzz's."

Without lifting her head, she raised her right hand, forming the classic circle with thumb and forefinger. "Bingo. Give the man a prize."

"Too bad. I've already been in there. Then I peeked around the door and watched you sleep, so I went back to bed for another half hour. And now you expect me to listen to you tell lies about me snoring. Get up, lazybones. And dress for another warm day," he added as a parting shot before he closed the door behind him.

"All right, all right. I'm up." Her left foot emerged from the covers and flopped on top. Thirty seconds passed. He knocked on the door. "You're worse than the snooze button on my alarm! Can you see through walls, or something?"

"Molly…" he chimed in a singsong voice.

"I'm glad I don't have to put up with you every morning!" she pouted and stomped across the room, stopping to pound on the door. She shut herself in the bathroom against the intrusion of his hoots of laughter.

Sounds of an early morning news show filtered through the door and heightened her awareness that just feet away was a man she had spent the night with, in a manner of speaking.

And a man she had sheared. As she combed her hair, she wondered how Jordan's hair looked in daylight.

I may never know. She watched from the doorway. Sitting beside the table, engrossed in the weather map on the television screen, Jordan was dressed for the day, wearing a brimmed hat. She smiled and quickly bit her lip.

"Okay, I'm ready."

"Pancakes. I hear about six of them calling my name."

"Nope, it's waffles. Two waffles. Whipped cream on one, blueberry syrup on the other," she challenged.

Luggage bumping against their legs, they walked out the door to the already warm car. "I'll drive, and you're in charge of keeping a lookout for a cafe that won't mind if I keep my hat on."

"Nice hat. Colorful."

"Thanks."

"Will you wear it all day?"

"Is the Pope Catholic?"

"I didn't think your hair looked that bad this morning."

"Uh-huh. Personally, I plan to wear this hat, or one of its magnitude, until my hair grows back."

"I thought golfers only wore those visored dealy-bobs."

"I thought you didn't know anything about golf?"

"I've seen pictures!"

Jordan was one of three men in the cafe wearing hats, as he hastened to point out from their stools at the counter. Wrinkling her nose at him, she grinned. Soon they were on their way again. "Well, are you going to continue to sneak peeks at the hole where I used to have hair, or shall we play hide-and-seek?"

"What?"

"Hide and seek. You know, one hides, the other seeks."

"I'm familiar with the game, and equally aware that we're driving. Or did you get me up at the crack of dawn," she raised her voice to drown out Jordan's loud imitation of a morning rooster, "to drive me ten miles outside the city limits, stop the car in the middle of nowhere and play silly kid's games?"

"You sure have a limited interpretation of the rules for hide and seek, Molly! We *can* play it while we drive, you know."

"Right." She rolled her eyes.

Jordan blew away her scorn with one breath of air. "Just for that, you're it. I'll hide. Count to ten."

"1, 2, 3, 4, 5, 6, 7, 8, 9, ready-or-not-here-I-come-10."

Silence.

"I said, 'Ready-or-not-here-I-come.'"

Silence.

"Oh. That's right; you're hiding. Okay, are you in the ashtray?" She pulled it open and wiggled her fingers inside. "Nope. Clean as a whistle. Glove compartment?" She opened the door and bent to peek inside. "Wrong again."

Jordan jiggled in the driver's seat. "Hurry, guess again," he said through pinched lips.

"Are you in the trunk?"

He shook his head.

"Nope. Three guesses, you're out. Ha! I was hiding in that tree right there!" He pointed to a huge elm as they sped past it. "Your turn to hide. I'll be nice, even though you didn't find me."

She bit her lip in concentration. "Okay, come find me."

His eyes whipped across the countryside. "Under that log?" he asked, pointing at a field.

She shook her head.

"On the hood of the car?"

"Cold."

"Are you behind that wreck of a red barn?"

"Too late! I was sitting on top of that billboard; you never even looked."

"Good spot! My turn again. Close your eyes. I'll be in the car this time."

She squeezed her eyes shut. So tight she saw rainbows like she used to when she had played the game with Mara. She giggled.

His hand slid across her mouth. "Don't they teach librarians to be quiet anymore?"

She shook her head beneath his hand, "Ats of ut ee oo aeyor! Yoo an alk ouwoud an airying in…"

"I swear, you'd think a librarian would speak more distinctly." Molly licked his hand. "You little minx!"

"Talk about preconceived ideas!"

"Just for that, you'll never find me this time."

"I'm very good. I'll find you wherever you are."

"Is that thunder?" Jordan asked abruptly.

"I don't know, what's the sky look like?" Molly pushed against the door and peered up at the sky. "Clear."

"Oh, no!" He jammed on the brakes.

She lurched forward, her seat belt breaking her move. "What?" No answer was needed. As they came over the crest of the hill, their game was forgotten in a hurry. The Volvo was surrounded by a herd of cattle coming up out of a ditch and on to the road. "Jordan!"

"Yeah. I see them. I guess they knocked down their fence. And we're at a dead stop in the middle of a major highway!"

"Along with some others," Molly pointed out, seeing cars already stopped ahead of them and forming a line behind them. "Yikes, help!" She jumped as a huge brown face pressed against her window and let out a bellow. His breath fogged the glass.

"How many little buggers do you think there are?"

"Little? They must weight a thousand pounds each! If they decide to sit on the car, it is all over for us." As if on cue, the car rocked while three of the cattle butted each other. "Jordan!" The single word was couched in fear.

Their hands met between the seats.

"What do we do?" Several hundred beasts milled around the cars stopped on the road and more were pressed tight outside the fences on each side of the highway.

"I think we are doing it. We wait."

"That is not the most comforting thing I have heard lately, Jordan. If they knocked down their fence, which I would assume is not a garden variety picket fence, think what they could do to this car if they stampede again?"

"911 is no doubt pretty busy right now with all the cell phones calling this one in. At least we're not alone out here."

His tone calmed Molly. "They scared the bejeebies out of me!" she said.

"Aw, we can handle it, we are from the Wild West, you know!"

"Do you know any rules for what to do when you find yourself caught in the middle of a stampede?"

"Hmm, cannot say that I have, but it could come under the principle of When in Rome, do as the Romans." He rolled his window down an inch, threw back his head and bellowed, sounding very much like the cattle just inches away.

She watched in fascination. So did all the beasts within six feet of the car. They stopped bumping against the car and peered in at the couple they held captive. "What did you say to them, Jordan? I think they understood!"

"It seems so. Well, then," he rolled the window down another inch, "I say, old chap, how long will you be keeping us here? We are on a bit of a tight schedule, you see." The steer opened his mouth in a loud, low rumble. Jordan responded curtly, "Well, ask your leader if you are not free to comment."

Molly laughed nervously. Jordan whispered sternly, "Shhh, it does not pay to be rude." He looked the animal in his big brown eyes and listened to the ensuing roar. "You can't tell your leader apart from the rest in the shuffle? Well, I can certainly sympathize with you there! Never saw so many look-alikes in my life." He was interrupted by an angry howl from a choir of mouths. "I beg your pardon. I am quite sure you all have distinct personalities!"

Tears rolled down Molly's face and even Jordan lost his straight face. "Whew! Those guys have bad breath! Must come from not brushing and flossing after their morning hay."

"Jordan, quit! My sides ache from laughing. What are we going to do?"

"Well, schweet-hot," he said, tipping his hat low over his eyes and peering at her from the shadow, "choices are momentarily limited. But I must say, it is good to see you enjoying yourself."

She wrinkled her nose at him. "Would they move if we honked? Turn the key and let's try it."

It was hard to say who was more scared, the animals or the car's occupants when the cattle jumped. "Well. Do you know CPR for a cow with a heart attack? I do not think honking is going to move them. We could sing to them, Molly."

"Sing, you say? How can you think about singing?"

"Why not? Why do you think there are cowboy songs?"

She eyed the herd cautiously.

He leaned his head against the car window and began to croon. The din outside the car diminished as Jordan's rendition of "Oh, Give Me A Home" edited out the roaming buffalo in favor of cattle. So effective was Jordan as Calmer Of The Angry Mob that Molly entertained and dismissed a wild thought of rolling her window down to pet a big brown body outside her door.

"Your turn."

"I cannot think of one more song about cows."

He grinned and said, "I am willing to bet they would not complain if they heard repeats!"

But before she had a chance for her debut, Jordan spotted a pickup in the rear view mirror. "Here comes help."

The truck approached the live road block and slowed to a stop. Jordan and Molly turned in their seats to watch the driver, brave soul, get down from the cab in disbelief. Several cattle broke away from the herd and lumbered toward the truck. The driver was back in his seat in record time and plunged across the median in a cloud of dust.

Jordan and Molly looked at each other with wide grins and Jordan said, "Did you see the look on his face?"

"I hope he saw us. Next time remind me to buy a color of car that has been tested to stand out in a herd!"

"Hey! Look behind again. He either called for help, or somebody just realized they are missing some four-footed friends."

"Horses?" Molly said in disbelief.

"Just like the movies."

Each man on horseback made his way through the herd to a section of the string of cars that had collected on the highway. From stride his mount, one called out, "Everything all right with you folks?"

Jordan did as others along the line did and waved. Lowering the window, he said, "We're fine in this car. You have sure got a mess on your hands. Wish we could help."

"Thanks. Sorry it took us so long to get to you. We had to stop traffic back there, and call the highway patrol, and get the next ranch to come help us. Gotta move along. You are safest in your car."

With a wave of a feathered hat, he whirled his horse around and called a command to the dog nipping the heels of the cattle as he rode toward the next car in the line.

Molly and Jordan sat in silent admiration as the cattle responded to dogs and horsemen. Within minutes the herd was moving as one unit back to the fenced-in prairie field they had escaped. At a signal from the cowboy, Jordan started up the car and drove cautiously between the last few lingering wanderers.

Other cars started their engines and rolled slowly along. Occupants of each car waved as their vehicles passed each other. Grins gave hints of the brief camaraderie born of the strange event.

"Wouldn't you know it? We missed an opportunity to take pictures. Or even better, to record that wonderful concert you gave for the herd! Too bad you didn't have your video camera, huh?"

"I will have you know, they were calling out requests when I sang."

She nodded in mock solemnity.

"Kind of puts me in a mood for a steak dinner."

"Jordan, you shock me!"

"Well, if we take a rest stop in Lincoln and go on to Omaha for dinner, we could be fairly sure that the steaks on our plates wouldn't be from a relative of any of those guys."

If the residents of Lincoln were observant that evening, they saw a man and a woman munching apples, deep in conversation, sometimes holding hands, sometimes with his arm draped around her shoulders, sometimes stopped by statues in the park, or with faces pressed against store windows.

Looking at many things, but seeing only each other.

The Kiss, that third traveler from California to Minnesota, added to the memories of that walk along quiet streets.

The waitress in Omaha's restaurant with the motto *The Only Fresher Steaks Are Still On The Hoof* reported to the kitchen crew, "I had to ask them twice how they wanted their steaks." But she happily waved a healthy tip in the air after she had cleared their table and announced, "That meal was wasted on those two. We could have fed them medium-rare shoe leather for all the attention they paid to the food."

As she went back to reset the table, she muttered under her breath, "He stared into her eyes, she stared into his eyes…criminy, just eat up and quit wasting good money!"

A gentle rain was beginning to fall as Jordan and Molly returned to their car still parked in the restaurant parking lot. When they left the lights of the city behind them, they needed the windshield wipers. The monotone beat of the blades on the window was hypnotizing. "Well, Minnesota, one important thing was accomplished today."

"What's that?" she asked lazily.

"I saw you laughing like you must have when you were a child."

"You must consider me a real sour puss."

"Not sour, just serious. Life cannot be that sobering, can it? Or do busy, organized people only laugh if it fits into their schedule?"

"Maybe I am a typical librarian and don't know it. You know, never smiling, always saying 'Shhhh' and chasing noisy people out of our sacredly quiet domain."

"Well, I am sure glad I stay out of libraries then! I would spend most of my time leaving on the toe of your boot!"

"Is there anything sober about your life, Jordan?"

Even in the darkness she could tell he clenched the steering wheel. "Nope, I live a carefree, jovial existence. Even work is play, by most people's standards." His voice gave no clue to his body language.

She reached over to trace his tight knuckles. He loosened his grip under her gentle touch. They drove through the rain, the car like an umbrella that brought them closer together. But beneath the night noises his words echoed in her doubting mind. *Carefree?*

It was late when they crossed the Iowa state line. "There is a good motel just off this exit ramp," Molly volunteered.

"A good enough recommendation for me," Jordan said and soon pulled in under the canopy. Rain drops splattered when Molly closed the car door behind her. She took a deep gulp of the fresh, clean air and hugged herself as she walked along beside Jordan into the motel lobby.

They squinted in the light and signed up for their rooms without any unnecessary conversation. Both rooms were around on the quiet side, the clerk assured them.

Jordan waited with Molly until she had the door open and then he whispered, "G'night, Minnesota. I'll see you in the morning on my way to the coffee shop. Sleep well."

"You, too." As he turned to move away from her, she caught her breath and called softly, "Jordan?"

He paused expectantly as she moved toward him. Lightly touching his cheek, she cupped his face and lifted her lips to offer a kiss that grew from hesitant to hungry. Breathless, she murmured, "Thanks for the laughter."

Obviously moved, he nodded as he slowly released her from the embrace that had naturally followed the kiss. She stood in the dark doorway and watched until he disappeared into his room.

She closed the door and sank into a chair a few feet into the room, letting the muted light from outside the room silhouette her pensive stance against the carpet before she rose to the pull the drapes.

Laugher is not the only difference in me on this trip.

The sight of the telephone on the bedside table was a nagging reminder. Tomorrow they would reach Rochester. Mara's house. Her calls throughout the trip had been infrequent and short. Infrequent, because she had much else on her mind, and short because she couldn't trust herself to keep from spilling the beans any sooner than she needed to. Now that time was at-hand: She would be at Mara's house with Jordan tomorrow.

She sat on the bed and drew meaningless circles on the motel's note paper before she lifted the receiver.

"Hello?" Mara's familiar voice jolted Molly back to reality.

"Hi. It's me. Are you ready to see me tomorrow?"

"Molly! You bet! We have wondered when you would call. What time will you get here?"

"Just in time for dinner. I would say we have got at least seven or eight hours of driving until…"

"We? Who is 'we'?"

This was why she had called so few times along the trip. "Uh, I have a passenger. A paying passenger. Royce lined it up; he's a friend of Royce's. The fellow, uh, is kinda stressed out, so he can't fly so much…"

"And you're his nursemaid?"

"No, Goofus! He's not sick, he's just…never mind. It's late and I'm tired. I just wanted to let you know we will, I mean, I will be there in time for dinner tomorrow night."

"Well, no need to make the paying passenger sit on the curb. I can probably rustle up an extra serving. Where do you drop him off?"

"Minneapolis."

"Okay. Get some sleep and we will be waving the Minnesota flag when the native child returns. Tell the old fella he is more than welcome here."

"I will. Bye." Molly eased the receiver back into place.

Tomorrow.

Jordan. Mara and Matt. All at the same table. They were bound to notice there was no "old fella" in sight. Whoops.

So what? No big deal; he is a paying passenger on his way to a golf tournament. He is just a guy who has made me laugh. A lot.

And we have left a trail of kisses from the West Coast to the Great Plains.

After an early breakfast, they left, Molly driving this last stretch. "We have almost made it, Molly. We get to Minneapolis today, right?" He did not mention their parting the evening before, but unspoken words formed a foundation for all their conversation.

Why couldn't I be driving him to New York, not just Minnesota? We need many more miles to talk. "We are close enough to make it there, but I usually stop in Rochester where my sister lives. I called her last night and she said to tell you that you are more than welcome to have dinner and a bed for the night at their house."

"So Rochester comes before Minneapolis, huh? Can you tell I fly a lot and do not have a clue what is going on down on the ground?"

"I guess I should have mentioned it. You should not be expected to know Minnesota geography. Do you mind an overnight stop?"

"Mind? No. Hey, it sounds good. I can get a motel room. I will enjoy meeting Mara and Matt. The kids are Emily and Toby, right?"

"Excellent memory. Emily is five, and Toby just turned three."

"That's right. I remember now from the house-painting story you told when we were in the mountains. Hey, that could catch on as a new memory device; if you can associate people's names with the part of the country you were traveling through when you first heard of them, you always know them!"

She grinned. "It could work, Jordan. I will remember your cousins' names by the truck stop in Nebraska. And if I ever meet your grandparents, I can say, 'Ah, yes, the drug store in Wyoming'!"

He laughed, and stretched in his seat. She pulled her eyes away from the long expanse of tan slacks and shirt that were molded around his body more carefully with each movement he made. "So, we eat dinner there, spend the night, and head out in the morning."

"If you have that kind of time."

"No problem. Would you normally stay longer with them?"

"Not necessarily. I will stop there again on my way back to California, and they are likely to make a trip to Duluth while I am around."

"Good. I hope you will not cut your time short with your sister just because of me." He slid his sunglasses down his nose to look at her over the top. "This week has gone by so fast. Have I turned you against having passengers on future trips?"

"No, not at all. Have I made you decide to fly from now on?"

"No, but I may try to put nail clipper manufacturers out of business!" he said, pushing his hat up and running his fingers across the stubble above his ear.

She blew out a puff of air. "Yeah, sorry."

"Hey, this look could catch on. We could name the style after you. After the camera zooms in on me, hairdressers from all across the country will take note."

Molly groaned, "I forget that you are on television. Maybe you can convince them your left side in your most photogenic!"

"Either that, or I could hang a sign around my neck saying, 'For a haircut like this, call area code 209…which number will we list, your cell phone or your house phone?"

"You're just trying to find out my home phone! I know your type. If you think I would tell you now, forget it!"

"How can I call you if you don't tell me your number?"

"I'm in the book."

"Right. For almost every man in the world to call." His eyes grew dark. Minnesota's sky before snow.

Is he jealous? Good grief. "How was your room last night?" she asked.

"Absolutely without excitement. The bed just sat there. There was no one to talk to. I almost felt like complaining." His smile eased the threat of storms from his eyes.

"Yeah, what did we pay for, anyway?"

"You know," Jordan said, "I think we have almost got this travel business down to a system. We remembered to get fresh coffee in the thermos, our plans for tonight are set and it is still quite early in the morning, and our gas tank is full. What a pity the trip is almost over."

"How long will you be in the Twin Cities?"

"For a couple days. Then it is off to Colorado. Then Florida and Georgia. Why?"

"I wondered if you need a ride back to California."

"Afraid not. You will be in Minnesota for what, two weeks? By then, I'll be history. Funny, huh? With all the things we have talked about, there are still things we never got to. That is one thing I've enjoyed about this trip, Molly. Talking to you."

She tried to imagine the return trip without Jordan sitting next to her. *Sheer depression.* She reached into the back seat and pulled a newspaper up, dropping it on Jordan's lap. "Luckily, I remembered to get a paper this morning. Read to me and help me cram for the inevitable exam my family will give me on Minnesota news. They accuse me of knowing only about the Coast."

"We could just turn on the radio and listen to the news."

"Nah, they only hit the headlines. I need the nitty-gritty."

"Sorry, I could not possibly be party to such a massive lie!" he teased and folded the paper, wedging it into the door pocket. "Pull over and let me drive; you can read to both of us. You have had these tests before. I am the new kid in town and you should help me out."

"Okay, but it is *not* your turn to drive. I don't want to hear any complaints about how I made you drive more than your share!" She signaled a turn at an exit ramp and was reading aloud when Jordan pulled back into traffic.

Jordan's memory was astounding. Even when she was on the third section of the paper, he flawlessly remembered the details of the stories from the first section. "Ooh, you're good. This will be a spectacular homecoming! We will wow 'em at dinner. If I know Mara, she has called Mom and Dad by now and they will have 'just happened' to have come down to Rochester to see the grandchildren! They can never wait, once they know I am over the state line! So, you may have a chance to meet the whole crew."

Jordan's throat visibly tightened. He smiled stiffly at her. "Great."

Is he afraid to meet my family? "They are basically harmless. You will probably be subjected to endless questions, since it's not every trip that I have arrived home with a famous golf pro in tow, but you can handle it. They don't know much more about golf than I do," she said with a grin.

"Looking forward to it."

Like a trip to the dentist, if your face is an accurate gauge.

Jordan's mind was obviously somewhere besides the blue Volvo heading North on Interstate 35. When she pointed out the exit that would have them in Rochester in less than an hour, he drummed his fingers on the steering wheel in an annoying cadence. Following Molly's directions, he turned at the corner just six houses from the house where Molly's family waited.

"There is something that I need to tell you, Molly, before we meet your family, or before we go our separate ways. I should have told you when we first started out."

A cold river of fear rushed through Molly's veins. "What, Jordan?"

He did not look at her. "We have moved from strangers to friends in a relatively short time. But friends is where it is going to have to end." He pulled up along the curb across the street from Mara's house and reached across to clench Molly's hand in a bone-crushing grip.

"What are you saying?" Brown eyes followed elusive blue-gray ones.

"We have covered the miles between here and California, but we are still miles apart, Molly. Miles apart."

"What are you saying, Jordan?" Unexplainable fear ravaged her soul.

"You are a librarian, and…"

The silence lasted so long, she finally prompted, "…and…go on."

"…I am, uh, illiterate."

Her pulse pounded painfully behind her eyes. "What?"

"I can't read. I can rescue you from a dumpster," he clutched at his shirt, pulling it away from his chest.

There's that shirt-pulling again.

He continued, "I can play professional golf. I can make you laugh. But I can't read."

"Aunt Molly! Aunt Molly!" Four little feet pounded across the street and stopped beside the driver's door as four eyes bored into Jordan. "Who is *he*? Aunt Molly, huh?" childish voices asked as they ran around to her side of the car.

He's illiterate! He's illiterate! He's illiterate! The words were angry waves pounding on the beach of her soul, shifting sand, destroying the castles built along the shore of her heart.

She opened the car door and stepped out into Emily and Toby's arms. She buried her face in their hair. Looking over their heads she saw Jordan pausing in the car, pulling at this shirt. *The puzzling gesture suddenly makes sense.* She dropped her eyes to dam-up the tears.

"Mom! Aunt Molly's here! And she's crying. Why are you crying, Aunt Molly?"

"Because I am so very, very happy to see you," she said, forcing a smile to surface and give credence to her words.

Jordan walked two steps behind her up the sidewalk. Matt came around from the backyard, clad in a charcoal-stained apron that indicated his most recent activity. Mara swung the door open and bounded down the steps to engulf Molly in her arms. "Hey, big sister, welcome home! And look who is here to greet you!"

The door opened again to allow Molly's mom and dad and her three grandparents to join the group congregating on the lawn. An attack of hugs left Jordan standing to one side, watching and smiling woodenly. Mara broke away and called out, "Hey, folks, we are being so rude! Molly's not the only one who has just arrived." She extended her hand to Jordan.

"Welcome. I am Mara, Molly's sister."

"Jordan Kendall. Thanks for the invitation to join your family. I don't want to impose. Are you sure you have room? With all the motels we passed coming into town I could easily get a room elsewhere." His quick glance took in the larger-than-expected crowd in the yard.

"Absolutely not. Come, let me introduce you around this tribe. Molly seems to have left her manners in California! This is our father, Bob, our mom, Dorothy…and our grandparents, the Winsteads, and Grandma Bergen."

Molly watched, Emily and Toby pulling at her clothing, as each family member shook Jordan's hand. He dazzled the women.

Just like he dazzled me.

And developed instant communication with the men.

Yes, I know how that feels, too.

Toby left her side to run to get his newest truck to show Jordan.

The child in me loved him, too.

"Well, Molly," Mara whispered next to her as Jordan talked with Grandpa and the Grandmas huddled around him in an admiring circle. "You neglected to tell me your traveling companion was such a…" Her words trailed off in a subdued whistle. "What other secrets are you keeping?"

Molly pulled her sister into a quick hug as tears filled her eyes again. "It is so good to see you!"

Mara patted her on the back, unknowingly in rhythm with Molly's thoughts: *he can't read, he can't read.*

"Whoa, Mol!" She made a quick decision and said lightly, "Come on, Jordan is doing fine out here. Help me check the chicken on the barbecue so we can feed this mob."

Molly did not look back at Jordan but felt his eyes following her. This promised to be the longest evening of her life. As if to mark the significant event, the grandfather clock in the living room tolled six resonant booms as the door separated Molly from Jordan and her family.

Dad, the professor,

…and Mom, the teacher,

…Mara, the special education teacher,

...and Matt, the bookstore manager,

...Emily, already the proud possessor of an award in reading,

...Toby, who thinks going to bed without a story a worse punishment than a spanking

...Grandpa and the Grandmas, all in love with books—

May I have your attention, please? I, Molly, the librarian, would like to announce that I seem to have had an accident. I have fallen, with great damage to my heart, in love with a man who could not read a love letter if I were to write one.

He is illiterate. And I am inconsolable.

CHAPTER FOURTEEN

Emily stared at Jordan over a half-eaten drumstick. "Are you famous?" she asked during an infrequent lull in the table talk.

Jordan smiled as he gave the child his undivided attention. "Well, Emily, I do not feel famous."

"Are you on television?"

"Sometimes."

"You're famous." This settled, she took a healthy bite of chicken as the adults laughed and resumed their conversations.

Molly's father picked up the potato salad and sent it around the table a third time as he said, "Kids, this is an evening to remember. Mr. Kendall probably is the only celebrity you will ever meet at any of our family get-togethers!"

Jordan grinned and shifted the attention away from himself. "Mara, Matt and whoever is responsible for this fabulous meal, thanks for letting me crash your family gathering."

Midst the ceaseless chatter around her, Molly shifted back from the table, her food basically untouched on the plate. Her eyes moved from various members of her family to Jordan back to the precious ones who had peopled her life since she was born.

She watched as the men she loved and trusted interacted with Jordan. He seemed a natural part of the laughter and chatter as everyone joined in to clear the table in anticipation of homemade ice cream and fresh raspberries.

"This one is for you, Old Shoe," Bob said to Dorothy as he placed a brimming dish before her, "lots of berries on a little dab of ice cream."

Jordan's eyes captured Molly's as she flushed with memories. Fully at ease, he picked up the pitcher of lemonade and filled empty glasses; Grandma Bergen smiled a gentle approval. When he reached Molly, his hand rested lightly on her shoulder as he leaned to cap off her glass.

Time stood still until he moved on to the next empty glass. When Molly looked up she caught her father's eye and looked away quickly.

Evening came. Mara and Molly, winning over protests, took familiar places at the sink and looked out the kitchen window at the panorama of their parents, grandpa and the grandmas, two very excited children, Matt and Jordan forming a circle of lawn chairs in the backyard. "Nice guy," Mara volunteered casually.

"What?"

"Don't be so jumpy! He's a nice guy; Jordan."

"Royce lined him up for the ride. I will probably never see him again."

"I see."

"What is that supposed to mean?"

"It means, I see—you will probably never see him again."

"Right."

Glasses tinkled; steam rose from the sink. "Everything okay, Mol?"

"Sure. I mean, just tired and all. Long trip."

"You can fly again next time. But then again, you would lose your chances to drive all those miles with a man like Jordan!"

Molly smiled weakly.

"You do agree that he is an essentially well-constructed man, don't you?" Mara teased.

"Um, yeah."

"Try to contain your enthusiasm! We are talking about one of the best looking guys I have met, not counting Matt, naturally, and you seem quite reserved, to put it mildly."

"No, I agree. He is pretty good-looking."

"Who is pretty good-looking?" Dorothy Winstead stuck her head around the door frame.

"Hi, Mom. We're talking about Jordan," Mara responded.

"Do *not* tell your father I said so, but wow! Molly, you've done just fine."

"Mother! I have not 'done' anything. I gave the man a ride to Minnesota. Period."

"Ah."

Mara interrupted with a wide grin, "Molly is saying surprisingly little about Jordan, Mom! But, did you notice how his hand rested ever-so-lightly on Molly's shoulder when he poured her lemonade?"

"Did I? You had better believe I noticed! And did you notice how his eyes kept moving back to her? I have always said my girls have magnetic personalities, but really!"

Two of the three women in the kitchen chuckled.

"What's the joke out here?"

"Oh hi, Dad. Say, did you notice any significant differences in this evening's meal, contrasted with the first-night meals from other summers when Molly returns to Minnesota?"

He scratched his chin thoughtfully, "Well, let's see. Our normally coherent and communicative daughter enters the scene and shares approximately ten words with her family over a two-hour meal. And in her company is a handsome, intelligent, and very interesting young man. No, I do not think I noticed anything different this year. Why do you ask?"

Molly grinned in spite of herself and her father rested his chin on her head as he held her in a quick embrace. "Come on, you guys. You know The Plan. There are still almost three more years before I even think about falling in love, and marriage. I have invested too much time, effort and money into getting to this point."

"That you have, Sweetie. At least no one can accuse you of abandoning your goals, Sweetheart." He blew her a kiss. "Come on," he turned, circling his wife's waist with one arm, "Jordan's telling about his parent's catering business. I told him to wait until I got you back out there. They are quite a family!"

The screen door opened and closed. Molly held soapy dishes under hot water and added to the collection Mara was drying.

"How is Jordan going to get to his tournament?"

"I will drive him up there in the morning. Is it okay if he stays here tonight?"

"Of course, if he doesn't mind bunking with Toby. Toby will be one delighted little kid, believe me." She nodded her head in the direction of the backyard where the small boy had just climbed up on Jordan's lap. "That is no way to treat a guest, but…"

"Believe me, it cannot be any worse than some nights we spent coming out here."

Mara whistled, her puckered lips forming a grin as the sound faded. "I am willing to bet there are better stories from the trip than the ones he is telling out there!" She flicked water at her sister playfully. "My goodness, Jordan must have given The Plan quite a challenge!"

Molly ducked under the sink to search for a scouring pad to clean the grill and avoided her sister's eyes.

Within fifteen minutes all traces of the evening meal were gone and the two women rejoined the others in the dusky evening. "Kids, I hate to say this, but it's time for bed for anyone under four feet tall. Maybe Aunt Molly would like to help you."

"I would love to. Toby, I want to see your big-boy bed."

"It's a bunk bed cuz I don't wet the bed anymore!"

"Which reminds me," Mara interjected, "Jordan, you are more than welcome to spend the night here, with one hitch. You get the bottom bunk under a little boy, but he does come with a life-time guarantee that he is housebroken!"

"Oh, boy! Mr. Kendall gets to sleep in my room!"

Jordan nodded appreciatively at Mara and then turned to Toby, "Seems to me that if we are going to be bunkmates, you could call me Jordan, or BJ like my golf buddies do, if it's not against family rules."

Toby looked questioningly at his parents who nodded approval. "Aunt Molly, can BJ help you put us to bed?"

"If he wants to." His nod confirmed his answer.

"Will you read us our night-time story?" Emily asked him.

Molly's jaw tightened, but Jordan answered easily, "I bet your Aunt Molly has been waiting to do that. But I will listen with you." The four-some left the backyard, linked adult-child-adult-child, hand in hand.

Clutching a rabbit with one eye missing, Toby climbed up on Jordan's lap while Emily cozied up next to him and positioned four dolls on her lap. "Aunt Mol, move closer to BJ. I can't see 'way over here," the little girl fussed.

Jordan responded instantly, which put him so close to Molly that the warmth of his body radiated against her own, thigh-to-thigh, shoulder-to-shoulder. "My babies and I are ready now," announced the little mother. Molly began the story she had brought from California especially for this night.

Finally, two pajama-clad children climbed into their beds. Leaving a hugged, kissed, tucked-in Toby, the other three moved down the hall to repeat the process with Emily. Jordan and Molly each chose a side of the bed and met across the pillows. Two eager little arms reached out and encircled their necks, bringing them head-to-head over Emily's scrubbed and shining face. "I am soooooooo glad Aunt Molly brought you home, BJ. You're nice!"

"I am glad, too. Sleep tight, and we will see you tomorrow." He tweaked her nose and she giggled.

"Love you, Emmy," Molly said, burying her nose in the little girl's cheek before she planted a kiss on two rosebud lips.

As they pushed up from the bed, Molly and Jordan's eyes met and held for the first time since Jordan's curb-side announcement. Molly dropped her eyes first and smoothed the sheet around Emily's shoulders; Jordan headed for the door. "Are you going to marry him, Aunt Molly?" Emily asked in a stage whisper.

"No, honey. We're just friends."

"Like you and Uncle Royce?"

"That's right," Molly lied glibly.

On the steps heading back to join the adults, Jordan said softly, "I'm glad you still consider me your friend, Molly. I'm sorry about the last moments in the car. It was a terrible way to end a trip together. I knew on the first day of the trip that I needed to tell you, the minute you told me you are a librarian. But the time never seemed right. We need to talk about…"

"We had thousands of miles of talk, Jordan. Your timing stinks."

"So shoot me. As long as that's the only charge you have against me, that I have lousy timing." Jordan's eyes were pools of hurt, despite his joking tone.

Molly's answer was necessarily put on hold as they reached the bottom of the steps and were within hearing range of the others who had moved into the family room. Matt was in the kitchen. "Give me a hand, Jordan, this crowd just gave me a big order of popcorn to fill," he called when he heard them.

"In a minute. I'm going to stop in the bathroom first."

Jordan latched on to Molly's wrist and pulled her back into the dim hallway that led to the bathroom. Drawing her close, he splayed one hand across her back and tipped her chin up to meet his lips. This time, The Kiss held nothing back. Lust, love, longing. Pleasure, pursuit, passion. Anger, anguish, anxiety. All were there in the gentle touching, the insistent probing, the intense joining of four lips in the ageless rite of courtship, The Kiss.

It was their farewell. A cruel, final, crushing moment.

Molly sagged against the wall. Jordan released her and propped himself against the wall, one hand on each side of her head. They stood that way, in darkness, allowing their rocky breathing to stabilize. Finally, he spoke, his voice low, his words brushing across her face like a lake breeze. "I will always wish we could have ended on a better note. But maybe it's best this way."

She snagged enough of a breath to sustain life, and nodded.

"I just want you to know one thing. I did not mean to deceive you." He ran his hands along the wall to her hair, then followed the lines of her face, moved along her neck, down along her shoulders, finally spanning her waist. Her skin flamed beneath his touch.

A faint cry escaped her lips; helpless against her desire to touch him, she lightly ran her finger along the bridge of his nose, down to his kiss-bruised lips. Without warning, he dropped his hands and backed away. From an arm's length, he rolled forward on the balls of his feet and kissed her finger that still hung in the air close to his lips. With that, he turned on his heel and headed for the kitchen.

She slid down the wall to a fetal crouch along the floorboard. Every war has its casualties; she felt like the latest statistic.

"Just in time! Grab the butter from the refrigerator door," she heard Matt say.

"Man, after that incredible picnic, how can anyone be hungry? I guess popcorn is always hard to resist!" She could not imagine how Jordan could sound so normal; she felt like a limp dishrag.

"Tradition," she heard Matt say, "we always seem to end up with popcorn at any family event. If you like the stuff as much as the rest of us, you are in the right place."

Molly could take no more. She fled to the demilitarized zone of the family room. "Kids go down okay?" Mara asked.

"Like angels."

"Who finally read the story?" Grandpa Winstead asked.

Molly forced a smile, "I did."

"I could tell that was a hard decision for them! They had to choose between their favorite aunt and their new friend."

Molly sank down to an over-sized pillow on the floor and let the conversation form a cocoon around her, answering questions automatically, smiling mechanically, wondering how it was that no one else could hear the distant echoes of the artillery that had killed something within her and left her bleeding internally.

"First batch ready for the eating!" Jordan announced over her head. He stopped first beside the grandmas to let them dip into the big bowl of popcorn. He evidenced no wounds, but at least he wasn't playing the role of gloating victor.

Then, Matt appeared with a second batch. When all had been served, he said, "Okay, Jordan, now is your chance to educate this frightfully uninformed family about golf. Now that we know you, we will be glued to the television for your tournament, come Sunday."

Bob Winstead chuckled, "Actually, Jordan, if you could suggest a simple, authoritative book, we would not have to bother you on your time off with explaining golf to the relatively uninitiated."

Jordan tossed a kernel of popcorn in the air and caught in expertly in his mouth before he answered, "Well, Bob, golf is a pretty slow and quiet game. There is actually lots of teaching that goes on during the lulls when the sportscasters talk to fill the air time. You might be surprised how much you learn just watching."

He's already calling my dad Bob? Whew, talk about worming your way into the family. Her emotions took another dive. This made it even more difficult to explain to her family why Jordan would disappear from her life tomorrow, even without the rigid structure of The Plan.

She tuned back in as Jordan said, "Tell you what, I will get word to the announcer to be especially clear this week!"

Questions fired from around the circle received concise answers. Jordan spoke easily and confidently about the sport that was his life, his shield against the literate world.

Molly's thoughts wandered again. *I certainly would never guess that he hides a secret of such magnitude. He has a great vocabulary, and seems as ease with so many types of people. If there is a stereotype of illiterate people, Bartholomew Jordan Kendall slipped through a major crack in it.*

When the popcorn bowls were almost empty, grandpa and the grandmas began their good-byes for the evening. Grandma Bergen would go across town to stay at the senior Winstead's home, but before she left she clasped his hand and said, "Well, young man, it has been a pleasure to meet you. I hope we see you again."

Grandma! Enough!

The two grandmas hovered around Jordan much like the children had. Impulsively, he ducked down and lightly kissed each on her cheek. "Good night, ladies. It's been a most pleasant evening."

He got two kisses back in response and loving pats sealed them in place. Molly watched with a tightness in her chest.

"Molly, we will leave you and Jordan to visit with Mara and Matt," Bob said as Dorothy nodded. "We've spent the day keeping up with our parents, and quite frankly, we're bushed! Thank goodness Mother Bergen lives in St. Cloud and the Winsteads are here in Rochester or we would be exhausted most of the time!"

The two younger couples laughed as a bedroom door closed. Mara whispered, "That's *one* reason to head to bed early…"

Molly almost choked. "Mara…" She tipped her head in Jordan's direction and shot her sister a meaningful glance.

Matt chuckled as he explained for Jordan's benefit, "Bob and Dorothy are pretty obviously passionate in their love, even after thirty years of marriage. Their daughters tease them mercilessly!"

Jordan just grinned and Molly sighed in mock dismay, "They haven't changed much, have they?"

"We finally put a lock on the guest bedroom door so we will not need to begin sex education quite so young with our kids!" They all looked in the general direction of the closed bedroom door.

Two hours sped by while the four of them relaxed and shared stories. Sitting there, Molly almost managed to forget that she and Jordan were finished. A sort of healing began, leaving behind only a mute sadness.

Any tales Jordan told about their trip were carefully edited so that Molly was never embarrassed or compromised. Matt laughed so loud over the episode with the tent that Mara smothered him with a pillow. When Molly told about Jordan climbing in the back seat with the tribe of kids, Jordan demonstrated his part of the story with hilarious physical contortions until all four had to escape through the patio door into the outdoors before they woke the rest of the family with their raucous laughter.

As they stood under the brilliant stars, Matt and Jordan talked softly and Mara plucked dead roses off her prize bushes while Molly stood quietly by. *Why couldn't his terrible secret be dandruff or a fear of snakes, instead of illiteracy? Why, why, why? And why didn't I guard my heart?*

"It hardly feels like we just met you this evening, Jordan," Mara said as she tucked a rose into Molly's hair. Jordan smiled at Molly; fragrant memories crossed a bridge between them and the sadness inside Molly cut sharply against her heart.

Matt nodded, "You feel like an old friend. Which gives me the courage to mention something that Mara probably will kill me for saying. Whoever cut your hair last, Jordan, should lose his license."

Molly kicked at a rock on the patio. Jordan laughed easily and said, "If it had been my regular person, I probably would never go back, but traveling around as much as I do, you have to take your chances."

He didn't tell! Gratitude warmed Molly's eyes as she smiled thankfully at Jordan. The grandfather clock in the house chimed in the house and startled the foursome, signaling a need to end their evening.

With order restored in the living room, Matt led the way to Toby's bedroom and opened the door quietly. The rabbit with one eye stared at them from the floor; Toby's face was a picture of contentment in the moonlight streaming through the window. Jordan tiptoed to the bed and quietly placed his suitcase on the floor before he turned and saluted the three in the doorway.

Matt eased the door shut and Mara gave Molly a quick hug and whispered in her ear, "Glad you're home, Mol. Your same old room downstairs is ready for you."

Propped up against the pillows of the single bed forever known as "Aunt Molly's bed," she imagined Jordan lying on the bottom bunk staring up at Toby's mattress. She grinned. *He is probably sincerely hoping Mara's housebroken guarantee holds true tonight!*

She undressed and slipped into her robe and curled up with an afghan around her shoulders and a book from the shelf above the bed. The night was still and the house quiet as she turned pages trying to entice sleep. For the first time in her life, holding a book in her hand felt unnatural; Jordan's voice echoed in her mind: "I'm illiterate." She futilely fought back tears and finally gave way to sobs that she muffled with the pillow until they diminished. Even then, sleep refused to come.

She tiptoed upstairs and headed for the comfort of a cup of hot chocolate. She stood ready to catch the microwave's buzzer before it could alert anyone to her late-night kitchen prowl.

Pulling out a chair in the breakfast nook, she curled up, chin on her knees, and sipped carefully. When a shadow cut across the light cast by the street light, she jumped and then felt foolish when Matt whispered, "Can I join you, Mol?"

"Sure. It's your hot chocolate, so help yourself!"

"Sounds good."

As Molly watched him prepare his cup, she thought sadly, *Matt can read. Mara loves a man who not only can read, but enjoys reading. Gee, Molly, you need some sleep!* She blew across her cup, dividing the marshmallow sea.

"You're a good night watchman, Matt."

"Didn't hear you at all. I was just checking on the kids and decided to get a drink of water. But this is better," he said and dropped into a chair across from her. "Couldn't sleep, huh?"

"Haven't really tried yet. I was reading and…" Her face felt tight from all the secret tears; she was glad he didn't turn on a light.

"I think Jordan is a great guy, Molly."

"Yeah."

"He is real easy to get to know. No ego, or anything that could go along with his career. It sure was a good thing you guys could drive back here together."

Molly nodded thoughtfully.

They sipped in comfortable silence for a few moments. "He has some great stories, doesn't he? I have not laughed so hard in I don't know how long."

He's got one story that won't make you laugh, I guarantee it.

Matt tipped his head back and drained the last swallow from his cup. "I had better head back to bed or Mara will wake up and wonder where I am."

"'G'night, Matt."

"See you in the morning. Whoppin' big breakfast in honor of our favorite sister and her honored guest. Be there or regret it."

Molly sat in the darkness for several minutes, listening to the ticking of the clock in the stillness. Clues that should have been forerunning clues to Jordan's pronouncement now played in her mind like words of a haunting song.

He never read a menu; I always read the billboards.

When I mentioned books I have read, he talked only about movies he has seen.

This is why he grabbed frantically at his shirt at the oddest times—any talk about books or reading is threatening to his dark secret; it's like an inescapable stranglehold to a helpless victim.

When the clock struck a melodious quarter-hour, it roused her from her dismal thoughts and she rinsed out her cup in the sink. As she walked past Toby's bedroom on her way to the steps going to her room, she paused. *Jordan, why didn't you ever learn to read? And why did you, of all people, have to show up in my life?*

CHAPTER FIFTEEN

Molly leaned against the kitchen door frame, stifling a yawn. Breakfast was over; a fresh pot of coffee was almost ready. Bob looked up from his paper and smiled at his oldest daughter, "Good morning, Sleepyhead."

Three other heads turned her way as various sections of the paper lowered. "Bob! She has every right to sleep in after the long trip she just made!" Dorothy chided mildly. "G'morning, honey!"

"Coffee, Mol?" Mara asked, already on her feet. Matt pushed out a chair with his foot and Molly slid into it, nodding at Mara, and including them all in her sleepy smile.

"Where is everyone?"

Four sets of eyes darted around the table and shared a glance that fairly dripped with humor. "Everyone?" Mara teased. "Well, the grandmas and grandpa haven't touched base yet this morning, and the kids are biking around Silver Lake with their newest friend, your paying passenger. Is that 'everyone'?"

Molly wrinkled her nose at her sister and breathed in the wonderful aroma of every first-cup-in-the-morning-coffee. "Yeah, that pretty much covers it." She refused to be baited any further.

"Brave man, that Jordan," Bob said, shaking his head ruefully. "We offered him a section of the paper, but he left, instead, with one five-year-old on a bicycle with training wheels and a three-year-old who thinks his tricycle is a Jeep."

"Yes," added Dorothy, "he actually seemed excited over feeding bread to the geese. He is quite a guy."

Molly spread jam on a piece of toast and listened to Jordan's praises being sung around the table.

"I drove him to the phone store bright and early this morning, and he was able to get his cell phone fixed which impressed him no-end. I told him that in this town, cell phone owners expect that kind of service!"

"Oh, I'm glad. I hated to think he would be without a phone until he got home," Molly said.

"He asked me to take him to the airport later this morning," Matt added a few minutes later. "He said he will catch a flight up to Minneapolis. Or maybe he was going to rent a car. I can't remember. Whatever. We're going to the airport later. We zipped down Broadway without looking left or right, so we missed the obligatory spin past the Mayo Clinic and IBM and any other Rochester tourist attractions he might have heard about out there on the left coast. I think we will leave early enough for the quick tour."

Molly breathed jaggedly. *Jordan is leaving. In just a few hours.* She dropped her toast onto the plate.

"I told him we could drop him off in the Cities when we head home, but he was adamant about not wanting to put any of us out or wear out his welcome here, even though I told him no one was complaining about his company," Bob said, winking at his West-coast daughter.

This is it. Two thousand miles coming to an end and Jordan is walking around Silver Lake with two little kids. And I am choking on toast, guarding his life's secret.

"Looks like they survived their adventure." Five heads turned toward the kitchen window. Jordan walked between the two children who were beaming as they pedaled and shared the morning sunshine with their tall hero.

"Mommy, mommy! We fed the ducks and Jordan talked to them and they didn't peck me this time! Not even once."

"Mommy, mommy! Jordan said that he will wave at me when from TV! Can we watch?"

"You better believe we will watch, Sweetheart. We will all be sitting there watching Jordan win the tournament."

So now this is suddenly a family of sports fans? Molly could hardly disguise her amazement. *This from a family who rarely knows who plays whom in any given sports event?* Molly stared at Jordan in wonder. *What magic does this man possess?*

They said their public good-byes in the middle of the driveway. Molly swallowed hard as the familiar suitcase and briefcase were loaded into the back of Matt's car, and the suit bag and hand-tooled leather golf bag were transferred from the Volvo. Emily and Toby bounced with excitement in the back seat of the car, eager to leave for the airport.

Jordan shook hands full circle. "Mara, thanks for your warm welcome and superb hospitality...Dorothy, it was my delight to meet you. Enjoy the rest of your summer away from the classroom...Bob, I hope you get hooked on golf! It's been so good to spend this time with you. Please say my farewells to grandpa and the grandmas."

He turned to Molly who was trembling inside, steeling herself against any outward sign of it. Jordan smiled gently and caught her in a neutral embrace. "Molly, thanks for a very special week. Have a great time with your family. Maybe we will see each other in California again." Rain-washed-spring-sky eyes seemed to memorize her face before he turned away.

Wait! She ached to toss her well-ordered life to the four winds. *We need to talk...but it won't help, will it? Talking is no magic wand.* She smiled tremulously. "'Bye, Jordan. Good luck in the tournament. Thanks for coming along on the trip."

And it was over.

Molly felt six eyes boring into her back and turned. She shrugged, "Well, they are off like a herd of turtles."

Bob dropped an arm across her shoulders as they walked toward the house. "What a great guy, Molly. I am glad to have gotten to meet him. He is what Grandpa Bergen called a regular guy."

Dorothy's arm came around her waist from the other side. "And we are glad to have you home, too, Sweetie."

"Claim spots on the porch while I grab the coffeepot," Mara said, letting the kitchen door slam behind her. Molly sank into the wicker swing, beginning to rock with a thrust of her foot.

Numbly, she accepted a mug from the tray Mara held in front of her and sank into despondent silence amidst the idle chatter around her until a loudly honking goose landed in the front yard.

Bob laughed, "That fellow is lost! Hey, buddy, the lake is that-a-way!"

"Maybe he tried to follow Jordan back…and didn't make very good time!" Dorothy offered.

"What a guy. Even ducks leave their course to find him!" Mara added with a teasing wink in Molly's direction. Molly pushed against the floor of the porch and set the swing in vicious motion.

"Sounded like Jordan wouldn't mind seeing you again, Molly."

"Mom, it is not likely. We have…nothing in common."

Bob snorted, "Well, shall we place bets on that?"

Molly's lips tightened. What had happened to the two parents who had always carefully kept their opinions of her male friends to themselves? The parents who were so proud of her, so supportive of The Plan?

"Dad, Mom, Mara," she blinked back scalding tears, "before you all say things you will regret later, there is, uh, something you need to know about Jordan." She stared across the lawn; trees and fences suddenly blurred. "He can't read." The angry rasping of the swing as Molly rocked was the only sound for a full minute.

"Cannot read, or doesn't read?" Dorothy asked softly.

"Cannot. He is illiterate."

Mara held her coffee cup in both hands; her knuckle-whitening grip was the only clue to her emotions as she asked, "When did you find this out, Mol?"

"Oh, sitting out at the curb, about ten seconds before he met the troops yesterday," answered Molly with a voice that trembled beneath the burden of unshed tears.

"At least it's nothing terminal," Bob said softly.

"Dad! The man is 34 years old and he cannot read. I, on the other hand, come from a family I do not need to describe to any one you, and I make my living working with books, and reading, and readers. We are miles apart. What could be more 'terminal' than that?"

Mara muttered a most indelicate word and neither parent batted an eyelash.

"Honey, did you like him before you found this out?"

Molly chewed her lip until she tasted blood. She looked into her mother's love-filled eyes. "Yes. I started to. A lot," she said sadly.

A neighbor strolled by, walking a dog. Mara waved and they made light conversation for five minutes. Left alone again, no one spoke of Jordan. And no one thought of anything else, despite jokes about crab grass, questions about Royce and Brynn, and idle chitchat about family things.

The station wagon rounded the corner; each detail of Jordan's boarding the plane had to be covered before any other plans for the day could be made. "Jordan is gonna look out the airplane window and try to find our house," Toby beamed.

"We are going to climb a tree in the back yard so he can see which one it is," Emily called and followed her brother behind the house.

"Dad, he showed me his golf clubs while the kids were looking at the centrifugal force display," Matt announced with a grin. "I hate to say it, but those clubs we have are sorry excuses!"

"Your clubs? Since when do you two have golf clubs?" Molly asked in amazement.

"Ever since your mom told me I was getting too sedentary!" Bob replied with an exaggerated sigh.

"And Mara decided that I should keep your dad in line," Matt added, "and so we have taken to hitting a few balls once a week or so. Believe me, it is *not* as easy as it looks on TV."

"It will be more fun to watch the tournament this time now that we know Jordan," Dorothy said.

"*Et tu*, Brute?" Molly said, laughing in spite of herself. "I do not believe this! And if Mara says she's..."

"Hey, no pointing that accusing finger at me is allowed! I will stick with the torture of aerobics. No golf until I sprain something major going through those antics!"

"I cannot believe this is the same family I saw last summer!"

"We felt it was about time this bunch did something physical before we all turn into a reader's equivalent of couch potatoes!" said Bob.

Next thing I'll hear is that the grandmas and grandpa are playing touch football in the park every weekend. Molly's lips twitched in amusement, despite her jangled emotions.

Come Sunday, dinner dishes were left to soak, eight chairs circled the television in the family room, and two children sat on pillows, all eyes glued to the set.

The excitement at the scene of the live tournament was no less real than that in one home in Rochester. A cheer went up at both sites when the camera first caught Jordan's smile. "There he is! Mommy, that's BJ."

"Yes, it is. Sit down so we can all see, okay? Isn't it fun to know somebody on TV, Toby?"

"He is famous, isn't he, mommy?"

"I would say so, Emily."

The announcer's voice effectively quieted all conversation in the room. "...and from California, here's everyone's favorite, BJ Kendall. How about this weather we ordered especially for you to play in today, BJ?"

Blue-gray eyes. The camera effectively brought him into the room. "What a day! It's beautiful. I hope everyone watching has the same terrific weather. I am pleased, as always, to be part of a celebrity tournament for such a worthy cause like Kid's Wishes Anonymous." He smiled as if seeing directly into their circle. "I hope everyone watching enjoys the afternoon, whether they are in a hospital bed, or in a family room." The camera turned to pan the crowd, but not before it showed Jordan talking seriously with the announcer, out of the range of the microphone.

"What's he saying?" Emily asked curiously.

"Maybe he's telling him to explain the game to us!" Grandpa Winstead chuckled.

"I'm sure he is," Grandma Bergen defended stoutly, "because he said he would. He's a gentlemen of his word. What a nice man to play and donate all his earnings from the day to that charity."

Molly stared at her grandmother. *She remembered him saying something about playing for charity, but it had not registered. Jordan had made a trip back to Minneapolis, not for more money for himself, but solely for a charity cause.* It was obvious he really cared about the sick children. Molly watched the screen with interest heightened while prerecorded interviews with several excited, heart-breakingly ill children told their wishes that would be granted after today's tournament.

Most likely the announcers' comments were evenly distributed, but coverage of BJ Kendall seemed prominent. "...breaking with tradition, as he has gained a reputation for doing, today BJ uses a persimmon driver on this hole..."

Bob jotted a note on the pad beside his chair. Persimmon.

The announcer almost whispered as Jordan moved into place for his next shot. "What we are seeing here, ladies and gentlemen, is a great player who is renowned as a recovery player. Watch as BJ shows us his competitive nature. Friends and critics alike say of him that he never gives up. This persistence gets him high-powered results."

Jordan stared at the ball at his feet as if willing it to follow his wishes. Molly hid a smile, remembering the windmill.

"He is going down the handle a little, but other than that, there are no clues that this is a difficult shot."

The microphone picked up the whiz of the club as it cracked the ball through the air.

"Perfect! A clean hit. The sure sign of a fine golfer coming out of a difficult recovery."

Applause rose spontaneously from the sidelines and from the circle around the television in Rochester.

The announcer's soft, riveting voice broke into Molly's reverie, "Perhaps many watching do not realize this, but BJ has a handicap that would keep a less ambitious man out of the sport altogether."

Molly's nails pressed half-moons in her palms. *No. He would not dare tell the world that Jordan is illiterate! But how did he find out? Jordan said no one knows.*

"…BJ is several inches taller than the average pro golfer. Height is as much a disadvantage in golf as it often is a desired trait in some other sports. But, as you're seeing today, BJ plays well, whether with woods or irons, despite his height handicap."

Half the adults in the room blew out pent-up air, falling back against their chairs in relief; the rest curiously stared at them.

"In talking with BJ before today's tournament action began," the announcer said, "we learned something that will come as a shock to the golf world. Over the next few months he will decide either to continue with professional golf competition or to settle into business with the golf club back in California's San Joaquin Valley where he has worked for years between public appearances. It is hard to imagine pro golf without BJ but we wish him well in whatever he decides. More later on that late-breaking story."

The camera focused on Jordan's face and upper torso while he relaxed in a chair, the greens behind him for this taped segment. His familiar voice spoke, "It is a tough decision. I enjoy both aspects of the sport, playing and teaching."

The announcer said, "Many spectators along the sidelines today have had the opportunity to work with BJ at his club. They are torn between wanting him to continue his meteoric advancement in pro golf, and wanting him at the club where he can work one-on-one with them when business or pleasure land them in California. We now move along the bunker to where BJ is beginning…"

If Jordan's decision was to be influenced by his success or failure in the Minnesota tournament, the charity was considerably richer when the sun turned pink behind the trees around the course. The camera in Molly's mind held the memory of a jubilant Jordan with his club raised in one hand as well-wishers crowded around him after the masterful stroke that sealed his success.

His smiling face was on all the early and late newscasts of the evening; his name was in bold headlines on the sports section on Monday. His previously scheduled upcoming Florida, Colorado, and Georgia tournaments quickly became the focus of the sports world. And black ink filled white newsprint as columnists speculated on his news-worthy decision.

Monday, Molly drove to Duluth behind her parents who honked their horn each time Jordan's name was mentioned on WCCO radio.

After a rest stop just North of St. Paul, Dorothy climbed in to Molly's car and said, "Your father said he is willing to share me until we get to Hinckley!"

It was obvious she wanted to talk and equally obvious she had a subject in mind. "Did Jordan go to high school?"

Molly kept her eyes on the road. "Yes. And graduated."

Dorothy nodded with a triumphant gleam in her eyes, "Good."

"Good? I think it stinks. It smacks of what is wrong with our educational system if people can get diplomas without being able to read."

"Molly, we do mot know all the details. And he is not the first, nor will he be the last person who reaches success in their careers with a secret of this magnitude. My assessment is that he somehow missed out at a crucial stage, maybe through an illness, or some crisis at home. Whatever it was, he just could not keep up, or grasp the concepts, and he got farther and farther behind. The farther behind, the more embarrassment it caused him. Some people are good at beating the system. Or perhaps he had a teacher who wasn't prepared to catch the problem."

Molly searched her memory for clues. With all the stories they had told on their trip, she could not remember anything about an extended illness or a family crisis.

"But he is smart, Molly. Surely, you noticed that he has an excellent vocabulary. This can only mean that he has a good memory, a keen mind, and a great deal of pride. To say nothing of a desire to appear educated. Those are strong characteristics."

"But he can't read, Mom. Even if he learned how..."

"I think he wants to read. And meeting you might be the needed spur to get him to enroll in an adult reading program."

"I don't think so. He is very opinionated about reading, Mom. We had some major, uh, discussions about it. He basically feels reading is a waste of time, and totally removed from real life."

"Sounds like the gentleman doth protest too much."

Molly stared at her mother in surprise.

"Can't you see, Honey? He is defensive, and afraid. I think he wishes, maybe more so since meeting you, that he could turn back the clock and be a reader."

Tears welled up in Molly's eyes; her breath escaped in a sob. "Mom, ever since he told me, I keep thinking back to the times I acted like a jerk on the trip. I said some pretty awful things. I must have made him feel like scum."

"Not on purpose, Molly. He knows that."

"It must be awful not to be capable of reading. He cannot even read a menu, or a road sign. Or a newspaper, even though he pretends; maybe he just looks at sports scores. He has developed a pretty good system for getting out of reading without losing face," she ended grimly.

"There are many people out there like him."

"I know, but until now they have just been statistics to me. I never thought they would be so…"

"…much like Jordan?"

"He is pretty terrific, isn't he, Mom? Except for the lie he lives."

"He is pretty terrific, period."

Molly accelerated and pulled around a slow driver. "Could you love Dad if he didn't know how to read?"

Dorothy's eyebrows raised slightly. "Oh, yes, Molly. Or if he only had one leg. Or if he were suddenly impotent. Real love is funny that way."

"I feel so sad. Mom. Sad that Jordan can't read. Sad to have discovered that I am such a prejudiced boor about it. Sad that it is over between Jordan and me before it got a good beginning."

"I know, honey. What do you like best about him?"

Molly's eyebrows hiked up this time. "Best?" She weighed the question for a minute. "He makes me laugh. I think that is something I have forgotten how to do lately. He is so much fun to be with, Mom."

"That's important, Honey. What else?"

"He is a great person to talk to. We talked for hours at a time on the trip. I have never talked with any guy I've ever gone out with before like Jordan and I were able to talk. I *thought* I had really gotten to know him."

Dorothy watched her daughter's face carefully.

"He can tell stories so well that you feel like you are right there, part of the action. And he goes to great lengths not to embarrass me in front of other people."

"How did you meet him? Through Royce?"

"That is a story for both you and Dad to hear. Hold on for a few miles. We are almost at our traditional exit. I think I can finally tell it without blushing."

They pulled off the highway at the familiar spot in Hinckley. After they ordered coffee and warm, giant caramel rolls, Dorothy said, "Mol's got a story to tell, Bob, about how she met Jordan."

"Fire away!"

Molly covered the dumpster scene and the lunch with Royce and Jordan in the next half hour. They unknowingly attracted smiles from around the restaurant while they wiped tears from their eyes and erupted with laughter throughout the story.

Then she hit the crisis points of the trip. When she got to the part about Jordan and the empty gas tank, Bob held up his hand, "Wait!" He massaged his aching cheek muscles. "Give my cheeks a rest. What a story, Molly! And what a trooper Jordan is!"

Dorothy erupted in a giggle again, "To think you accused him of being a lazy gardener! He *does* work on greens, but not with a mower!"

Molly topped off their coffee cups with the pot the waitress had left. "Being with him makes me realize that I have become all too serious lately. And the fact that he did not tell any of these stories on me in front of the family, well, I really appreciated that." She paused, and then asked with a sheepish grin, "Did you notice his hair?"

Bob and Dorothy glanced quickly at each other before Bob said, "Well, yes, we did. We talked about it and figured maybe he has some condition that makes his hair grow, um, well, strangely."

Molly took a deep breath and said, "No. It is from where I cut his hair to get him loose."

Bob grinned broadly and signaled the waitress. "Could we get another pot of coffee? I think we will be here for a little while longer!" He added, to his wife and daughter, after she moved away, "Wild horses couldn't drag me away from this table yet!"

Molly dug around in her purse until she found her nail clippers; she dropped them on the table before she began. When she got to the part about Jordan wearing the cap in the next morning, Dorothy pushed back her chair and begged, "Stop the story until I get back from the rest room!" Heads turned to watch the graceful, dignified lady who giggled like a first-grader all the way to the ladies room.

As they were heading for the cashier, Bob teased, "I hope the rest of your vacation can compete with the excitement level of the first week! Duluth may seem a little tame after that trip."

Molly led the way to the port city alone in her car. She changed to a Duluth radio station with her first glimpse of the expanse of Lake Superior from the hill and sighed resignedly when BJ Kendall was mentioned twice within the first ten minutes.

He will haunt me for the rest of my life, I just know it. She groaned aloud.

Tuesday. Molly shopped with her mother at the mall. They separated for an hour while Dorothy got her hair done. Molly wandered aimlessly, enjoying the relaxed pace of the day, stopping outside a sporting goods store when golf clubs caught her eye. An enterprising manager had capitalized on Sunday's tournament. A sign read: *Get a grip on the clubs used by BJ Kendall.* Blue-gray eyes sparkled beneath maple syrup hair in the life-sized photograph on a poster in the window. Molly stared, oblivious to time or her surroundings.

Wednesday. The evening breeze off Lake Superior drew the three Winsteads from their home for a walk. When they passed the library, they went in to spend a few moments reading magazines. Molly found it difficult to concentrate and left her parents with their noses buried in the pages of news magazines.

She talked shop briefly with the reference librarian, then strolled by the new books and thumbed through one on golf personalities. The section on Jordan was positioned near the front; this alone showed the author's bias that BJ Kendall was one of the decade's best pro players.

Molly bit her lip. *I wonder if Jordan even knows about this book?* Dismally, she returned to the magazine reading area.

Thursday. A lazy day; Molly and Dorothy sipped iced tea and watched Bob putt in the back yard. The telephone call came as a complete surprise. Bob ran inside and talked for quite a while before coming to the door to call Molly. "I have already told him how proud we all are of his performance in the tournament. You can cover other stuff, Mol!"

"It's Jordan?" she whispered.

"So he says. The one and only," Bob said with a chuckle as he closed her fingers around the receiver, saving it from a fall to the floor.

"Hello?"

"Hello, Molly. How's Duluth?"

She swallowed hard. "Fine." She leaned weakly against the wall. "Where are you?"

"At the airport. I am heading to Florida for two days, then off to Colorado, and then back to Georgia."

"Sorry you have to fly."

"I could never find a travel partner like my last one! Are you having fun?"

"Umm. Pretty low-key. I walked along the Lake by the aerial bridge; that's always fun."

"Wish I could be there, too. Oops, they have announced my flight. Got to run."

"Thanks for calling, Jordan," she said softly.

"Say hello to your mom for me."

"I will." She could hear the loudspeakers in the background. "You had better go, Jordan."

"'Bye, Minnesota. Later."

Later? Slowly, she hung up the telephone and dropped into a nearby chair, hugging her knees to her chest, lost in thought.

CHAPTER SIXTEEN

Friday. Golfing day. Molly moodily drove a cart as her parents played eighteen holes with friends. In the lounge, Bob and Dorothy exchanged glances over Molly's head as she swirled the cherry from her genuine cherry coke by its stem, creating a sticky mess on a cocktail napkin.

Saturday. Molly attacked the flower beds with a vengeance. Any weed that survived the war she waged that day deserved to live. Exhausted, she dropped into bed early in the evening and slept fitfully.

Sunday. The Florida tournament was an assault on the senses. Jordan interviewed. Jordan at every hole. Jordan in commercials. Jordan's every move was newsworthy. Jordan, Jordan, Jordan. Molly had no fingernails remaining by the end of the televised broadcast.

Monday. Molly woke to the sound of rain. *Perfect.* It fit her mood exactly. She pulled the Volvo into the garage to clean it out for the trip to St. Cloud to pick up the boxes of books from her grandmother's house, and then on to Rochester where she would finish her vacation. The plastic bag on the passenger door held poignant memories: dried flower petals, a receipt for the motel room that first night when Jordan had paced in his room above hers, a napkin with a smear of blueberry ice cream in the shape of lips.

Vacuuming out the crumbs, dirt, and reminders of the trip, Molly backed out the rear door and hit her head on the door frame. She leaned against the car as tears rolled down her cheeks and a sob turned to crying with abandon.

"Honey, what's wrong?" Dorothy asked from the door connecting the garage to the kitchen. When there was no answer, she let the door slam behind her while she slid her arms around her oldest daughter and dried away the tears with a dishtowel.

"I hit my head on the stupid car."

Dorothy smiled above Molly's head and pulled her closer. "Well, that about corks it. Let's sell the car, alright?"

Molly sighed and smiled morosely. "Must be hormonal! Sorry; got mascara on your dishtowel."

"Pffffft. How's your heart, I mean, head?"

A smile tugged at Molly's lips, despite the tears that still clung to her eyelashes, "Mom, will I ever be wise like you someday?"

"I think you are one smart cookie right now. Come inside. Your father and I are having coffee. You look like you could use a cup."

Molly nodded and obediently followed her mother into the kitchen. "Yes, Doctor Mom. There's nothing a good cup of coffee can't cure!"

Bob was sitting at the kitchen table with a map of the Central and Western states spread out before him. "Triple-A says this route is still good. Where do you plan to stop the first night after Mara's? I will call and verify your reservations for you."

"Omaha. I'll leave Rochester early enough to make it."

"That's a pretty long first day, Honey. How 'bout Des Moines? That way you could leave Mara's later in the day."

"Okay. Whatever. I'm sure there are lots of good places in Des Moines to choose from." She tucked her leg beneath her as she bent over the map with her father. From across the table, Dorothy smiled at the two blonde heads as they calculated distances and jotted down cities and motels from the guide book.

After lunch, Bob packed the car, checking the spare tire, fluids under the hood, and giving the vehicle his pat of approval. Dorothy refilled thermos, cooler, and packed a shoebox with treats for the eventual trip back to California.

Molly selected a few paperbacks from her parents' collection and replaced them with those from her luggage. She would get more reading done on the return trip than she had coming East. Jordan had certainly interrupted her reading patterns.

"Remember, your Grandma Bergen is still in Rochester, but you can get her key from the neighbor. She told you all about the boxes for you being labeled and right inside the side door. Too bad you have to make the trip to St. Cloud when there's no one there to see, but she did *not* want to miss out on the Elder Hostel week in Rochester with your other grandparents."

Bob and Dorothy hugged their first-born and waved from the curb as she rolled away. Traffic was light and Molly began to put Jordan behind her by selecting tapes to listen to, rather than subjecting herself to the radio announcers' whims of discussing every known and speculated facet of BJ Kendall's life.

The side trip to St. Cloud was uneventful, even though it felt strange to be at her grandmother's house without her grandma to welcome her. There were still signs of Grandpa Bergen, too. Theirs had been a love that lasted close to sixty years, and as she saw her grandfather's leather-covered footstool beside his matching chair and his hat still hanging on the front coat rack, she knew his love sustained her grandma even now. It was a love that had served as a model for both Molly's parent's and sister's marriages; that powerful love had given each generation of her family a true sense of stability.

Love, however, was something she was better off not thinking about in great detail right now. She turned her attention to the task at hand. The boxes of books that had filled so many wonderful childhood hours now filled the trunk of the car and forced all other possessions into the back seat. She covered them with the stadium blanket and actually managed to grin when grass fluttered off it.

When she reached Rochester, she felt more like herself than she had for days. Except for a jagged moment when Mara informed her that they were painting "her" room downstairs and she would have to sleep in the bunk bed below Toby, she hardly even thought about Jordan.

Except for each person in Rochester who had met Jordan and now felt obligated to acknowledge his recent successes, no one said his name for over four hours.

The national newscast highlighted its upcoming stories: "BJ Kendall's surprise decision. Stay tuned for the report, live from Florida."

Molly was alone in the room with the television when his face filled the screen. An unseen interviewer asked, "What is behind your decision to take the next three months away from the circuit, BJ?"

The familiar smile. Molly's fingers stole to cover her lips. "There are going to be some major changes in my life that require time away. I apologize to the sponsors and fans, but this is an important time for me. I will be happy to answer further questions when I know more of the answers myself."

"Does the timing have anything to do with this tournament, BJ?"

"No. Even if I lose the Florida tournament, or the ones in Colorado and Georgia that I will fulfill for my contract, I plan to be off the course for the next few months." It was obvious, despite Jordan's friendly smile, that he had said all he would say on the subject.

"So, golf enthusiasts, you have heard it here, such as it is. The news, in recap, is that BJ Kendall, who can add another trophy to his burgeoning collection from today's win, is beginning an extended hiatus from professional golf following the much publicized Florida, Colorado, and Georgia tournaments."

Another voice informed viewers that the interview segment had been prerecorded at noon that day.

Molly closed her eyes and leaned back against the chair. In the fog of her thoughts she heard more voices but she pushed them into the background. She was glad Matt and Mara were busy in the kitchen; she needed time to sort through this latest information.

"…will you elaborate further on these plans of yours, BJ?"

"I will enroll in adult literacy classes back in California."

Molly's eyes shot open and she stared at the screen. It was the Network News anchorperson talking about the Persian Gulf, not Jordan's face that she saw.

"…and what is your extended plan?"

"I hope to be married to a librarian, if she will have me."

This was nothing from the television. Molly leaped from the chair and flung open the door to the hallway.

Jordan. In the hallway with a grinning Matt, Mara, Mom, Dad.

"She's stopped breathing, Jordan!" Dad's voice sounded from a cave within her head.

"Step aside. I can administer First Aid." Lips that she had never expected to touch again now closed around hers. Helpless, she let herself go limp in Jordan's strong arms. The hallway mysteriously emptied.

"What…? How…?" She clung to him.

"I love you, Molly." His caress was gentle, yet intensely possessive.

Her lips opened, but no sound came out.

"Do you love me, too, Minnesota?"

She nodded, her eyes locked to his face like a prisoner in stocks.

"You must really love me; you haven't stopped nodding!"

"How did you get here?" she asked, unconsciously reaching up to follow the cheekbone she had memorized with a light finger.

"I flew." His hands cupped her body close to his.

"I mean how…"

"That's a long story. We'll talk on the plane to Colorado."

"Colorado? Plane?"

"Is there an echo in here?" Jordan teased. "Yes, my Love. Will you fly with me to Colorado? I have missed you so much. I want to be with you." Molly felt positively giddy, listening, trying to absorb all the love that ricocheted around her. "Then we could fly to Georgia if you can arrange more time off work, and then fly back here for the car, and drive home to California. I believe we have some more talking to do. And that's what car trips are good for, right?"

She looked back into the family room where the TV still played to an empty chair. "Was the reporter's story true about you taking time off from pro golf?" she finally asked coming out of the fog she floated in long enough to form a coherent question.

"You bet it was, and so was the hallway story about what my plans are. I need time off to get a good handle on reading before I go back to the circuit. I know it will take longer than just a couple months to become a full-fledged reader, but your mom says that will give me a good start, right?"

"...Right..."

"I never want to be miles apart from you. In any way. Ever again."

Molly began to cry. No, this was full-fledged weeping.

Jordan stared at her patiently.

Patience was a fading commodity beyond the hallway. Mara, Matt, Bob and Dorothy could wait no longer. "Did she say yes?" Matt hissed from the kitchen.

"We haven't gotten to that part yet. She's busy crying now. I think she said she would go to Colorado with me, though."

"Well, I would hope so!" Dorothy puffed indignantly, steering the loiterers back to the hallway.

"Were you all in on this?" Molly asked, brushing away her tears, now crying and laughing simultaneously.

"Questions later; coffee's ready!" Mara sang out and ushered them out to the kitchen table.

Words tumbled over each other as the story unfolded.

"You must have logged quite a few long-distance minutes over the past week, Jordan!" Bob chuckled.

"Well, you will have some pretty hefty phone bills, yourselves, unless you've got a good long distance plan!" said Jordan as he homed in on Molly's hand under the table.

Molly managed a stunned, smoky whisper. "You have all been talking on the phone to each other?"

"Every day!" Bob announced with a broad grin. "Sometimes taking the cell phone outside when you would *not* leave us alone for a private phone call!" Jordan has our cell phone and house phone numbers memorized, I'm sure!

"Sometimes we talked twice a day. Each of us!" Dorothy added. "It has been just great!"

Molly looked at Jordan as if in apology. "Jordan…"

"Hey, I called them first. I wanted to be up-front about telling them that the man who loves their daughter, sister and sister-in-law is not on a par with this family in reading. I learned an unforgettable lesson on the curb out there about coming clean with secrets like that. No more walls between us. I could have lost you."

"I told him that I had never seen you so whipped over anyone who *could* read, so I surely did not think it was such a big deal!" Mara chimed in.

After the laughter faded, Dorothy said, "Hopefully, your dad and I have assured Jordan we are delighted with him as he is. Any changes he makes will be icing on an already terrific cake."

Molly bit her lip as fountains of joy threatened to spill down her cheeks. She had never loved her family more.

Matt said, "I told him your family welcomed me, even if I wasn't a coffee drinker back then. Now *that* was a pretty suspect trait, believe me! More coffee anyone?" he asked with a grin, lifting the pot in anticipation.

"What it comes down to is that any man who can win the heart and affection of one of my daughters is a special fellow, believe me. My girls are so picky!"

Conversation stopped. It was suddenly as if Molly and Jordan were alone.

"In the presence of these witnesses, I ask the most important question of my life. Will you marry me, Molly Winstead?" Jordan asked softly.

Blue-gray eyes magnetically held shining brown ones willing prisoners.

"Yes." The simple word carried deep emotion.

"We will have happiness for a lifetime together," he vowed.

"I know."

Bob pounded the table. "Yes! She said yes!"

Instantly, Jordan and Molly welcomed The Kiss that topped all its predecessors in sweetness, passion and intensity.

*   *   *

Molly watched from the golf course sidelines, part of the sometimes silent, often cheering crowd. She was more conscious of her unique role there since Jordan had kissed her unabashedly, in full view of the rolling cameras.

Not surprisingly, the news media latched on to the news that someone special to the star of the day was in the crowd. Cameras flashed when Jordan, holding his trophy high, pulled her close to him in a one-armed embrace that told the world all it needed to know about their new-found love, if the earlier kiss had not been clear enough.

Back in California, Jordan began his pursuit of reading with the purposeful passion of a thirsty man in sight of an oasis. "I do not believe I am saying this, but you really don't have to learn to read all in the first month, Jordan!" Molly chided gently as she poured a cup of coffee for Jordan in her kitchen.

"My tutor says I am doing really well and why not? After all, my goal is in sight. It's just three months until we get married! Now *that's* motivation!"

"I had better marry you fast, before you are hopelessly addicted to words on a page leaving me lucky to get a sliver of attention!"

"Fat chance of that happening, Minnesota, when you're around to, uh, shall we say, create a diversion?" Jordan said with a grin.

"Hmmm. What an interesting idea…" She let her hands travel down his chest and shivered with the realization that this delicious man was all hers. "This kind of diversion?"

"Temptress!" He pulled her around and nuzzled her neck and met no resistance on her part when he tugged her down on his lap. She leaned back in his arms, remembering the first time he'd held her. As if reading her thoughts, he said, "Know what we need at our wedding? A big old dumpster."

"May I suggest that we least park it out in the parking lot?" she asked and arched an eyebrow over a pseudo-frown.

"Provided we get to pose by it!"

"For memories of our humble beginnings?"

"For memories of when our love began." He nibbled her hand and gently kissed each fingertip.

"Uh-uh. Don't start that stuff or we'll be terribly late for lunch with Royce. Does he suspect anything?"

"Nope. All he knows is that this is the lunch he ordered so we could show him we didn't explode on the desert! Remember, he's been hiking in the wilderness, so he has been out of touch with newspapers and even television news."

Molly smiled broadly. "This is going to be great. The poor guy has probably developed an ulcer since we last saw him!"

They had staged it to be as similar to the original lunch as possible, even calling ahead to assure that Bones would be their waiter. At precisely noon, Molly entered the Club wearing the same outfit; it didn't take lavender today, though, to do interesting things to her eyes. They glowed consistently these days.

Royce was seated at the predictable table and Molly walked in first, Jordan waiting outside long enough to add authenticity.

Royce rose at the sound of Molly's footsteps. He gave her a quick hug and held her chair for her. "It is so good to see you at last! You didn't even send a postcard this trip!"

She shrugged apologetically. "Sorry, Royce. It just got, uh, busy, I guess."

"'Busy'? On vacation? Doesn't sound like much fun to me. But didn't you add an extra week or so?"

"Sure did. You know me. I'm happiest when I'm busy, with a schedule to keep, a plan to follow. Where's what's-his-name, that Jordan fellow?" Molly asked nonchalantly.

Royce rolled his eyes and said pointedly, "*Beej* will be here. Gee, woman, if you can't remember his name after driving all the way to Minnesota with him, I give up on you! Didn't you guys even *talk* to each other? Oh, there he is now. Beej, over here!"

Jordan and Royce pumped hands, slapped shoulders, tossing the predictable macho insults back and forth, and then Jordan finally acknowledged Molly's presence. Bowing solemnly at the waist, he said, "And hello to you, too, Minnesota!"

"Hello, Jordan," she replied coolly. "How nice to see you." Out of the corner of her eye she caught Royce's seemingly off-hand observation of this casual exchange.

Bones trotted up then with his pad and pencil poised and all three chimed, "I'll have the Special, please," prompting awkward laughter that quickly faded into electric silence.

"So. Here we all are." Royce said uneasily. "Tell me all about the trip. I gather you found a level of civilized behavior that preserved you for this lunch."

Molly eyed Royce and then Jordan. "We promised you we would behave; you would have been so proud of us. We had a few awkward moments, but basically..."

Jordan snorted. "'A few awkward moments,' she says! That's what she calls running out of gas on the hottest day of the year in the middle of the desert? Or how 'bout *forgetting* that motels just might not have extra rooms available on a moment's notice? Royce, this ride you landed for me was something else. No stress? Ha!"

Royce shifted nervously in his chair and took a flying leap at trying to redeem the situation. "Sounds like it was an opportunity to create memories..."

"Oh, yes. You can say that again." Molly said dryly.

"Well, you're back home, safe and sound, and you can get on with the summer," Royce said desperately, beads of perspiration forming on his forehead. "I'm sorry, you guys. It seemed like a good idea, but from the level of tension around this table, I guess that…"

Jordan interrupted, "Royce, you're right about the tension. Both at that first lunch, and today. Let's just say we owe you a big one for what you put us through."

Royce's cheek twitched nervously. "I just wanted to give you each a chance to meet each other, maybe become friends, but I was wrong to meddle. I'll be honest; I had hoped it would be, uh, the beginning of, well," he twisted his napkin into a tight ball and finished in a rush, "I worry about Molly not spending time with guys except for me." He was a picture of dejection and despair.

"Don't persecute yourself, buddy. We came through it with some memories, that's for sure." Jordan nudged his tennis partner. "The stories we could tell you about how your plan of sending me, an illiterate, freestyle guy, cross-country with a full-fledged, list-keeping, card-totin' librarian are the backbones of legends!"

"And there was no way you could have known that Jordan and I would have already met under, let's say, compromising conditions."

"Wha…? Did you say illit—…compromi—…"

Jordan cut in on this startled explosion. "Got your calendar handy, Royce? I want you to mark off a weekend in September."

Royce patted his empty pocket, shook his head in response, and never once took his eyes off Molly. "Sure…I mean, no, I don't have my calendar with me, but I'll jot down the date. Got a pencil?" He ripped a corner off his placement in preparation.

"No pencil, but maybe this will help you remember." Reaching into his hip pocket, he said, "Hey Minnesota, this is something I neglected to give you on the trip." He handed her a golf ball.

"A golf ball? I don't need a golf ball, Jordan."

"Sure you do. Squeeze it and you'll see why."

"What?"

"It's magic." He closed his hand around hers and she felt the ball move. When she opened her hand and held a golf-ball-turned-box.

A velvet-lined golf ball that held a solitaire diamond.

"Ohhhhhh…"

Royce spoke first. Actually, he sputtered. "That's a diamond ring, Beej! An engagement ring."

Jordan nodded agreeably. "Yes, it is. I believe that's the traditional jewelry a man gives the woman he plans to marry."

This time Royce squawked. "Marry!"

Molly stared, dewy-eyed, at Jordan. "This wasn't part of our plan for today!" she whispered.

"Well, there was *our* plan, and there was *my* plan!" He reached across the table and met her hand mid-air. "Sorry I didn't have it when I proposed, Old Shoe." He shoved back his chair at the same time she rose from her side; they met behind the empty chair.

Royce rocked his chair back on two legs and watched, his head wagging loosely like a balloon on a string, while Jordan slipped the ring on Molly's finger and his lips sealed it in place for all eternity.

Bones chose that moment to appear with three plates balanced on a tray over his head. "Royce," Molly said once they were alone again, "one thing we need to tell you is that somewhere along the trip, we fell in love."

"No," Royce said softly, but with a firmness that made them both turn toward him. "That's where you're wrong. You did *not* fall in love on the trip."

"Hey, man, we know it seems a little unbelievable, but it's real," Jordan said. "You sent two strangers out on a trip, and two lovers returned."

"I don't doubt the last part. What I'm saying is you didn't fall in love on the trip. That happened whenever and wherever it was that you first saw each other. The tension around this table at that first lunch was incredible; and it's back here today. It never *was* the stuff wars are made of that I felt that day. It was then, and is now, love. Powerful, sexual, riveting, life-changing love. I have just one more thing to say: Wow!"

"Will you be Best Man at our wedding?" Jordan asked. "That is, if you can remember the date without your calendar handy!"

"Please?" added Molly. "There's no one else we can imagine beside us."

"Absolutely. By then, I may have recovered from my shock!" He dropped one hand on Jordan's shoulder and squeezed Molly's hand simultaneously. "I'm incredibly happy for both of you. And just a little relieved that you're not going to sue me for setting up the trip!"

Suddenly they were all ravenous. Over lunch, Royce heard the story of the dumpster, the trip, and the love that had swallowed up all the miles that separated them.

Back at Jordan's house, Molly laughed and said, "I wasn't sure how we would pull it off, but I think we genuinely surprised Royce." The diamond on her finger was captivating. "But his shock pales beside *my* condition when that golf ball popped open!"

"Well, I proposed to you in front of your family, so I didn't want to ruin the tradition of Important-Moments-In-Public that we started, so giving you the ring with Royce in attendance seemed appropriate!"

Molly smiled. "Life with you, whether we're crammed in a hot car or painting the fence or making crepes at midnight, will never be dull. And to that, I say a resounding yes! How about you? Can you face life with a librarian who may need reminding from time to time that plans are never as important as people, or that schedules are made to be broken, or even the lessons you've taught her about laughter and living on the light side of life? Do you—can you—love someone with all those faults?"

Jordan hooked her close to his chest and tilted her chin so that brown eyes found gray blue ones. "Hey, Minnesota, I love you. More than words. F-o-r-e-v-e-r."

"D-i-t-t-o, in reverse, Jordan. F-o-r-e-v-e-r."

*   *   *

API & UPI PRESS RELEASE

San Joaquin Valley Press/ Professional golfer, Bartholomew Jordan Kendall and Molly Bergen Winstead, a librarian from the San Joaquin Valley, wed today at the chapel in Yosemite National Park in a private family ceremony. The couple read vows each had written.

About the Author

Hadley Hoover lives in Rochester MN with her California-native husband and a 140-pound Bernese Mountain Dog. She works as an editor for a medical certification board, and is a former English teacher and librarian. This is her first novel.

www.hadleyhoover.com